THE
SWEET
BY AND BY

TODD JOHNSON

wm

WILLIAM MORROW

An Imprint of HarperCollins*Publishers*

This book is a work of fiction. The characters, incidents, and dialogue are drawn from the author's imagination and are not to be construed as real. Any resemblance to actual events or persons, living or dead, is entirely coincidental.

HarperCollins books may be purchased for educational, business, or sales promotional use. For information please write: Special Markets Department, HarperCollins Publishers, 10 East 53rd Street, New York, NY 10022.

FIRST EDITION

Designed by Susan Yang

Library of Congress Cataloging-in-Publication Data

Johnson, Todd.
    The sweet by and by / Todd Johnson.—1st ed.
        p.   cm.
        ISBN 978-0-06-157952-3
        1. Female friendship—Fiction.   2. Older women—Fiction.
    3. Reminiscing in old age—Fiction.   4. North Carolina—Social life
    and customs—Fiction.   I. Title.

PS3610.O3836S94   2009
813'.6—dc22   2008015740

09 10 11 12 13   OV/RRD   10 9 8 7 6 5 4

To Mabel Barnes Langdon and
Mozelle Woodall Johnson,
my grandmothers

He who binds to himself a joy
Does the winged life destroy;
But he who kisses the joy as it flies
Lives in eternity's sun rise.

—WILLIAM BLAKE, *Eternity*

THE
Sweet
By and By

CHAPTER ONE

LORRAINE

I barely have got in the door good and it's already three thirty in the afternoon. Church seemed like it lasted too long this morning and I didn't come straight home like I usually do. Althea was determined to take me over to her house cause she had fixed collards and was bound for me to have some with her cornbread and dumplings, so now I'm 'bout to pop wide-open. She said she might not go to church so much if it wasn't for me, it takes so much time out of a Sunday. I told her, "Don't be puttin the burden of your soul on me, girl. You're too hardheaded to change, and I'm too smart to try and make you."

Althea used to decorate cakes for a livin out of her own kitchen 'til it 'bout killed her it got to be so much work. She did birthdays, anniversaries, weddings of course, retirements, and a couple times she even made a cake for a funeral, but I don't think there was much decoration on those. Now she works in an insurance office, mostly houses and cars is what they do. She picks me up on Sunday mornings for church sometimes, I think she likes to have some company ridin, and there ain't no way her husband is gon go unless a meal is bein served. She is one drivin woman, I tell you that. Wants to go, go, go every minute. This morning we had time to drink a cup of coffee cause she got to my house so fast. I pulled out the cups and put four big spoons of sugar in hers or else she woulda asked me if I was tryin to put her on a diet.

"Well," Althea said, raising her eyebrows when she took the hot coffee from me. "Lorraine, I've had a revelation."

"Was it the Ten Commandments?" I asked. "Cause I ain't so sure you got em the first time around."

She ignored me. "I had a dream last night. I woke up sweatin to death, and I remember every bit of it. There was a circle of candles and me sittin in the middle of em."

"Is this voodoo, Althea, cause if it is . . . ?"

"You're bad for interruptin somebody, you know that?"

"I'll hush." I took too big a sip and burned my tongue.

Althea looked around like she was about to tell a secret even though there wasn't a soul there but the two of us, sittin in my kitchen drinking coffee and gettin ready to be late for church.

She pushed her cup to one side so she could lean in across the table. "When I tried to step over the candles they flew up in the air like comets or something and disappeared, I mean poof." She lowered her voice to a whisper. "Then I saw a man with his shirt wide-open and muscles all up and down his chest and stomach. Fine lookin too. Standing in front of a big pond, no, a lake, big as Jordan Lake, and he was waving at me to come across with him, only there wasn't a boat or any other way to get across. Then he took a couple of steps backwards with his pants rolled up, water lapping around his ankles. He kept on waving at me to come down there, and I thought to myself I don't even know you, you might be tryin to drown me."

I got up and ran some water in my empty cup, then set it in the sink. I would wash it later.

"Are you listenin to me?" Althea snapped.

"I told you I would hush, that's what I'm doin."

"Well I woke up, Lorraine, and I realized. That mighta been Moses I dreamed. Do you think it was Moses?"

"Hmm." I must have made a sound even though I didn't realize it.

"That's all you got to say?"

"Honey, what exactly's the revelation?"

"It's time for me to cross over, Lorraine. That's all I'm sayin."

"You gon die sometime soon?"

Althea shook her head and reached for her coat. "I don't know why I try to tell you anything. You don't have my kind of vision. Let's go to the car."

Me and Althea go way back. She helped me just about raise my daughter, much as anybody did besides my mama. That's how come she feels like she can act like a second mother to April. Some people might not like another person tellin their child what to do, but I like it all right. Having to make all the rules all the time wasn't never my idea of a party. I'm grateful for the help. There's one thing about gettin somebody to help you though, you got to take whatever it looks like, their kind of help, and you can't be choosing what you like and don't like. Help is a take it or leave it kind of thing, and if you can't take it like it comes, might as well leave it cause it's gon be more trouble than it's worth. Or you're gon lose a friend in the process.

When April was little, we stayed at Mama's. She didn't have many rules in her house except for one, and I made it my rule too. No matter what else was goin on, we had to sit down and eat breakfast together every day unless one of us was sick, and I mean so sick you couldn't get yourself up out of the bed. Mama fixed food for me and April while I got ready to go to work. There was one morning, I remember cause I had just started my new job, I heard her call April in from her bedroom for about the third time. Breakfast was on the table, and knowing my daughter, she was probably readin something or other, still in the bed.

"Sit down baby, and eat your oatmeal," Mama said when she saw April leaning against the kitchen door, rubbing her eyes. It was a cool morning, especially for October in eastern North Carolina, and April was in long flannel pajamas, way too big for her, probably handed down by somebody, I don't remember who. I can see those pant legs wadded up around her feet, lookin like they were gon make her fall down any time, but she liked em that way, she liked slidin around on a wood floor in those old pajamas. She could make herself skate four or five feet if she got a runnin start and hit a slick spot just right.

"You want something to drink?" Mama added, pouring orange juice into a jelly glass with cartoon characters on it cause that was the only one April ever wanted to drink out of. Mama was glad to fix breakfast, she was always the first one up anyway, it didn't matter how early I had to go to work. It was like she made a contest out of beatin everybody to the start of the day, even though she wouldn't admit it, like she was racing to an invisible finish line. You couldn't have caught up with her if you was a jackrabbit.

April just stood staring at the table. She was expecting to see butter and syrup, and instead there wasn't even a plate. "It's Saturday!" she pouted. "Why aren't we havin pancakes?"

I had started that habit a long time ago. I tried to fix breakfast myself on Saturdays since April didn't have school. And she did love her pancakes. Sometimes I made em plain but usually I put in a little somethin extra like some overripe bananas or pecans I picked up out of Althea's yard, anything I could put my hands on. If I wasn't in too big a hurry, I'd heat up the syrup on the stove, and April said she thought that was how rich people ate their pancakes, with hot syrup.

I came flyin into the kitchen tryin to leave on time and saw her sittin in front of her bowl, stubborn as a knot on a log. "I'll make you some pancakes tomorrow, honey, before we go to church," I said. "I don't have time to this mornin."

April knew something was different because she saw me wearing a bright green dress instead of my uniform, and I had my nice black pocketbook. I think she also might have saw my eyes all swelled up, I'd been crying some.

"What happened?" she asked. "Aren't you going to work?"

"I've got to go to a funeral first. Now go on and eat so Grandma can finish cleanin up."

"Who died at the funeral?"

"Somebody I take care of, honey," I said. "Mr. Whitty Holcomb. He was an old, old man."

"Is everybody at your nursing home gonna die?"

"Baby, everybody everywhere is gon die sometime, but you don't need to be studyin that now."

Mama didn't take much to that kind of talk and saw that her granddaughter hadn't even picked up her spoon. She got up and opened a cabinet. "Look here, April," she said, "I'm gon put some brown sugar on it for you."

My daughter wouldn't be sidetracked. "Mama," she said, with a change in her voice, "you're a nurse, aren't you? Etonia's sister came up to me on the playground, and she said you wasn't a real nurse so why didn't I stop pretending like you was. I told her you are so a nurse so shut up."

Mama heaped so much dark brown sugar into April's bowl that it looked like wet dirt. "You got a lot of questions this mornin, girl," she said, still scooping. "You need to eat and leave your mama alone. Lorraine, tell her to eat."

"I'm an LPN, April," I said. "Licensed Practical Nurse. That's what it stands for. You can tell Etonia that."

"Why'd she say it then?" April said.

"There's other kinds of nurses that got more school than I got. I did what I could do, and here we all are. Now I got to go or I'm gon be late."

"Well I'm gonna be a real nurse, and I might be a doctor too," she stuck out her jaw.

"There ain't a whole lot of black women doctors, baby," I said, tryin to get into my long gray wool coat, worn out, but the only dress coat I had.

"Well I can be one if I want to!" she yelled. I thought at the time she was only tryin to get my attention as much as anything else, but I bet you I've thought about that conversation a thousand times and that was almost twenty years ago. Those kind of words stay with you. You think about your child and how you want everything to work out and be the best it can be for them, and then you wonder if even one thing you say might either raise em up or push em back down. God knows I tried to raise that girl up in spite of everything. I did my best.

Althea's probably already back home by now if she didn't get herself a speedin ticket. I hate to say it but I'm glad she didn't stay long once she dropped me off. I'm gon change out of these church clothes and sit down a few minutes. I need to clean up the house some before I go back to work tomorrow, but I might be too tired to do much. I still got the morning shift most days. That's all right, I like the morning, I choose it when I can. I like getting up in the dark and having my eyes open to see the sun come up. I start my morning, every morning, pouring urine from one container into another. I ain't gon say I don't mind it. Sometimes what's in a bedpan is bright yellow and stinks, and other times it's clear as water, especially when somebody can't eat solid food no more or don't eat at all. But that's my work. For some of them, I'm the only face in this world they know. I can't hardly stand hearin one of them cry out, "I'm ready to go home now, Lorraine," when all I come in to do is take out a plastic bag of trash or soiled bedsheets rather than wait for a nurse's aide to do it when we don't have enough of em to go around. That's my day, doin what needs to be done. I guess some people get to where they don't hear it, the sound of those voices, but that ain't me, I can't help it. I hear it every single time.

CHAPTER TWO

MARGARET

It's Christmas time again!" That's what everybody keeps on saying. I hear it on television too, somebody always selling something with a verse or two of "We Wish You a Merry" or "Jingle Bells." I've always hated "Jingle Bells" myself, except when there are children around, which in this place there clearly are *not*. And nobody is likely to ever go dashing through the snow any time soon in this part of Carolina, I'd bet my last nickel on that. When it comes to carols, I myself like a good slow hymn with a little bit of a sad sound in it like "It Came upon a Midnight Clear." At least with a song like that you don't have to put on a happy face just because everybody thinks you ought to. I put on enough as it is just getting through.

You can't blame me too much if I'm not in the mood, the holiday spirit. My daughter Ann says I can be ill as a hornet sometimes, and I don't deny it. Plain old mad. And it's nobody's fault either, nobody's done one thing to me. But I wish to God they'd stop flitting around like spring butterflies, like I ought to be overjoyed at the prospect of somebody feeding me every bite I eat and changing my clothes like a baby. I've heard them say I can be "difficult," and so what if I am? I didn't ask to be here, surrounded by linoleum, blinded by fluorescent lights, or left alone in pure black darkness. They think I complain all the time anyway. And I'll tell you another thing. There are an awful lot of busybodies around here—I have to be on guard. You might not know it to look at them, but they traipse up and down these hallways, all hours of day and night, listening in at your room. Peeking in at the inmates. I think they want to know one of two things: if you're crazy and need to be put somewhere else, or if you're dead and need to be put somewhere else.

Lorraine is at my door at the crack of dawn, just like every day. She's not a regular nurse, meaning the kind that gives medicine all by herself, but she does everything else in the world there is to do for me. She wears something like nurse clothes, except instead of serious doctor white, her smock usually has red and blue balloons or fat little teddy bears on it. I'm not asleep this morning but she thinks I am. I don't know how anybody can sleep after daybreak when all you can hear is Mathilda rolling a medicine cart down the hall like she was on I-40. I asked how one person could make so much noise, and Lorraine told me she was mashing up pills so people could swallow them better mixed up in a little juice. I told her, "Honey, I don't know what kind of pills she's mashing up, but she might as well be using a jackhammer." I crack my eyes open at Lorraine, but she doesn't know it so she tiptoes, moving potted plants and old boxes of candy, not that there's very much to move, because Ann comes every day and picks up. She thinks I don't remember it, but I do. She's my one and only child and I love her, but she's one of those people who, if you leave something sitting out for more than two minutes, swoops it up never to be seen again, either thrown in the garbage or put somewhere that you would never in your whole life think to look, so it might as well be thrown away. She thinks I'm "out of it" sometimes, that's what she says under her breath to people who come to visit from church, and she may very well be right.

"You're not thinking, Mama, you know better than that," she says in a voice so sweet that it's irritating, and I feel like I want to reach out and slap her.

"No I don't know better," I want to say. "I don't know anything but what I say right this minute!" But I stay silent and let her go on. Go right on. Today, tomorrow, the next day. I'll be right here.

While Lorraine is sneaking around like a mouse, and she is neither a small girl nor mousy, I notice she has gotten her hair done up in little curly-cues on top of her head. She looks like she ought to have on a church dress, not a nurse's smock and squeaky white shoes that you can hear a mile away. I open both eyes all the way, but I don't say anything, just wait for her to notice I'm not dead yet. After she's through pushing poinsettias around for God-knows-what reason, to do something quiet to wake me up I guess, she turns around to the bed. "You don't have to be quiet Linda, I'm awake." I don't know why I call her Linda because I know just as sure as I'm telling this that her name's Lorraine. It's awful to know things in your mind that won't come out of your mouth. Sometimes I give up, but most of the time I go ahead and say whatever comes, and if it rubs you the wrong way, I'm sorry.

What do you expect me to act like? Wake up smiling every day like some soft gray-haired church lady when I can't do one damn thing I used to? I can't even cook a piece of toast because they won't let me have a toaster. Can't work in the dirt planting vegetables like I used to, good enough to put on anybody's table in this world. Can't drive, and *that's* a big one. Ann used to let me drive on short runs to my cousin's house and to Creech's Store, but Lizzie's dead now, and Creech's burned down. I do admit that I did one time go all the way to Smithfield, but it came back to haunt me because somebody called Ann and told her they saw me drive straight through a red light without taking my foot off the gas. It doesn't matter that it was a pure lie, my wings are clipped now anyway. I haven't driven for five years, it may be longer than that, I couldn't tell you. But I will tell you this, they better not even think about selling my old Plymouth. I don't care if it sits under the carport and rusts all the way down to a pile of metal dust. I paid good money for that car, and I might need it. I wish for things all the time that I can't use, but I need to have at least some things that are mine. It's a way to say to anybody, "I can do something if I want to. I can decide things."

I don't want to start thinking about that car now, I might never see it again. Sometimes my mind has open window spells. It's as though a wind blows through and scatters everything all over the place, trash flying in while other things get sucked out. Then I'll say something crazy, out of the blue, and even while I'm talking foolishness, I know full well it doesn't make a bit of sense. Yesterday lying right here in this crank-up bed, I told Ann to go into the kitchen and check on my sweet potatoes. She looked at me and smiled, and said, "Mama, you're not cooking anything today." Now I know damn well I'm not cooking. I know I'm not home. But sometimes when I picture myself in my living room, it *is* me. I'm turning on the TV, making a phone call, or walking around with a magazine. And the whole time I'm here in bed half asleep—the thing I do best—until somebody comes to drag me out to eat or take a bath or just to sit up in a chair for a few minutes.

It's not a very cheerful picture, so you can see why I don't know what kind of Christmas party they think they are going to have in a place where nobody even knows what day it is. I guess they have to do something for the holidays so it still feels like some brand of "alive" around here instead of like the waiting platform for the last train out of this world.

Lorraine perks up when she sees me awake. "Well good morning, Miss Margaret, how you feelin? You 'bout ready for some breakfast?"

"Yes ma'am I am, thank you," I tell her, even though the only breakfast I like is when they bring Frosty Flakes. Everything they have the nerve to cook tastes like it's been on the stove for two days, boiled to death. I know they're afraid we'll choke if they don't make everything into mush, but try eating something that feels like slime on the top of a pond going down your throat. There's nothing like it to put you off eating altogether.

Lorraine pushes over a tray with dry cereal on it, Cheerios, not exactly the kind I want, but thank God for small favors, at least it's something I can actually chew. There's also a glass of orange juice, coffee that looks like what comes out the bottom of your car, and a little cookie in the shape of a star with green sprinklies on top. I never have cared much about something sweet. Just a little sugar in my coffee, that's all. Not that I haven't made some cakes that are the best thing you've ever put in your mouth though, but I don't eat them. I never have. Maybe a sliver right after they come out of the oven good and hot, but that's all.

"Today's the party, Miss Margaret, are you ready for Santy Claus?"

"I reckon I'm ready as I'm going to be. How about you?" Please Lord, don't let her start going through drawers pulling out everything red she can find and trying to make a Christmas outfit. I told Ann to get rid of that sweatshirt somebody gave me with big appliqués of candy canes all over it, but I'm sure there's plenty of other tacky mess in those drawers if she looks long enough. I don't want to be all in red, and I don't want to be all in green either. And most of all I don't want to wear any sparkly gold loafers on my feet. Just a plain black or brown shoe with a little bit of a heel, that's what I have always worn, and that's exactly what I plan to continue wearing. But you just let me say something when somebody comes to visit. They'll say, "Oh come on Mrs. Clayton, don't you have any Christmas spirit? You look pretty as a picture." Good Lord, I know I really do—*that's* a picture I don't want to see.

I push the bowl of Cheerios back after a few mouthfuls. I'm hungry just about all the time, but I don't eat much. I guess I don't want it when you get right down to it, plus there's nothing to make you lose your appetite like worrying about whether everything you put down your gullet is gonna make you sick. Lorraine takes away my tray but leaves me some juice because she knows I like to have something to drink sitting close all the time, something besides water. I must say I have never liked to drink water. Dr. Shiraka says I'm supposed to drink six glasses a day, but I told him I've never drunk six glasses of anything in one day and I'm not about to start. I prefer something that has some taste, and not too cold, just a little ice. Tea or Co-Cola suits me all right.

Lorraine reappears after putting my tray on a trolley in the hall. "What you want to wear to the party? I know Ann's got some pretty things in here in these drawers."

"Honey, I don't care one bit so long as you don't fix me up to look like a whore."

"What?" Lorraine wheezes. "Now what am I gon do to make you look like that? You don't even know what you're talkin about."

"Yes ma'am I do, don't you think I don't."

"Uh-huh, all right." Lorraine cuts me off. "I ain't gon argue with you right here at Christmas time." She opens the closet, puts her hands on her hips, and stares for a minute. "How 'bout this outfit? Does this look all right to you?" She pulls out a navy blue knit jacket with gold buttons, and blue slacks to match.

"I've never seen that before in my life."

"Still got the tags on it." She places the clothes on the end of the bed as carefully as if they were her own. "See there, we'll get you all fixed, and then I'll come back and take you down to the party room a little bit after lunch."

"Do I have a choice?"

"Not while I'm on duty."

"Go on away from here, you stubborn mule." Lorraine offers her characteristic grunt and squeaks out into the hallway.

I have to say I am very curious to go to a Christmas party where most of the people there cannot or will not speak even if you held a gun to their heads. Some of them are bound to be crazy too. I know full well that Bernice Stokes, across the hall from me, wanders out all the time to say she's going to smoke a cigarette, even though Lorraine says she's never smoked a day in her life, which in North Carolina is saying something. If they don't watch her, she'll be out on 50 Highway sure as day, trying to get somebody to take her to downtown Raleigh and offering a hundred dollars for the ride. She doesn't have five dollars, but Lorraine says she used to have money and now her son's got all of it, the one that's left. I feel sorry for her, thinking she's got what she hasn't. I guess that's the way it happens a lot, which is why I'm thankful I've got my mind, at least most of the time. Ann has all the money she needs, she sells houses like nobody's business and buys anything she wants whenever she wants it. What little I've got I plan to keep as long as I've got sense enough.

I only have time to watch a little bit of *One Life to Live* when Lorraine comes back, but I tell her to go on and turn it off, it's not worth seeing. Viki has lost her memory for about the tenth time, and even I am getting tired of it, and I love that program, I really do. Television can be a great thing when you're in my shoes. Some of it's trash, but so is most of what we spend our time on, so I figure it balances out. If you don't watch it all the time when you're young, then you can have it on all the time when you're my age if you so desire. At least it's some talking, people's faces, moving around and laughing and trying out new products and not spending every day in a bed.

"Anybody in here ready for a party?" Lorraine starts singing down the hall and she's not bashful about it. *Here comes Santy Claus, here comes Santy Claus, right down Santy Claus lane!* I hear her singing into Bernice's room in the highest, squeakiest little voice you've ever heard. It's not humanly possible that a voice like that could come out of anything except a baby. The concert stops abruptly when she steps into my doorway. "Come on, Miss Margaret, I can take you and Bernice at the same time. If you don't feel like walking you can go in the chair and Bernice can hang on to one arm, is that all right with you?"

"Yes ma'am, but before we go down there, would you please make sure Bernice has her yellow monkey doll, because she will no doubt have a conniption without it. And then you'd think the world's going to end 'til somebody gets it, which personally I would rather not witness."

Lorraine calls out into the hall, "We got ole Mister Benny right here, don't we Bernice?"

Lorraine plops me as soft as she can into the wheelchair that's parked full-time beside my bed in case I need it, ever since I fell and hurt my hip. With her as the engine, we roll out the door, first time I've left this room in four days—last time was when they had a fire drill. In the hall I get an eyeful, I mean right now. Gold garland hanging in scraggly strands above everybody's door. Red plastic shiny balls with the color chipping off at the top. I know it all came from the dime store, and I'm all for working on a budget, as long as something doesn't *look* like it came from the dime store.

I try to get comfortable and tap Lorraine's arm. "Okay, let's roll, honey. I don't want to miss anything."

"You know nobody's gon start nothing without you," Lorraine lowers her voice, "there'd be hell to pay."

There are already ten people in the party room in various states of sleep, propped up on multiple pillows, falling over, or sitting straight as sticks except with their eyes closed. Lorraine takes Bernice and me over to the wall nearest the refreshment table, away from the door, which I know means that she intends me to stay for the whole affair.

Ada Everett, the all-too-pleasant woman who is in charge of this entire operation, walks up to the front of the room once everybody has gathered and says, "Well I'm just as pleased as I can be to be here with y'all so we can say 'Merry Christmas' all together. We have some special music planned and some presents to open, and we might even have a visit from the North Pole!" she chirps like she's talking to a bunch of six-year-olds. "And we're going to enjoy some of these fine refreshments that Twin Oaks Baptist has so kindly provided, but before we do that, I thought we might play a little game to get us all in the Christmas spirit, okay? Have any of y'all ever been in a spelling bee?"

There's dead silence in the room. She might as well be talking to trees. And I myself am one of the few who could answer her if I wanted to, but that's one true pleasure about being old; you realize every day how many things are more trouble than they're worth, and how much time you could have saved yourself over the years if you had only had that precious knowledge at a time when you could have actually done something with it.

"Well here's how it works, we'll just all take turns spelling holiday words, and the last one in gets a prize, okay? Okay. Now. The first word is . . ."

She reaches into a box wrapped in shiny red foil and pulls out a small light blue strip of paper.

". . . 'Joy.' How 'bout that? There's a simple one for you."

An old lady on the end of the row yells out, "J-O-Y, J-O-Y—that was my grandmama's name, J-O-Y!"

"Good for you, Mrs. Bain!" Ada chirps. "How 'bout another word? Let's see . . . 'mistletoe'! Mr. Tart, do you want to give that one a try?"

Vinnie Tart used to be a history teacher and he's smart as a whip, but he had a stroke and it's harder for him to speak now. He also some-times gets words and names mixed up. So when he spells "mistletoe" with two S's, I know darn well that it isn't because he doesn't know how to spell it. They ought to let it go, but I reckon rules are rules.

And so it goes on for a while—I get out on "potpourri," which I've always thought was one of the most stupid things I could think of anyway, especially since some of Ann's Realtor friends insist on giving me something just that useless on every single occasion when they feel like they ought to bring a present. After me, there are only two people left, the hard-of-hearing woman they call Miss Inez and crazy Bernice, who has somehow made it all the way through without having to spell anything harder than "eggnog."

Ada looks to Miss Inez and says, "Okay now think hard, the next word is . . . 'Christmas'!"

"'Liquor'?" Miss Inez scrunches up her face like she doesn't understand Ada.

"No dear, 'Christmas'!" Ada smiles.

"'Liquor'?!" Miss Inez repeats in a loud voice.

"No, not liquor, Miss Inez. Now listen. 'CHRIST-MAS!' Like 'we wish you a MERRY CHRISTMAS'!" Ada is almost yelling at this point.

Miss Inez looks at me sharply, "Is that girl yonder saying 'liquor'?"

I shake my head, and Ada, clearly exasperated, replies with a testiness in her voice which delights me because I know the veil of her patience is lifting, "Honestly, Miss Inez. Go on and spell it. That's what Christmas is to some people anyway."

Inez starts spelling. "L-I-Q-U . . ." She pauses. ". . . E-R."

"Oh no, honey, I'm so sorry." Ada fake pouts, reveling in her private victory. "Bernice, how about you? Spell 'Christmas.'"

Bernice grins and yells, "L-I-Q-U O-R!"

Ada Everett is dumbstruck for a second because that isn't the word she was supposed to spell, but I start clapping immediately and cry out, "Hurray Bernice, you won, sweetheart!" and then other people wake up and start clapping too. Ada, clearly dismayed that she has somehow lost control of the situation, says simply, "So she did," then looks back over to Miss Inez whose head is now over to one side, sound asleep.

Never missing a beat, Ada pipes up like a North Pole elf. "Well now, that was just fine, wasn't it, everybody? And congratulations, Bernice," she nods as she hands her a box of chocolate covered cherries with a bow on top. The pitch of Ada's voice kicks into an even higher key. "Now I think it's about time we had something to refresh ourselves a little, don't you?"

She walks in the direction of the punch bowl and cookies. I'm staring at the door, thinking about going back to my room for a nap, when
Bernice punches me in the side, not so gently, with her elbow. When
I turn my head to snap at her, I see that she is holding in her hand one
of those little whiskey bottles like you get on the airplane, Jack Daniel's
or something else brown. God knows where she got it, maybe her son
traveling all the time. Let me be clear about one thing—I myself do not
touch a drop of spirits. Only a nip of dark rum in my eggnog, that's all. I
push Bernice's hand back down into her lap before Ada can see what she
has, but I am too late. Ada snatches the bottle away from Bernice, and
knocks Yellow Monkey Benny onto the floor, and unfortunately that
one careless gesture throws Bernice into an all-out hissy fit.

"My Benny Boy," she wails. "That's my Benny! You've killed him.
See, he's dead!!!"

She is sobbing for all she's worth, and I reach over to put my arm
around her, but she knocks it away.

"Ada, I know she'll be all right if she can go lie down for a minute,"
I offer. "Just wheel me on down the hall with her and I'll sit in her
room to keep her peaceful, honey."

Ada motions Lorraine over and tells her to do exactly as I suggested, but Lorraine sort of squints one eye at me. "Miss Margaret, I
know just as good as you that you don't want to be at this party a bit
more than the man in the moon."

I look up at her and don't have to say a word, but she sees a smile
forming at the corners of my mouth. She grunts, hands Benny back to
Bernice, and off we go, Lorraine pushing me, with Bernice holding
on to one side of the wheelchair, pacified now down to a few little
sniffs and snorts rather than screaming bloody murder. When we get
to her room, Lorraine settles her into a chair and pushes me right up
alongside of her, then turns on the television to a Christmas music
special with a group of four teenage boys that look like criminals singing "The First Noël."

"Now y'all behave in here, you hear?" Lorraine half scolds and squeaks back down the hall toward the party. Before she's out of sight good, Bernice is pulling on Benny's head all over again.

"Now hold on a minute, shug." I touch her arm lightly. "You're going to tear him all to pieces if you don't mind."

She is not to be deterred by anything I do and keeps on tugging until she finally has her hand down inside that monkey's mouth, all the way up past her wrist.

"What in creation are you doing, Bernice? You need to leave Mister Benny alone and settle down or they're going to send Mathilda down here to give you a pill."

Bernice lets out a loud laugh and yanks her hand out of Benny's throat, holding up her blue ribbon prize, another baby whiskey bottle. I nudge the door closed with my foot and wheel back around. She unscrews the tiny bottle top with her eyes set on me, grinning all the time. Now as I've already said, I do not touch a drop of whiskey, never ever. I do, however, partake of Bernice's miniature offering just to keep her sane and make sure we're left alone. Bernice grabs the remote control off her bed and uses Mister Benny's dirty yellow hand to turn the volume up as loud as it will go. The Christmas show has switched now to an ancient gray-haired man, perched on a stool, croaking his way through "Jingle Bells," while trying to snap his fingers along to a jazz band behind him. It's pitiful. He looks as bad as I do and can't snap worth a flip. Bernice takes the bottle back from me, gulps the rest of the liquid down, and stuffs the empty down into her housecoat. Without missing a lick, she reaches down into that poor monkey's intestines and pulls out another. "Christmas!" she screams out like a cheerleader, waving the bottle above her head. She kisses Mister Benny square on the mouth and holds him out to me to do the same.

I lean in close enough to give him a peck. "Merry Christmas, Benny! Merry Christmas, Bernice." I can't believe I kissed a monkey doll.

It startles both of us when Mathilda bangs on the door and pushes it wide-open with her usual tractor-trailer load full of medicine. "Sounds to me like you might want something to help you rest, Bernice, is that right?" she bellows.

"No ma'am." I speak up. "We're fine, thank you. In the Christmas spirit, that's all. How about you?"

"The party's over," she says without even trying to hide her sarcasm, then backs out of the room, an eighteen-wheeler on an interstate highway. Roll on.

"I'm going to go on to my room," I say to Bernice. "You lie down for a little while, don't you want to?"

"Benny's plum worn out." She sighs, pulling down the covers on her bed.

"I know he is. I'll see you after while."

Bernice blows me a kiss, then cackles, waving her fingers like a movie star to her fans. I wheel myself across the hall. I honestly feel like I can get out of this chair with nobody's help except Jack Daniel's, but I think better of it and ring the nurse's bell.

"Do you need anything else?" Lorraine asks after she gets me situated on the bed.

"No ma'am I don't," I say matter-of-factly. "I'm full of Christmas cheer."

"You're full of something else too, and you better be glad it's me that came down here." Lorraine turns off the light, squeaking down the hall like she always does. I'm not worried though, she's all talk. She'll be back in the morning, same as always, and I'll be where she left me.

CHAPTER THREE

RHONDA

M y car is one helluva sight, it looks like somebody's living in it. I haven't quite got to that point yet, but I did see a car yesterday at the Food Lion that made me wonder if somebody hadn't beat me to it. That thing was filled up to the windows with newspapers, magazines, clothes, and McDonald's bags, along with what looked like some T-shirts and underwear sprinkled around a pint-sized hole for the driver to sit in. I was tempted to sit there in the parking lot and wait and see who came out and got in that trash pile, but after about ten minutes, long enough to find my billfold and brush my hair out a little bit in the rearview mirror, I went on into the store. I loaded up my cart with the usual stuff, sugar, milk, eggs, a can of Maxwell House, but in the back of my mind I was still thinking about that car. Somewhere inside this store with me was the owner of all that mess, walking around just like I was, looking at hamburger buns and cereal and Cool Whip. A secret slob, and you probably wouldn't even know it to see her. I know it was a her because of the underwear. Unless it was a him that likes lace better than Jockeys. Now *that* made me real curious to figure out exactly who it might be by looking up and down at everybody I passed in the aisles. Especially their eyes. I started wondering if I coulda picked out Charles Manson before he ever killed anybody just by looking at him doing something innocent, you know, like picking up packs of chicken thighs.

Right now I ain't doin a thing but killing time, I know it, sitting in another parking lot about to freeze to death in my own filthy car. At a rest home, for God's sake. Hey, sometimes you do what you gotta do, isn't that what they always say? Well some people say it. And I keep telling myself that, especially today. Of all the ways I could spend my day off, you'd think this would be the last place I'd want to go. I don't know a soul in here. But I got a few ideas, that's my problem, and my ideas are gonna cost me some money, so I figure this is as good a way as any to get some. So what if I'm having some second thoughts, anybody would, thinking about working in a place like this. I'm gonna take my time. I don't want to go in yet, I'm gonna wait a little bit. It's just a job, right? No need to make it into more than that. Shit, I'm gonna have to get myself a better attitude.

There's a ring of bushes around a brick sign with white letters that spell "Ridgecrest" and the "i" is dotted with an orange sun. I was able to find a parking place way down on one end of the semicircle of a driveway. I ain't bothering nobody sitting here for a minute. How bad do I need the money anyway? I could work at the Target or somewhere, but I can't really see myself standing at a cash register selling eye makeup to high school girls and family-size boxes of Huggies to tired women in sweatpants. And the truth is too, I'll make more here, and I'll be doin what it is I do. Hair. That's my job. That's what I do the other six days of the week. This is about one thing to me. Cash on the barrelhead. All so I can have my own shop, and I will too one day, you watch. I got lots of ideas about how to design it and everything. I started pulling pages out of magazines and putting em in a drawer by my bed.

Damn, it's cold. My breath is steaming the windows up. I should get out and go on in, but I need to look around some more from where I am, out of the way, here behind my wheel. A black man in a uniform is sitting at a picnic table off to one side of the building, smoking and laughing with an older man in coveralls holding a rake, both of em without any coats on. I see their breath just like it was smoke, in between puffs. They're laughing awful hard at something. They get up when an ambulance backs up to the sidewalk. The doors open, and a bearded young guy and heavy woman in white get out and unload a gurney with somebody on it, blue-looking with a wild shock of white hair on top of his head. They're heading for a set of double doors at the front entrance. The coverall man grabs one of the doors for them, and the gurney disappears inside.

Last week sitting inside that building, I told the woman who interviewed me that I was comfortable around old people, and then I thought, hell I don't even know any old people. My grandma was definitely old, but I ain't so sure she was a person. More like a rattlesnake. Or an alligator. I don't think I'll freak out around any of em, unless they act crazy or wet themselves or something like that. Or if they die, that would be pretty bad, I'm really not into somebody checking out while I've got my hands in their hair.

There's prob'ly gonna be a bunch of em that can't even talk. That's all right with me. Might even be better that way. The last thing I need is a bunch of half-dead people trying to get into my business. And you know that's how they'll be. Asking am I married and do I have any kids. Well I can spare em the breath. One big old "NO" to all of the above and anything else they want to know about me.

Okay girl, do what you came here to do. I twist my body around with the seat belt still on and start grabbing plastic bags full of everything you can think of from the backseat. I have to bring my own brushes, blow dryer, curlers, all my equipment. The only thing they supply is shampoo, conditioner, water, and a couple of second-hand hair dryers that sound like they run on Chevrolet parts. And I know they're gonna have the cheapest shampoo you can find, but I can't afford to bring in the stuff I use at Evelyn's, where I work. She wouldn't give me a discount anyway even though I'm in that salon six days a week. She's like that. Nice to strangers but stingy with the people close to her. I never have understood that, oughta be the other way around. And there ain't no telling how long it's been since some of these women had their hair cut, much less colored. The director flat out told me that they'd been looking for somebody for three months because the woman they used to have got a divorce and moved to Tennessee with her three-year-old. "The patients thought a lot of her," the director said, sighing like she was talking about somebody who died, twirling her index finger around the rim of a red coffee cup that said "NC State Wolfpack." I thought she was trying to rub off the lipstick smears but she wasn't doing much of a job of it.

I do manage to get myself out of the car, but I open the door one more time and drain the last of the coffee from my travel mug. I could turn around and go home. I say out loud, "Rhonda, you can go home and open a Corona anytime you want to, it's your day off. You're the one who wants to have her own salon." That thought alone, sounding like a mean schoolteacher in my head, makes me move in the direction of the front door. It's weird, I can feel my feet on the sidewalk but they're going real slow like they're not attached to me. I wore boots with heels and I shouldn't have, but I'll change once I'm in there. I don't never wear heels this high except on a date, and even then I don't like em cause they hurt my little toe on both feet. I wish I had asked if they've got a drink machine. I always like to get something to drink about halfway through the morning. I'm usually coffeed out, but I do like a Sprite or something with no caffeine. They're bound to have a drink machine, they got a ton of people working here, and then the families too that come to see these people. Everybody gets thirsty.

There's nobody to open the door for me. The smoking men are long gone now. I wish I'da been smoking with em. I push my way through the first of two plate glass doors with a tiny foyer in between. A woman in a wheelchair is sitting in there, and how she got herself into that little room I don't know except by wedging her chair against the door to keep it open while she inched herself in. She smiles, she ain't got no teeth, then she reaches for my arm. I feel like she's a monster in a haunted house trying to grab at me. She makes a moaning noise that sounds like either "say" or "safe." I don't look back at her. I pretend I don't notice but she don't buy it and so she yells again. "Same!!!" it sounds like. I ain't got no idea what in the hell she's saying so I keep walking up to the nurse station. This whole thing is gonna suck, I can tell already. There's a couple of nurses inside a high circle of a desk messing with stacks of paper and file folders. I can't see a door in it right away and I wonder how in the world did they get in there, it's like a playpen.

"Can you tell me please ma'am where Ada Everett's office is?" I say to a woman with short cropped gray hair. She ought to color it and let it grow out some, she ain't that old, I think. She ought not to be walking around with those stubs on her head, she looks like she's been at Dix Hill, which is where they put crazy people who ain't got nowhere nicer to be put. I saw a picture of somebody with hair like that in a magazine, living up on the side of a mountain in a convent or some kind of a monk building, and I'll tell you one thing, that is not for me. The woman acts like she's waiting for me to say more. What else do I need to tell her? "I was here last week," I say, "but I can't remember where that office is to save my life." I'm trying to be pleasant even though it ain't exactly how I feel.

The woman points several times like she's stabbing air, puncturing something with a straight pin. "First door," she says, adding a few more quick finger points. What's she got to be so ill about?

Ada Everett is sipping from the same NC State mug I remember, flipping through pages of a date book. I bet she's looking for whatever it is she needs to fill in on the big plastic wall calendar outside her door. Last time I was here she was erasing off all the stuff that was either already over or canceled. She uses all different colors for movie night, art class, bingo, and I guess whatever else they can come up with for these people to do stuck in here.

"Mrs. Everett?" I move all my plastic bags into one hand and tap real light on the door frame. She does not look up at first. The phone startles her, and she answers, sort of pissed before she even says anything. I can tell from the way her nose is curled. It reminds me of Evelyn's Pekingese, Miss Dolly, named after Dolly Parton of course, that she brings into the shop sometimes.

"Yes. Yes." Ada Everett sounds impatient with whoever is on the other end. "I already told him we needed Dr. Hammond's approval." She rolls her eyes. "All right. Yes, please do." I wait in the doorway. Her expression changes like turning on a light in a dark room. "Oh hi," she says. "Rhonda, right? Yes. Welcome, Rhonda. Listen, you don't really have time to sit down. I believe I showed you the salon, didn't I?"

She is the most polite person I ever saw, even though she's trying her best to push me out the door. It sort of scares me, that kind of cheerfulness. I don't know why. You can't be part of it. Like maybe she's just had sex in a closet or something and is dying to tell somebody the secret, only the somebody ain't me.

"I wanted to check in with you first, that's all," I say. "I remember the way."

"Well that was kind of you dear, but you need to run on down there and get yourself organized. They'll start lining up in the hall soon, and I know they're all going to be so glad to see you. They'd much rather see you than me!" She laughs but it sounds like letting air out of a balloon in short spurts, a few short squeaks followed by a low sigh like she wore herself out.

I say, "Well I'll go on then," but I think, like hell they want to see me, they don't even know me, and I don't really want em to. I'm here for work, not to find a best friend. I already got one of those.

Outside the salon, there's a line starting to form exactly like she said. This many heads means I'm gonna be here all day. Damn. A woman with a cane stands up on thin legs, but she looks strong. She's got a strong mouth, it shows from the way she sets her lips. Her hair has been taken care of, that much I can say. I can't help it, I always notice hair, it's one of the first things I see, man or woman.

"Excuse me," she says. She is holding out her hand, and the veins make it look more blue than white. Pale blue like faded jeans against skin that looks like it ain't never seen the sun. I shake her hand. I've never shaken hands with a woman before, and her skin feels like it's barely hanging on the bones, saggy and thin. Her knuckles are big, she must have arthritis. She acts like she shakes hands with anybody in the world she takes a notion to, sorta proud and prissy together.

"I'm Margaret Clayton," she says. "You must be the new hair girl."

This woman's gonna make my life harder than it needs to be, I can tell. I don't think I like her. I want to use some shampoo and scissors, collect the cash, and get out. In fact, I meant to tell Ada Everett that I need to be paid in cash.

This old woman must be able to tell she's rubbed me the wrong way. "I don't mean any harm, honey, I call everybody a girl, doesn't matter how old they are. I call that woman right over there a girl too. The girl who lives across the hall from me."

She points to a woman only a few years younger than herself, clutching some kind of pillow to her chest. Maybe it's an old doll. I think she's talking to it. I'm thinking I'm gonna do just this one day since I'm already here, take the dab of money that goes along with it, and find me some other kind of job. Nobody told me there was crazy people in here. Just old people who can't no longer take care of themselves, that's what the job notice said. Now I already see one crazy one, and there's the one who's standing in front of me who might not be crazy but is bound to be trouble, I can smell it. Hey, I don't give a damn what people do as long as it don't cramp my style none. Live and let live, that's what I tell everybody.

"You waitin for a haircut?" I say. What a stupid thing to come out of my mouth seeing that we're getting ready to go in a beauty shop.

"I do need one," she answers. "Along with the rest of the state of North Carolina from the looks of it. Listen shug, you think you might be able to take my friend and me a little bit early? I know you don't open for another half hour, but it sure would make my back feel better not to have to sit for so long, and my friend there, well she's marching to the beat of her own drum, which right now, is a little tom-tom, but could turn into the timpani at any given moment if you know what I mean."

"Timpani?" I say before I think. I don't want her to know I don't know what that is. She's kind of fancy-acting for my taste.

She ain't even fazed. "We've got to take advantage of the peaceful moments. That's true for all of us, don't you think? What's your name?"

"Rhonda." I follow her into the salon and put on my apron. I reckon she thinks she's gonna be first come hell or high water.

"I knew a Wanda once." The woman sits herself down in the shampoo chair and starts to lean her head back. Her friend, the crazy one, is lingering in the doorway without coming inside. "Bernice honey, come on in," she says. "This is Wanda, come on and sit down. She's the new hair girl."

"Rhonda," I say, but she doesn't let on that she even hears me. What do I care if she knows my name, or if any of em know? They prob'ly can't even remember what day it is or who's the president.

"I'm going to stop talking, sugar, you just relax and do your work." She closes her eyes. "You don't have to worry about me distracting you for another second."

"No problem," I say, sort of automatic. The friend is sitting in a dryer chair, still whispering to her pillow with a face. I'm gonna get through today, that's it. I'm not making any promises about next week. I've got a good six days to think about it, I'll see how I feel then. This ain't nothing but a trial run.

The warm water splashes my hands and the old woman's forehead. I think she's fast asleep with a smile on her face, but she surprises me.

"That feels divine. We are so glad you're here, you have no idea," she says. "Thank you for doing this, we know you don't have to."

I *don't* have to, I think. But I'm here. My voice sounds softer. "I'm sorry, I forgot your name already."

"Margaret, you call me Margaret. You'll have plenty of time, honey, don't worry. We'll be here. That's an understatement, right Bernice?"

Her friend laughs and says, "Fine, thank you, and you?"

CHAPTER FOUR

MARGARET

One of the ugliest things God put on this earth is a tobacco worm. I know this from direct experience, as does anybody else who's ever seen one, so I'm not being judgmental about a fellow creature. One of my first memories is of just such a nasty thing as that. I am five years old, sitting in gray dirt between rows of tall tobacco with the flowers still on the plants, waiting to be topped. I am using a twig to poke at a big green worm with a pointed horn on its tail. It looks like a stinger, but it's not. Tobacco worms won't hurt you but they can sometimes be five inches long, and stepping on one barefooted in the summer is a disgusting mess. The workers have to pick them off the leaves by hand, they can't just brush them off or shake them loose. They might as well be glued on. I am hiding in this field from my sister Catherine, called Callie, three years older than me, because I have stolen part of her stash of candy out of her underwear drawer where she hides it. Why she hides it there I don't know because I always steal it. It looks like she'd have sense enough to move her treasure around, but some people would do exactly the same thing their whole life even if it were to kill them, which, depending on what the thing is, it sometimes does. When she finds me I will throw the worm on her, which will ruin her by leaving her in tears, and me too, because Daddy will punish me by making me sit in the chicken coop. I hate it in there because it smells like chicken shit, which should come as no surprise, but somehow is easy to forget until you find yourself sitting in the middle of it.

My daddy was the Reverend Reuben Driver Barclay. He owned several tobacco fields, all handed down to him by his own daddy who farmed his whole life. A couple of the bigger ones were near our house, but the rest were scattered patches of land all over Johnston County. Daddy was also a Baptist preacher, alternating Sundays between two or three churches. He had a man, Ardor Lee, who ran the farm and lived out in a shack way back on the edge of the field behind ours, but Daddy still went to the fields some part of every day. Ardor Lee didn't have a wife or children, he was a loner. His hair was a mixture of gravy brown and whitish-gray, along with raggedy whiskers, you couldn't really call it a beard, it was more like he only shaved once every two months. Callie said he wasn't right in the head, not bad enough to be put away, but still not right. Mother said, "Ardor Lee may not be as bright as you girls seem to believe you are, but he works harder than either of you ever will, so don't speak ill of him." Mother always chose to think the best of people and wanted us to at least try and do the same.

The fact is Ardor Lee did not like us. We didn't pay him any mind when we were little, but once we were older, he thought we were watching him all the time, and we were, because of his strangeness. I often saw him talking to himself when he was harnessing a mule, having a full on conversation like he thought that animal could answer him back. Ardor Lee didn't talk to any person much except Daddy. He might tell a field hand what to do, something Daddy had already told him, but not much beyond that. I never saw him say one word to Mother. He looked at the ground like he was scared of her, and my mother was the last person in the world anybody needed to be scared of unless they'd done something mighty bad. Ardor Lee did however yell at Callie and me if we even got close to his place. He'd been known to throw a rock at us too even though we never did anything but look. His house only had one window and he couldn't afford any curtains so it was wide-open all the time. Callie said one evening she looked in there and saw him with no clothes on and his hands on himself with his head back and eyes closed. She stepped on a dead pine branch that snapped and he saw her and yelled. I asked her if she told Daddy and she said no, didn't I know what Ardor Lee was doing, because if I didn't she sure wasn't going to tell me. And I didn't know exactly, but ever since then, he said things to scare us, like "Y'all girls better mind where you're poking around, there's a old woman lives in them woods who ate her baby, cooked him, and carved him up and ate him, and she's liable to do the same to you." If we told Daddy that Ardor Lee was trying to frighten us, Daddy said, "I don't know why you all don't leave that poor man in peace with all the work he's got. He hasn't got a soul in this world, and this farm is lucky to have him."

I knew we were not poor. We didn't have any money, nobody did, but even as a girl I could tell we had more than a lot of country people. My mother's maiden name was Raynor. Her father owned and ran O. D. Raynor Dry Goods store and saved every penny he ever made, so when he died, Mother sold the store and hid away all that she got out of it, pretending like she never had it in the first place. Her father did not at first approve of her marrying my daddy. He didn't envision his daughter as a farmer's wife, the only reason he gave in was because Daddy was also a preacher and that meant he was more educated than most of the country boys that would be hanging around Mother. Education meant something to Mother's daddy. Even though he didn't have more than a few years himself, he could add numbers like they were going out of style when he was buying and selling in his store. Mother says sometimes he didn't even write them down, he might look up at the ceiling for a minute and then come out and tell a customer what his total was.

My mother loved the land as much as she loved Daddy, she said she had to be on it. She said she was never as happy as when her hands were in dirt. That's what makes a woman born to be a farmer's wife. Also being a preacher's wife, she had to wash the dirt off herself every Saturday night and then, on Sunday morning, put on a long stiff dress and high boots, both of which suited her because she could have a kind of high and mighty way about her. Not that Mother looked down on people, far from it. I think it was her one aim in life to make folks feel like they all could do better if they only tried hard enough. My mother honestly believed that, and at times I saw that resolve as the hardest thing about her character, primarily because even as a young girl I knew that what she preached was simply not true. Some people try as hard as they are humanly able, and their lives never change at all. They are as empty-handed when they die as they were the whole time they were alive. Mother couldn't abide it; she could not accept that people couldn't rise above their lot in life with enough willpower, hard work, and faith.

When I got old enough, I worked every summer in one of Daddy's fields. I never did the backbreaking work of priming, but I helped at the barns, handling sticks at first, then learning from the black ladies how to grab handfuls of tobacco and shake them, looping them with thick white string onto a stick so they could be hung up on the rafters of a tall barn to dry out. I loved to watch those women pull the tobacco off the wooden sled when a mule sauntered up. They shook out their tobacco leaves like big fans in a rhythmic dance, and I tried to copy them but the leaves were huge and I shook so hard that I ended up dropping them all over the ground. The white women would have liked to scold me but they couldn't cause it was my daddy's farm, but the black women laughed out loud, especially the oldest one Glendolia, who had worked for my daddy's family almost her whole life. "Child, your daddy ain't gon have no crop left with you 'round here," Glendolia said and then swatted me on my rear end with her kerchief. The men worked harder than any person was ever meant to. Bending over pulling tobacco leaves, their hands covered in black gum that wouldn't come off, under July and August sun that was like a furnace planted square on top of their heads. More than a few times, I saw grown men fall over in the field. Daddy insisted that Ardor Lee carry water around to everybody, but the sun was not interested in the frailty of us living down here. Its one purpose was to burn, and an eastern Carolina summer is still proof positive of that. I prayed at night for rain so the workers could have a day out of the fields, but it never rained during those summers, never ever. Daddy only stopped work once that I recall, when one of the primers had a heart attack. Daddy didn't think the heart attack had anything to do with the heat, but he told everybody to go home anyway, he knew they'd all be thinking that it could have been any of them who died out there.

We always started before the sun came up. Mother stormed into Callie's and my room and woke us up at about five because we had to eat something and go with Daddy straight to the fields so he could start the morning out there before coming back at dinnertime and doing his preacher duties later in the day. I never liked to eat anything hot first thing in the morning and I still don't, but there was no arguing with Mother. The smell of breakfast wafted through the house in no time. Mother made her biscuits in a big rectangular pan. Daddy wanted fresh ones at every meal, so she threw the leftovers out three times a day. She wouldn't give them to Tally our retriever because she said that dog was already too fat to be as young as she was. I could have learned to put the biscuits in the oven by myself, but Mother always stopped me and took some buttermilk on her hands and patted them, all around the pan because it made the tops brown better.

She said to me, "Maggie, you can't forget the buttermilk if you want them to be pretty."

"What's pretty about a biscuit?" I answered, and Mother's face looked like I'd just told her that she was an ugly woman, suddenly sad and faraway. I understand that now. Whatever she was doing at any moment was not only the most important thing she could possibly be doing but she did her best to enjoy it and couldn't understand why other people might not feel the same. Most mornings I'd take a biscuit with some jelly on it for later on, once my stomach started growling. By the time the summer was over I was brown as a chestnut, just from being in the fields. Mother didn't particularly like us to be so tanned because while we were farmers, she didn't like the idea of us looking like field hands, especially as we got older. By the time she was thirteen, Callie was starting to look more like Mother in her body than like me. She left me behind with my flat chest and bare feet. She brushed her hair, showed signs of small bumps of breasts, and started wearing underwear on top as well as bottom.

A mixture of heat, dry dirt, tobacco, and bugs at night sums up all of my summers as a girl. Once in a while there was swimming in the pond if Daddy agreed to watch us because Mother was deathly afraid of water. More than once she warned my father, "Reuben you know exactly how I feel about those girls in that pond and yet you choose to let them swim in it. Lord have mercy on you if anything ever happens to one of them, I swear."

"You ought not take the Lord's name in vain, Sallie," Daddy answered.

"It's not in vain, I mean every word of it."

That was usually the end of it. We'd go to the pond with Daddy anyway, but what Mother said had definitely made an impression because anytime one of us put her head underwater, Daddy squirmed around on the bank until he saw us come up again, even if it was only a few seconds.

I have no doubt our parents had as many fights as anybody else, but the only other time I remember was when Daddy brought home a caramel-colored pony. I don't know where he got it, maybe I did at the time, but it seems like somebody gave it to him because they couldn't take care of it anymore and Daddy being the preacher, people gave him things lots of times. He was a pretty pony, but I didn't like to go around him because he made a snorting sound through his nostrils which sounded hateful to me. Callie on the other hand wasn't afraid at all and was ready to ride him first thing even though she had never done it before. That's where Mother stepped in and declared that no child of hers was getting on a strange pony that we didn't know and so help her if Daddy let one of us, he better plan on sleeping on a church pew because the only way he would step into the house was over her body lying dead in the doorway. Daddy did not challenge her. He ran the house and made every important decision as far as I could tell, but on the rare occasion that Mother put her foot down, he understood that the battle was not worth the casualties and simply moved on. Callie did not ride the pony, and within a couple weeks the pony was living somewhere else.

Every fall, I couldn't wait to go back to school. It was all I thought about the whole month of August. By the time I was fourteen there was no one else left in my grade. Farm children, if they went to school at all, only stayed long enough to learn how to write their names and read a little, then went back to work for their families. Daddy had taught me to read before I ever started school, mainly because I was always curious and asking questions when I saw him studying and writing notes for his sermons. I don't think he ever wrote out a whole sermon, if he did I never saw it, but he always made notes to help him think about what he was going to say, which is more than I can say for some preachers I have heard since. If I asked him, he would stop what he was doing and let me sit on his lap, and we would sound out words together from the Bible. I know now that he picked easy ones because there are still some Bible words I couldn't sound out if I had to, names of places, and people and rivers. I read anything I could get my hands on, which wasn't a lot because there wasn't any such thing as a library. The only books I got were presents now and then and the ones our teacher, Mrs. Eloise Grimes, would let me borrow. Her husband got killed by lightning in a bad storm and she never married again, but she had family up in Richmond and she went to see them about twice a year, which was a lot of traveling back then. She always brought back books. I think my eyes would be better now if I hadn't stayed up many a night squinting by a kerosene lamp. Callie only went to school because Daddy made her but had already stopped by the time she was my age. She could read as good as anybody, but she didn't care two cents about it.

Callie grew into as pretty a girl as ever lived. She had long light brown hair, almost blond, sometimes she braided it and other times wore it up on her head. To have spent her life on a farm, her skin was as pale creamy as a dogwood blossom, almost white. I myself had skin the color of ruddy earth, and hair to match. Some people still say I've got good color, I guess that means they can tell I'm alive. Callie's skin was so unusual people talked about it at church when she was dressed up or if we went into town. Callie was looking to get married if she could find someone she would have, and there were plenty of boys that took an interest in her. She wanted her own house and a bunch of children to go with it. At the end of the summer, picky as she was, after many a picnic and Sunday afternoon visit, she had decided on who it would be, Lawrence Adams, the son of Sanford Adams the banker. Lawrence hadn't asked her to marry him, but I could tell it was coming once he felt comfortable that she would say yes.

Ninth grade would be my last school year according to Mrs. Grimes. She said I had already done all the work and there wasn't anyone else at my level. After a few hot days, leftovers from summer, the leaves started to change. I loved seeing a patch of fiery red or shiny yellow in the middle of a thick bunch of pines. The greatest change was about to come in a way that my family would never get over.

I had been back in school for only about a month, and I was reading on my bed before supper. Callie came running into our room, wild-eyed, scared to death. She had dirt on her face and one sleeve of her dress was torn so her shoulder showed through, scraped and bleeding. "Callie?" I said, sitting up.

She threw her arms around me, "I didn't do anything, this is Daddy's farm. I can go wherever I want to, can't I?"

"Ardor Lee," I said. It came to me like daylight.

"I didn't do anything," she cried.

"Wait for me. I'm going to get Daddy." Mother was digging in her vegetable garden by the henhouse and shouted at me when I ran past her to the barn where Daddy always was at the end of the day before supper. When Mother saw us running together back to the house, she dropped her hoe on the ground and ran too.

The sheriff told Mother and Daddy they had been to every farm around, and that nobody had seen him. Ardor Lee's house still had everything that belonged to him in it, like he had gone to the outhouse and planned to be back any minute. Daddy said he wanted that shack burned to the ground, and he hired a man and his son to come haul off anything that wouldn't burn. Callie stayed in our bedroom and wouldn't come out; I wasn't allowed to go in either. Mother made me a pallet on the living room floor to sleep on, and every morning she got whatever clothes I needed and brought them to me.

I never saw my father look so sad, it was a sadness that would stay on his face for the rest of his life, in lines across his forehead and sunken eyes. He didn't preach that Sunday or the next. Nothing had to be explained to the congregation. What they didn't know they figured out. Weeks passed and I had the feeling that our life was different but didn't know how, it was like we were caught in a place where nothing happens except waiting, and everyone sucks in their breath and holds it, feeling like they might explode. Ardor Lee was gone.

In the middle of a November morning while I was at school, Mother found Callie lying at the foot of her bed. She had swallowed most of a bottle of poison. They did not let me see her, they thought the way she looked would be too upsetting for me, even after the undertaker got her ready to be buried. Daddy insisted on preaching his own daughter's funeral, even though Mother tried to get him to reconsider. I thought it might be the only thing that would ever make it real to him. Seeing the faces of the people in church told me they weren't listening to him, but feeling sorry, amazed that he could stand in front of them and talk about the love of God with what his own family had been through. We buried Callie when the leaves were all gone, and not a cloud was overhead, only plain blue sky going on forever. After the funeral, Mother went to bed for a month. She didn't speak to anybody, including Daddy, and didn't eat one morsel that I ever saw. Daddy went in every evening and sat with her by the light of a lamp. Sometimes he held her hand and read to her from the Psalms, then he'd leave her and come back into the living room to ask me about my schoolwork, and we would talk for a few minutes before both of us went to bed. There wasn't anything else to do once it was dark.

Mother's grief was a well that dried up so slowly that it eventually became useless to her, meaning that it had run its course and no longer had a purpose. With one of the first frosts of winter on the ground, she got up, bathed and dressed, went to the kitchen, and started cooking collards, the most pungent of greens. The whole house smelled horrible for days. The end of her sadness came because she willed it. She had taken a part of her heart and boxed it up for storage, sealed against damage or further wear, like a cherished bridal gown. The contents were still there, still took up space, but she would never open it again.

I miss my sister. I miss her in the summer. There aren't any more tobacco fields, at least none I can see. Farmers can't make a living. The same fields I worked and played in are shiny neighborhoods with twenty or more houses on what amounts to no more than a postage stamp of land. I can't catch up with all the change. I don't want to catch up. When August comes, hot as it ever was, I would give anything to be hiding from Callie, sitting in the dirt, digging my bare feet in deep enough to find a place that's cool and damp, eating candy as fast as I can so I won't have any left when she finds me, hearing her rustling through rows of tall tobacco, mad as a wet hen, looking for me. I can feel my heart speeding up as she gets closer. I don't move, don't breathe, I keep chewing. I can't wait to be found.

CHAPTER FIVE

LORRAINE

I get to church early when I can. April knows I like to have some time to myself before the service starts, so she don't make me late when she's home from school. If you'da told me I'd have a daughter in college one day, I would have said you'd lost your mind. Where was I gon find enough money for anybody to go to college and me working as a LPN? But the good Lord provides, because she didn't need my money or anybody else's. She got herself a scholarship and is sittin up there on her own in Raleigh at Shaw University. Says she's gon be a doctor. I want to tell her, "Being a doctor is a long ways off, child," but I don't. I don't want her to feel like whatever it's good to want is always gon be slightly out of reach. It don't matter that I'm tryin to protect her from being disappointed. Too many people think that way, and where in the world has it gotten them? So I want to say right here in the house of God, why not? Why not a doctor? Why not anything? If God ain't a God of "why nots" then I say why bother? And I don't think that's taking His name in vain, I think it's tellin the truth about what people need. We're all people last time I looked.

The choir's in front now, behind the pulpit. I look over at April and she's staring straight ahead. She loves a good choir. She always says the music is her favorite part of church. Mine too a lot of times, but I do like a good preacher when you can find one. They're harder to come by than they used to be, seems like. I didn't notice 'til now that April and I have both got on yellow. Hers is brighter than mine. I must look like a big old sunflower beside the first daffodil of spring.

Our God is a migh-ty God!

The choir sings the word "mighty" so short and loud it feels like something punching you in the stomach. That's what "mighty" ought to sound like, powerful. Like it takes your breath away, which is exactly what I expect would happen if we could get that close to God, which we can't. Thank God. I am in my usual place; all the regulars go to their own places. We're in a pew on the right-hand side of the sanctuary, about halfway back. I crane my neck to both sides to look around. Everybody in here looks real good, as good as they can, and it makes me feel good to look at em. All these women in dresses and hats, some with a pair of gloves on and a nice pocketbook in their laps so ladylike. Old men sitting dignified, and little two- or three-year-old boys in coats and ties. I feel so proud I sit up straight and adjust my hat to make sure it's on right. I've always believed in dressing to go to church, April can tell you. Workin at the rest home, I've been to too many churches and too many funerals with people wearing anything they want. My Mama taught me that when we dress up for church we set our hearts on things above, things greater than we can see. She said, "We're singing 'Glory Be to the Father' and at least we can try to look like we mean it." I love the word "glory" because as soon as you say it, you know it's bigger than you are. It sounds exactly like what it's s'posed to mean. Glory. You can't say it in a whisper even if you wanted to, you've got to shout it out. I think it makes people hold their shoulders different when they hear that word. It don't describe anything of this earth.

Reverend Knowles stands up to pray. He's seventy if he's a day, but he looks good to have lived hard as he has. "Good morning, saints, we are blessed this morning to gather together in the house of God. We are blessed to walk in freedom and the love of Jesus Christ. We are blessed to come before the Lord in praise and thanksgiving."

The first prayer is long because he has to go over the list of everybody who's sick. I swear that list never gets shorter, only longer, and when you notice that is when you best start kissin your youth good-bye, because it's on its way out whether you know it or not. I take a Kleenex out of my pocketbook and a piece of hard candy that I will open as soon as there's some noise to cover it up, not during the prayer. I'm usually praying too, but this morning I can't set my mind on it. April is praying when I peep over at her, at least she looks like she is, but I probably look like I am too unless somebody sees me messin with this piece of candy. I've been looking for my friend Althea but she's not in here. She might be feelin bad; she gets sour stomach a lot of times. I don't know exactly what her sour stomach is, but I think it has a whole lot to do with her sour husband. Lazy and mean is what they say. I don't know myself, the only time I see him is when I go pick up Althea if her car don't start. All I know is he moves real slow for somebody strong as he is, and I ain't got no use for a slow man.

People have often told me I ought to sing in the choir, but I say "If I go up there, who's gon sing out here with the rest of this sorry flock?" I'm joking, but I mean it too. There's nothing more depressing than standing in a congregation where a bunch of tone-deaf people are halfway moving their mouths to some sad organ music. Margaret Clayton's church is like that, she grew up Baptist like her daddy but changed over to Episcopal after she got married. She invited me to go with her one Sunday when she could still get somebody to pick her up and take her. I asked her about it after the service, and I didn't say it mean either, more like "Y'all don't like to sing too much do you?" but she fired back at me that anybody knows that's the way Episcopalians are.

"We are part of the Anglican choral tradition, Lorraine. The choir does the real singing. Haven't you ever heard of that?" she said, and she turned on her heels on those stick legs of hers and clicked down the marble aisle. I don't think she knows what she's talkin about.

Miss Margaret don't care a thing about going to church service at the rest home. She said there's too much Bible yelling for her taste, which is not the same thing as Bible reading. She said to me, "Lorraine, I don't know why anybody thinks that something is more important by virtue of the fact that it's screamed at the top of their lungs. You would think that God doesn't have anything to say unless it's hollered. Well I say no thank you, I'll take my church right here in my room." I don't agree with a lot of what Miss Margaret says, and I don't make it no secret either, but I don't like that yelling part of church any more than she does. Now Reverend Knowles don't do that, he can get fired up from time to time, but he don't make a habit of bein mad up in the pulpit. Maybe he's too old, but I like to think it's that he knows better. You can scare somebody into something one time, but if you want them to stay scared, you got to keep findin things for them to be scared of. Eternal damnation works for a lot of folks. Looks to me like both good and bad things happen whether you're scared or not. If you don't think so, go work in a nursing home.

Reverend Knowles asks if there are any prayer requests this morning, and I raise my hand without even stopping to think. "Mrs. Bernice Stokes," I say. "She's having a real hard time. Her mind's not good." April looks at me like she's shocked that I said somebody's name out loud to pray for.

"All right then. Thank you, Lorraine. Mrs. Bernice Stokes." He goes on gathering up names until he probably has ten or so.

"Who is that?" April whispers, sounding impatient.

"I'll tell you later. A lady at the nursing home." I put my hand on her arm and pat it exactly like I used to when she was a little girl talking in church. I took her to services from the time she was born, and people said, "How come that baby don't cry? It's like she's a grown up lady, minding her manners." April used to lie there and smile and gurgle, and once she could talk, she always whispered. That child was born knowing how to act around people.

The name of the sermon is printed in the bulletin: "Blessed Are the Poor in Spirit." I don't need to hear a sermon to know about that. I live with it every day I go to work. When you look at old people as much as I do, you can't tell sometimes what's gettin ready to die, the body or what's inside the body. It's a struggle to the end, which one's gon go first. I myself believe God wants our spirits to live free, even when it looks like there ain't that much left of them. That's why I don't say nothin when Bernice talks to a stuffed animal toy. Her daughter-in-law tries to snap her out of it sometimes, and none too nice, but I think, that's where her spirit is, and who knows what's in there with it, best leave her alone. Let her go, she'll come back if and when she's good and ready. I can't say that to Ada Everett even though she's my boss because she'd say mind my business and she'd be right, but when I'm by myself, I do what I think is the best thing for right then. That's how I find my peace, it might not be the perfect way, but I do what I can do.

Friday Miss Margaret wouldn't eat any lunch. When I told her she ought to eat something or she'd get sick, she perked up and said, "Lorraine, you and I have both been to church all our lives. Now tell the truth, what do you believe happens when we leave this earth? And I don't mean the Sunday school-approved version, so don't give me any made-up preacher talk."

"You don't have to worry cause I ain't a preacher."

"Well good, because I don't want the right answer. I want the honest one."

"I don't know nothin about heaven that you don't know."

"Tell me and I'll decide the truth of that statement."

"All right then. I don't know if it's a reward, like something you get when you retire. I think it might be going back to the way things always were, the natural state of things."

"That doesn't say much about saving souls, Lorraine."

"God knows who needs to be saved and from what. I don't."

"You haven't answered the question."

"When we die we're in one place and we go to another place and that's it. That's all."

"That certainly doesn't sound like what I hear preachers say on TV."

"I don't get my religion from TV."

"Well thank God. You are one of the few people left in this world who actually thinks for herself, Lorraine, and I simply could not stand to have that ideal shattered."

"My friend Althea believes that when we pass on, the rules are all different all of a sudden. Everything we thought we knew is either a whole lot more or a whole lot less complicated. Up is down, and down is up. No rules that we can recognize."

"I like the sound of that. I'm tired of the rules. We live with ones we make and too many that are made for us, and I'm ready to do without. I think the trick is knowing when you're where you're supposed to be, and letting go of everything else long enough to be there." Then she waved her hand in front of her face like she was erasing a chalkboard full of scribble. "Give me one of those Reese's Cups, will you, honey?"

I reached into the glass cookie jar that's her goody stash. "What makes you want to talk about God and dying, in the morning of all times? You've heard as many preachers as I have."

"Because Lorraine," she said, her mouth full of chocolate, "you've got faith." She stuck out her hand with part of the candy still in it. "I don't want the other one, it's too much. That's why I like the single Reese's Cups better, but seems like you can't get them anytime except at Halloween."

April is unwrapping my last piece of hard candy for me, I must have been rattling paper and didn't know it. She taps my arm and reaches out to me with candy in her open palm. It's about time the sermon's finished; my left leg is asleep so I pull myself forward with my hand on the back of the pew in front of us and uncross it. I can't tell you what Reverend Knowles talked about this morning, I'm thinkin too much. Mama used to tell me, "Lorraine, you think too much when you're in church, that's not the place to think, just listen and learn." I disagreed with her then and I still do. I am proud to death to have April here. She looks so content and happy. I think she really is happy. I look at her hair, her hands folded in her lap, my heart feels like it's gon bust open.

"Sing, choir." Reverend Knowles's arms are raised, his robe draping down makes him look like an angel wearing purple.

I don't feel no ways tired . . .

Everybody in the front is swaying to the music, some people in the congregation have got their hands up.

I've come too far from where I started from . . .

"Sing children, praise God." Reverend Knowles keeps on talking over the choir.

Nobody told me that the road would be easy . . .
I don't believe He brought me this far . . .
I can't believe He brought me this far . . .
I won't believe He brought me this far to leave me.

"Oh no I won't, no. I don't feel no ways tired." Reverend Knowles's voice is like medicine. "We've all been through more than we ever thought we would. And some of us have suffered more than anybody ought to have to. I have seen my share of suffering in the faces of many I love, some of them sitting here this morning."

I spot Althea way in the back, I don't have any idea when she came in. She points to her watch and makes a frown, mouthing "I'm sorry" real exaggerated so I can see her. That's all right, she made it. Everybody in here this morning got up and made it.

"Will you keep on walking, children?" Reverend Knowles has left the pulpit and is standing down front. "When your hope is gone, will you hold your head up and walk? When it's time to move, my sisters and brothers, as long as we've got legs, then praise God let us learn to use them. One more step, one more day. Sing now, choir."

I don't believe He brought me this far to leave me.

I do love the sound of this song. Althea's arms are up in the air over her head, swaying back and forth with everybody else, her gaze is lifted and eyes are closed. I reach over and put my hand on top of April's and when she looks up, I stare straight out in front of me, smiling like I'm encouraging the choir. I am, I reckon, in my way.

CHAPTER SIX

MARGARET

I have been sitting in the dining room cutting hearts out of pink paper and gluing them to squares of red construction paper for two hours. I've only done five. It takes me a long time to use scissors, my fingers don't go into the handles the way they're supposed to. I know how scissors are supposed to feel. Something's wrong with these. It's good for me to move my hands; if I don't, arthritis is going to take over completely and then I won't even be able to write my name. Bernice is making small hearts out of paper lace and gluing them onto flowerpots with tulips in them. I don't know where they got tulips this time of year. They don't look that healthy but any kind of fresh flower is nice. I have never been someone who liked silk flowers. Part of the whole reason for flowers is not just the way they look, it's bringing the outside inside, the smell, even the occasional bug that comes in with them. I've never seen Bernice so focused on anything, she is taking her time, cutting the shapes perfectly, putting just the right amount of glue on, and lining the hearts up evenly all around the outside of the pots. It makes me think that she must have kept a beautiful house when she was able. Her work is so neat it makes mine look like a five-year-old's. Ada Everett asked me to help with the Valentine's decorations and I said no, I was sure I didn't have anything to offer, but she told me Bernice was helping, and I thought if Bernice is doing something then I have no excuse.

Candy hearts on the table say things like "Be Mine" and "Hot Stuff." Neither of these sayings speaks to me. I'm past both of them, for different reasons. There are also ones that say "Cutie-Pie" and "Kiss Me," both of which are truly wishful thinking in this place. I would love to find one that said, "Massage My Feet" or "Hot Soup." Those are some meaningful messages. I tried to eat one of them, but they're too hard. They don't taste good enough to suck on, and if you try to chew one you'll break a tooth or a denture or make your gums bleed. Ada Everett ought to know better than to give us this kind of candy when we'd be better off with a coconut chew.

Bernice has changed projects and is making a heart that has tiny cutouts in the shapes of diamonds, clubs, hearts, and spades. It's like a Las Vegas valentine.

"Why are you doing those shapes, honey?" I ask.

"Anybody in here like to play poker?" she holds the nearly completed heart up to her face and peeks one eye through a club-shaped cutout.

"Not with you they don't because you always win."

"Alvin taught me real good. I can teach you."

"The only time I see Alvin is when one of the nurses is looking for him to do something that he was already supposed to have done. I guess now I know where he spends his free time."

"Alvin's real good at cards," Bernice goes on undeterred.

"Evidently."

"Have you got some valentines?" Bernice asks with her eyebrows raised, looking over at my pitiful pile of work.

"I'm sorry to say I've only got five, and only four usable." One of them is shaped more like a potato than a heart.

"No. Real valentines," Bernice giggles. "Sweethearts."

"You're my only valentine, Bernice, you know that."

"Well that's sad then because a valentine is somebody you hold in your heart. That's why I'm making hearts. I've got lots of hearts."

She is pushing for something and I don't know what. I search for what to say. My husband was a good man. I did not love him, but he was good. I reckon I was waiting for a real valentine, and what I found was Charles Clayton. We married; that's what a person did. And we made a life together, that's also what people did. My heart never changed, but it did soften, with time, and I found some room for him in it that I didn't know I had. I don't really feel like talking to Bernice in one of her crazy spells right now.

"Won't you be my valentine? I will be your valentine." Bernice is singing to herself a tune that sounds vaguely like "Old Dan Tucker." She sings the same two lines over and over and I think I might lose my mind but I don't want to tell her to stop because she's smiling and happy.

"Who is your valentine then, Bernice?"

"Mister Benny."

"I know that. Who else?"

"Everybody."

"That's not an answer." I try her out, not knowing whether she'll keep going.

"I love some people. They don't know but I love them."

We are silent now. It's as though she said something meaningless and profound at the same time. I look at her and see my sister. My Callie, whom I would like to tell that I love her. I focus all my attention on the construction paper and glue in front of us. So much paper, as many memories. Bernice and I are making valentines for people we barely know.

Down the hall, the same hall where we live, there's a sixteen-year-old boy. He was in a car wreck. No drinking, no drugs, he ran off the road with some friends late at night after a football game. One of them died. Jamie will never move anything but his eyes ever again. He will spend the rest of his life here. I know his brain works fine because I see him respond when his mother takes his hand and tells him "If you don't get a haircut I'm going to stop speaking to you."

I used to wonder why Jamie wasn't at some other place where there were young people, people like him, rather than in a nursing home with the ancients, but there's not such a place anywhere close by. This way, his mother is here every day like clockwork, lots of times his father too.

Once in a while, they put Jamie on something that looks to me like a combination of a wheelchair and a stretcher, and for a change, bring him out into the lounge. Yesterday his preacher came, I didn't know preachers made visits for Valentine's Day, but there he was, with his wife and a bunch of red carnations in a green vase.

"Are any of these nurses flirting with you?" she said in a real loud voice and then laughed even louder.

Lorraine looked at me with caution in her eyes. She knew what was going through my mind. I know they mean well, but when I hear something like that I feel like I'm going to cry. I want to scream out the truth that we make ourselves dance around because we don't know any other way to get through. Jamie will never flirt with anyone, not in a way that they will know it, and if anyone does with him, it will only be out of pity. That child, alert as he ever was, is trapped in a body, and I would trade my own body for him to get out of that withering shell and live like every sixteen-year-old should. He needs to be able to make his parents mad, figure out who he loves, find out what he can do and what he can't, make mistakes that he doesn't have to pay too dearly for. Instead Jamie lies still, his boyish skin touched by his parents or a rare visitor, or by the brash arrival of a cheap washcloth cleaning him up because he is authorized to be bathed in bed rather than taken in a heap down to a room where the shower and the tub are, stainless steel like a factory or a morgue.

"Won't you be my valentine? I will be your valentine," Bernice sings.

"Honey, I love you, but you have to stop. Please stop," I say, and she does, but I occasionally hear her humming under her breath. I have stopped working on my sixth valentine. I feel like a fool cutting paper. Why do holidays have to be parties, all of them? Not everything is a party.

"Bernice, there's going to be a change of plans. We're going to decorate Jamie's room. What do you think?" I feel excited, spontaneous.

"What are we putting up?" she asks.

I look around us at the crepe paper, hearts, and helium balloons blown up by Ada's husband using a big metal tank. "All this, every bit of it," I tell her.

"The whole party?" she asks, but she's not really asking because she is already gathering up all the decorations and some things that are not decorations like salt and pepper shakers and bottles of toothpicks in her arms and putting them in the empty cardboard box that originally contained all the supplies.

The door to Jamie's room is closed. That most likely means he's sleeping or getting a bath or having a diaper changed. We start to go back to the dining room when the door swings open and Lorraine puts a rubber wedge under it to hold it.

"What are y'all doin? I thought you was decorating the dining room this morning," she says.

"We'd like to decorate in here, Lorraine. Are you with us or against us?"

Bernice pipes up. "We're giving him the whole party."

Lorraine is standing in the doorway. "Ada Everett knows what y'all are doin?"

"No ma'am, without question, she does not," I answer.

"Hmm." Lorraine steps aside. "All right then." She can't help grinning in spite of herself.

Bernice starts riffling through long strands of crepe paper, while Lorraine tries to keep it untangled. I attempt to direct them. "Now don't put too much pink, Bernice, he's a boy." I hesitate. "I don't know, never mind, maybe he likes pink, so just do what looks good."

Bernice says to Lorraine, "We need you up high," pointing to the ceiling.

"Yes Lorraine, please," I add.

"I got to put on some lower shoes before y'all get me climbin up on things." Lorraine scurries out. "Y'all wait for me, I mean it now."

Jamie is wide-awake, his eyes darting, dancing. I could swear I see a smile. I lean down to him. "We're giving you all the valentines in this place, honey."

Bernice leans down too. *"Won't you be my valentine? I will be your valentine,"* she sings. Jamie's eyelids flicker, and Bernice takes hold of his limp hand and sings again. I tape our construction paper and lace cutouts all over the wall, and a potato-shaped heart onto my blouse. The party is starting early this year.

CHAPTER SEVEN

APRIL

The Asian woman at the desk said, "You go right back, it fine. You find her back there," without looking up from her work, which seemed to be dominated by a large chart and Sharpies in several colors, all very neat and orderly. "She working on B Hall. You find her."

"Which one is B again?" I asked, leaning slightly over the top of the high reception desk. I had forgotten the layout.

She burst into a giggle, then composed herself immediately, "Over there, no problem. You see?"

Whenever I came home from Shaw on a weekend, Mama let me use her car on Saturday to run errands as long as I promised I'd be on time to pick her up after her shift. On this rare occasion, I was early. I thanked the receptionist and pointed again to B Hall to reiterate, waving to her as I walked away.

The hall was lined with railing to prevent falls, and a linoleum floor was easier to clean than carpet, as well as being an optimal surface for wheelchairs. Some patients pulled themselves along in their chairs via hand over hand movement, clasping the rail as tightly as they could with arthritic wrists and fingers. Less skilled drivers often banged into the wall, which was why the floor molding was brown rubber, marred by countless bumps and bruises.

I had been here so many times that the smell didn't bother me the way it used to, as if it were something that one could ever really become accustomed to. The most pronounced odor was that of a strong citrus-infused bleach that masks the ubiquitous presence of urine. It is a smell that is found in this particular form of offense nowhere, as far as I can tell, except nursing homes.

On each door was a Magic Marker cartoon drawing—a star, a teddy bear, a rainbow, there may have been other shapes as well. Mama told me the importance of these when I was still in grade school after I had managed to take some of them off the doors and was adding my own creative expression via crayons. I understand now that they are a code to remind nurses and clue new staff into special needs or problems of the patients. A star means to check dietary notes before allowing them to eat anything other than prescribed meals. Mama said she had once seen a new aide sit watching reruns of game shows while a newly diagnosed diabetic man helped himself to a bag of bite-size Snickers bars that somebody had brought in. The teddy bear, if I remember correctly, means that the patient isn't ambulatory, often she can't get out of bed. And I definitely remember the rainbow because it showed up in at least one or two new places every time I came here. It is the code for a patient who has signs of senility or outright dementia. Mama said most of her coworkers didn't look forward to dealing with "the rainbows," but she didn't mind. She said it was harder on her nerves some days, but she wanted to think that she could help make up for some of the psychological health they might be lacking by making sure they were physically comfortable in any way she could and that the establishment allowed. More than a few times, I suspect she offered help in the form of things the establishment did *not* allow if she felt strongly enough about what kind of help was needed.

I was three-quarters of the way down B Hall when I heard Mama's voice. "Mathilda, are you out there? I need some help please."

I laughed. I knew enough stories to know that Mama didn't care for Mathilda. She called her "Mean-tilda." "Mean 'til da end of time" were her words.

"Sorry to disappoint you," I answered her. "I thought you'd be ready to go." I had started speaking while in the hall and turned into the doorway only to stop dead still. Mama was standing by a bed with an elderly white woman lying in it, or rather, sprawled awkwardly on top of it. The covers were pulled back and the woman's pajamas and underwear had been pulled down to her ankles. She was completely naked, gray flesh hanging on knives of bone that were her ribs and hips. Mama was wiping her with what had been a white cloth, now covered in near-liquid brown shit, as were the rubber gloves Mama wore. The stench hit me like a towering wall falling apart, I felt immediately nauseous. Instinctively, I turned away and saw that the sheets piled at the bottom of the bed were also stained all over with dark splotches of diarrhea.

Mama spotted me and did not say hello. "Honey, pull that curtain. Mrs. Clayton had an emergency." I was frozen in disgust. "Go on now. Pull it and wait for me in the hall," Mama instructed, sensitive but undeterred. I felt myself gag as I pulled the curtain around the woman's bed. Walking to the door, I heard Mama's labored moan. No more than a few seconds elapsed, and she grunted again. Instead of racing into the hallway, or even back to the car in the parking lot, I couldn't move, thinking something might be wrong. "Mama?" I meekly asked and took steps back toward the bed. I pulled the curtain back only slightly and saw Mama bending over the prostrate woman, using her full weight to try to raise the woman up far enough to pull off the soiled bottom sheet and replace what looked like a square thick pad underneath it. Mama, sweating glass beads on her forehead, succeeded in rolling the patient onto her side, at which time the woman's eyes landed on me. At first it occurred to me that she had died until I saw her face, leaking more humiliation than I thought possible for a person to feel, outside of being beaten or raped. I was sure she would speak. I prayed she would not speak.

I shouldn't be here, watching her, I thought. No one should watch this. I wanted to be invisible, but there was also a curious part of me that wanted to hear what she would say. Would she yell at me, rightly so, for intruding on her privacy? Would she cry out in pain, because even though my mother was strong and doing the best she could, it could not have been comfortable to be wielded and maneuvered like a side of beef? Maybe the woman would curtly tell me to help, anything to bring a more immediate end to her embarrassment and physical misery. Instead she said nothing, her large damp eyes fearful, like an animal going to slaughter. My mother couldn't hold her, and I watched her fall back onto the waterproof pad before Mama had gotten her cleaned up properly. I wondered why she had put a clean pad down, but no sooner realized that if she hadn't done so, a thin mattress cover that looked like wax paper was the only thing protecting the bed. The mattress should be covered in plastic, why didn't they plan for these things? Maybe it was covered, I don't know, my hands were sweating. I felt sick, I wished I had never eaten food. I wanted to touch the woman's hand, I had the urge to pull the curtain closed, but I couldn't make myself do it. Mama was wiping between the woman's legs, spread fleshy and gray with knots for knees. All the while she continued looking at me, her mouth slightly open, a fine line of saliva running from one corner. That spit made me mad, I wanted her to wipe her mouth. I understood that she couldn't help what had happened but at least she could wipe her own mouth. Then I immediately saw that she couldn't because one of her weak arms was pinned underneath her side while Mama stood between her body and the other arm, still cleaning her with moist baby wipes.

"I'm almost finished, Miss Margaret. You hold on now and don't you worry about it. You just need to get yourself cleaned up here and then you're gon rest and you're gon feel better. Don't you think one more thing about it. Maybe I'll bring you a Co-Cola directly and the bubbles might help your stomach some."

The woman sounded so exhausted that almost no sound issued when she finally managed to move her lips. "No Lorraine. I don't want it."

"That's all right then. I'll bring it and put it by your bed so you can have it later." Mama was drying her hands at the sink and returned to the bed to pull the woman's pajamas back up. "I know how you are and if I don't bring something, your mouth is gon be gettin dry, and you'll be buzzin that buzzer all night, only I won't be here."

"Where then?" the woman asked, barely a whisper.

"My baby girl came to get me, she's home from Shaw for the weekend. She's gon graduate, you know, come May."

"I declare I didn't know she was that old." The woman looked more comfortable now, covered in new sheets and a soft-looking blanket. She looked like she might fall asleep any minute, which was probably as good as anything for her.

I knew I would not leave without saying something. I needed to let her know that her privacy was a sacred thing, that I would never mention even to my mother what I had seen. I could only think of her searching eyes, scanning the room. I knew she wanted to flee. I also knew that she used to stand and dress and go out to dinner and chat with other ladies, and carry a purse and wear shoes. I knew that she used to send Christmas cards and wrap birthday presents. That she knew what it feels like to laugh until you start to cry. That she used to plan her tomorrows by herself. Her eyes revealed everything.

"Mama?" I pulled the curtain open slightly wider.

"I thought you prob'ly went to the car. You been waitin out there?"

"I wondered if I could help you."

"Baby, it's against the rules for you or anybody but family to help us. Insurance." The woman in the bed was looking at me to see what if anything I was going to do. My mother broke the silence of anticipation. "This right here is Mrs. Margaret Clayton, she's one of my patients. Miss Margaret, this is my daughter I was telling you about. She's home from college. Says she might be gon go to medical school, now ain't that something?"

The woman opened her eyes wider, more energetic. "She might have it in her, Lorraine, judging from looking at her. What's your name, shug?"

"April." I didn't like her calling me "shug." It was too familiar.

"You're April and you graduate in May," she continued, rather satisfied with her own wit.

"Nice to meet you." I started to put out my hand but retreated and I'm not sure why.

"Nice to know you too, April. Now y'all go and get on with your business."

Mama half snorted. "I thought we might go have us something to eat this evening, but April don't want a thing in this world but for me to cook, ain't that right, baby?" I didn't have time to answer.

"Well you need to bring me some of whatever you make, Lorraine, that's what you need to do, even though I can't imagine not wanting one of the delightful entrées that are on the menu here."

"You feelin better already, I'm gon leave you."

"If you don't, I'm going to start telling April the truth about you."

Mama dimmed the light and turned on the lamp by the bed. "All right then. You want to watch TV?"

"Put it on without sound. I'd rather look at them running around and try to figure out the story myself."

"I'll see you tomorrow."

"Lord willing. Come here a minute shug, before you go." It was clear she was talking to me. I looked to Mama, who nodded in the direction of Mrs. Clayton, and I obliged. I did not like a white woman calling me "shug," but I tried to relegate it to a generational difference and leave it at that. She crooked her finger and I leaned down to her, apprehensive.

"You take care of your mama, she needs to be loved back for all she loves. And I do like your name."

Mama knocked on the door to get our attention. "That's enough you two. April, don't you listen to a thing that woman tells you. She'd just as soon lie as look at you." Mrs. Clayton laughed like a teenage girl, and I could for the first time believe she had been one once.

CHAPTER EIGHT

RHONDA

I recognized Bernice at Ridgecrest as soon as they told me her name was Stokes. She woulda never known me, we never even met, but something clicked when I looked at her. I sure never dreamed I would know Wade Stokes's mother, especially not after so many years. And with what happened.

Evelyn's is closed Monday mornings like a lot of beauty shops, but I was going in by myself because I had a lady coming for an eight thirty appointment. I told her I'd do it because she was leaving a few hours later to go to a wedding in South Carolina. Mrs. Twiny Allen. She must have been in her late sixties then. First time I ever shampooed her hair, she told me her real name was Elaine, but that everybody had called her Twiny since she was in school. She was twiggy and tiny so they called her Twiny. It was easy for me to remember cause her hair had so many permanents it was like worn-out rope. Twiny, she made me call her that, started talking as soon as she walked in the door. She loved to talk and I was glad for it cause at that time of day I'm a better listener than I am anything else. "How you been, Miss Twiny?" I asked. "You want to hang your coat up?" That's usually about all I had the chance to say for the whole two hours I worked on her head.

"Thank you for coming in, Rhonda. Have you ever? This rain? A wedding on a day like this? Can you picture? I declare."

She always spoke real fast in a string of questions, firing at you like a machine gun. There wasn't any need to answer, you didn't have time to, and she didn't expect you to.

"I'm afraid we're going to have a sad bride, that's all. Sad on a wet wedding day." Twiny Allen clucked her tongue and looked out the plate glass window in front. I've never liked that window but Evelyn said she needed light in her beauty shop and that having it open would help attract new people because they could see us all in here talking and carrying on, and that's one thing people looked for in a hair place.

"You want color today?" I wasn't in the mood to talk about brides and flowers, I'da rather been still asleep.

"Yes darlin, I will wear chestnut brown to my grave."

"If I'm still here I'll make sure you do, Twiny."

She put her head back in the sink and I turned on the hot water, testing with my hand before wetting her hair. I looked down at her closed eyes. This is a position that is so familiar to me, seeing someone lean their head back into my sink with their eyes closed. They look peaceful, like they can let go of everything for a few minutes, not think about anything, and let somebody take care of them by running water through their hair and fingers over their scalp. The breathing changes too, the face changes. I take my position serious, I feel like they trust me. Twiny looked like she'd already gone to heaven, and it made me think what a lot of comfort you can give to somebody without doing all that much. Her eyes fluttered some, maybe I splashed her, so I wiped her forehead lightly before she sat back up.

"That's the best I've felt all week long," she said, trying to cover up a yawn.

"Well good, I'm glad. Good." I helped her up to the other chair where I cut hair.

"How've you been, Rhonda? I don't see you much."

"You know, Twiny, you oughta come every four weeks, I could do you a whole lot better if you wouldn't wait so long."

"I know, I know, I will. You're sweet."

I knew she wouldn't come more often cause she didn't want to spend no more money. When I raised my prices two years ago, Twiny was one of the only customers to say anything. "Well, this makes it harder doesn't it, to come so often I mean. I know everything in this world costs more, but I thought some of the more personal services would be more consistent. You know I heard at my bridge meeting that Hair Village only charges thirty dollars for cut and color. That's a good deal. Not that I would go there though. It's not convenient to where I live."

Twiny went on, flipping through a *People* magazine and not looking at it, much less reading it. "So, Rhonda, how are you, dear? Everything all right? Anybody special these days? Anybody I might know? Did you see the front page? It makes me never want to get in a car again. That man had everything in the world, college professor, book just about to be published. I think he was about your age, went to school right here before he went on to Chapel Hill."

Her hair was a tangled mess. It wouldn't have killed her to run a brush through it every so often. I only cut a little and got on with her color. "I don't take the paper," I said, working away. "Evelyn usually brings it down here."

"Did you know him, Rhonda? He looked about your age."

"I didn't see it, Twiny."

"Well it was horrible. He was a Stokes. His daddy's been dead for years. Gardner Stokes Contractors, very successful, he made a killing in construction. I thought y'all might have been in school together."

"Wade?" I said the name and waited for Twiny Allen to say, "no, that's not it." Instead she answered, "I don't know. I don't think so."

I took off my rubber gloves, tossed them in the sink, and left Twiny in the chair with color solution on her head. "Sit still, Twiny. I'm gonna run across the street to the drugstore. I won't be but a minute."

I saw the headline before I could get the paper out of the wire rack. NATIVE BORN ACADEMIC AND WRITER DIES IN HEAD-ON COLLISION. There was a picture of Wade from high school beside one of him from the present and I thought, "Why'd they put that old yearbook picture in there? He left, are y'all never gonna get it?"

The caption read:

> BENJAMIN WADE STOKES died early last night at the hands of a drunk driver in downtown Raleigh. He was traveling alone while visiting his mother, Mrs. Bernice Stokes, in the Cameron Village area. According to Mrs. Stokes, her son had gone out on an errand for her and never returned. The driver of the other car, a Virginia man in his mid-60s, survived with minor injuries and was taken to Rex Hospital. The survivor was accompanied by his two-year-old granddaughter, who was killed on impact (names withheld pending notification of the child's parents).

I stared at the picture and read the same words over and over like I was gonna see something new. Nothing though. Died. That was all.

Even now I hope he didn't suffer. I think Wade Stokes was somebody the world oughta have spared suffering. Somebody as kind as he was oughta be able to build up a savings account to pay off their own pain before it happens. I don't need nobody to tell me it don't work that way. But it makes me feel like I want to do everything right now, while I can. I got a long list of things I want to do. I'm gonna go to Mexico one day and I'm gonna ride a horse on the beach like you see in magazines. I'll tell em I want to ride a different horse every day, and I might even stay down there. Once they see how much I know about horses, they'll prob'ly offer me a job at the Club Med of Mexico, or I could be in charge of all the horses in all the Club Meds and get to travel around and show people how to train them, and teach people to ride. I'd be real gentle. I'd tell them, "Don't worry, it's goin to be fine. Nothin's gonna happen. I'm goin to stay right here beside you, just hold on." Sometimes the hardest thing is holding on, when you feel this huge force of movement under you that's not part of you. No matter what, you don't have total control of it.

Thank God there was a wall clock behind the pharmacy counter. I was in a total daze. I flew back across the street with the newspaper still in my hand and flung the door open, sending it slamming into the magazine rack in the waiting area. "Twiny, I'm sorry!" I shouted before I was even inside good.

"My scalp feels like it's on fire! Are you trying to skin me alive?"

"I know, I am so sorry." I was crying but she didn't see.

"Rhonda, you know I try to support you, I do, but you're making it real hard, you know that, you really are. Don't bother rolling it; just blow me dry with a brush. I have *got* to go."

"It won't take but two minutes, I promise." I ran warm water over her head, rinsing streams of dark color down the drain. I pushed the back of the chair up to towel her hair and turned towards the mirror, away from her, to wipe my eyes on a clean towel. I was thankful for the roar of the blow dryer. I didn't have to say anything else. The hot air felt good on my hands and face, drying everything off.

CHAPTER NINE

MARGARET

From the moment I woke up, I had the feeling something was off. Ann came in first thing in the morning with a Mother's Day bouquet of cut flowers. I usually like cut flowers, but I don't like carnations, and her basket was overflowing with them. Blue ones. A color of blue that doesn't exist in nature, only in a box of crayons. I think that's the reason I don't like them, nothing against carnations even though they are sort of the trailer park of the flowerbed. It's more that I don't like anything that doesn't look natural, and that includes food and hair color. I insist on still coloring my hair, but I try to keep it at least somewhat believable. It has never been gray, so I can't think of a reason to let it go now. Unfortunately, Beauty Shop Day only comes once a week, and if you happen to be sick or asleep during the allotted hours, that's too bad. It's usually on Sunday, starting first thing in the morning. Some people skip breakfast altogether to get there first. Those that can make their way by foot or wheelchair down to the Salon, and I use that term loosely, where we line up down the hall and wait our turns.

I used to get Rhonda's name mixed up for the longest time, but a few weeks ago, she stopped brushing my hair and leaned over a few inches from my face, tapping her name tag with a pointed orange fingernail. "It's Rhonda," she said flatly. "Spelled like Honda with an *R* in front of it." I don't think she likes that I might call her the wrong name, even though I don't mean to, because sometimes she's real rough when she's teasing my hair. Not that it's an easy job. My head is like a rat's nest after wallowing around on a bed for hours every day.

I do not skip breakfast on Mother's Day to go to the Beauty Shop line. I woke up with an appetite, and that has come to be something I do not take lightly. "I'll get there when I get there," I say to Lorraine when she brings my tray into the room.

"Fine with me. Long as you get your hair fixed cause you're too mean to live when you don't."

There are two sinks in the Salon. They do not match. One's pink and the other one is tan, leftovers I imagine from some closed-down hair place. There are also only two hair dryers, the old-fashioned chair kind that looks sort of like a spaceship that you could fly off in if you knew how to drive it. Most of my neighbors and I have the same hairstyle with only a slight variation. It's basically fluffed up and perfectly round, and a little hard to the touch. I like that way of wearing my hair because it looks like the hair of a person my age. There's nothing that'll take your breath away like a woman with the long blond locks of a twenty-five-year-old and the face of a mummy.

I watch a little TV while I eat my toast. I like to see the weather. It makes me feel like I know what's going on in other places. They always show what the day is going to be like in places like Portland and Denver and San Antonio. I love to travel and I have no idea where I got it from. My daddy never went anywhere in his life except one trip to a cattle convention in New York City. I can't imagine why there would have been a cattle convention in New York, but I think maybe because having a convention in a fancy city made it appear serious and important, much more so than it ever could have in somewhere like Topeka. I myself have been to New York two times. And I've been all up and down the eastern seaboard. I love that word "seaboard." I like any word that makes me think of the ocean. Dune. Tide. Gull.

Squall. They're all water words. Water moves and flows into every nook and cranny, and there's nothing you can do to stop it. I like that kind of flow. One time I went to London for a week with my husband Charles. We saw everything. The Tower, Parliament, Westminster Abbey, all the famous sites. I could walk a whole lot better then, and Charles said he couldn't keep up with me, which to tell you the truth, didn't bother me all that much. The tour guide, a pretty British girl, told us to be prepared, it might rain the whole time, but there turned out to be a heat wave. She kept apologizing for the temperature and I told her, "Honey, y'all don't know what hot is, come back to where I live in July and you'll get an education." That was my only trip overseas, but it was enough for me to tell Ann that she has absolutely got to go while she's young enough to enjoy it.

Lorraine doesn't have to come back for me, because Bernice shows up at my door with grape jelly in the corners of her mouth. "You're not finished eatin? We've got to go to the Beauty Shop. I need a hairdo, and so do you. Hurry up, or there won't be enough time."

"She's got all day, honey. We don't have to rush."

She looks annoyed. "Mister Benny needs a hairdo too. He doesn't like it cut, just shampooed."

If Rhonda is in a good mood, she will in fact wet the scraggly strands of yarn that are Mister Benny's hair, put a few drops of shampoo on it, and rinse it out over the sink. Seeing her do that for the first time made me like her, although that is still no excuse for being so rough on my head. At first, Bernice wanted Mister Benny to have an apron on for his shampoo, just like she does, but that is where Rhonda drew the line. She said, "Bernice, I don't have time for that, sweetheart. Put Mister Benny under that faucet right now. I've got about thirty more heads to finish today, and I am not staying late. I've got a date."

I push myself off the bed. It is going to be a walking day. That's a good thing. Some days are wheelchair days, and I never know which it's going to be until I take that first step in the morning. Then there's no going back, and if it's a wheelchair morning, then it's going to be a wheelchair afternoon and night too. The physical therapist told me, "Mrs. Clayton, you need more willpower. Just because you might not feel like walking one minute doesn't mean you can't walk the next." Have you ever heard anything so ridiculous? What is she going to tell me about willpower? I'm the one that's still here waking up in the morning and making the effort to put on lipstick. I'm all willpower, all the time.

"Let's go, Bernice. We need to tell Lorraine to make sure they've got enough folding chairs down there. Sometimes Alvin doesn't put enough out, and then waiting for him when he's on a cigarette break is like waiting for the Queen to show up here for tea. He's a handyman all right, very handy if you can find him. I don't know about you, but I'm going to take a pillow. I can't sit still for an hour without something behind my back."

"Mister Benny will carry it. He likes you." She waves a filthy, careworn yellow paw in my face. "We're neighbors!" Bernice breaks into cackling laughter like she's just now figured out that we live in the same place. Then the singing starts. *"Hey good lookin, what you got cookin? How's about cookin somethin up with me?"* All she ever sings is country music. She is surely in a happier place than most of us will ever be, and from the sounds of it, it could be Nashville. We meet Lorraine in the hall.

"Well hey, Miss Bernice. Happy Mother's Day to you. I know your boy Cameron's coming later on. That's real nice, it sure is." Lorraine doesn't say anything to me directly. We have an understanding. She doesn't speak to me like I'm a five-year-old, and I try to cooperate with her daily routines.

"Happy Mother's Day to you too, Lorraine." I follow. "Did you hear from that fine girl of yours this morning?"

"I did. You know she's on Dean's list this semester again. Doin fine." She walks on past, pants legs making a swishing sound.

"Well I sure would like to see her again one day," I call out behind her.

"Oh, you will. You will," Lorraine answers.

The Salon line is long, getting ready for a holiday. Bernice and I park ourselves along the wall. Alvin obviously got the message from somebody besides me, because there are enough chairs for a small army. Bernice doesn't like to sit down much, she stays too restless, so I save her place with my pocketbook. She would never leave Mister Benny in a chair by himself while she walks around. That is out of the question, because if anyone touched him and she happened to see it, she might do anything from scream to haul off and hit somebody.

Rhonda's already busy, but she waves as soon as she spots us. As a rule she has long, wavy platinum blond hair, but I think she's starting to let it go back natural, which would be somewhere in the dark brown or black family. This in-between phase leaves it looking sort of rough. She can't be more than thirty-five or so, but her hair looks like it's been used as a burnt offering. That's the danger of being in the beauty business. You can do anything in the world to hair, but you have to know when to stop. The possibilities are definitely not limitless. Doesn't matter, Rhonda's still pretty even though she's got a few hard lines around her eyes. I don't know if she's lived as hard as she looks, but I do know she rides motorcycles. I saw her once through the window of the dining room scoot off on one, holding onto the waist of a man in a blue jean jacket, beard flying out on either side of his crash helmet. I like motorcycles because they get straight to the point. Get on and go. They serve no other purpose than to fly as far as I can tell.

Rhonda takes me in first, but Bernice always insists on watching me get my hair done, so she drags her folding chair in behind me and sits down within a few feet of the sink. Sometimes Rhonda moves her back but most of the time works around her.

"Don't you get tired of talking to people, honey? I know I would," I ask Rhonda as I let her lower my head back in the sink.

"Shoot, most people don't talk. I reckon some of em can't talk, I don't know. My grandma had a stroke and she couldn't talk."

"Is that right?"

"She used to make moaning noises in her throat. I hated that. It freaked me out. Her moaning and groaning, trying to say something every time you looked at her. It was like she didn't know nobody couldn't understand her."

"I meant the people that can talk," I say. "There are a few of us."

"They always want to know if I'm married. Where do I live? Who's my mama? That kind of thing."

"That's all anybody talks about anywhere you go."

"I reckon."

"Honey, do you mind if I ask you why you work here?"

Before she can answer, Bernice stands up. "My turn now. Y'all are talking and you're supposed to be doing hair. It's my turn!" She has Mister Benny pressed by her cheek as though he is the one doing the talking. Rhonda finishes putting the last curler in my hair and helps me under a dryer to bake for a while.

Bernice jumps into the chair. "Is it my turn now?" Her demand has for some reason turned into a question.

"Bernice, if you don't calm down, I'm gonna make you wait 'til you're peaceful," Rhonda says. Her voice is firm but soothing.

Although it sounds like an air raid going on around my head underneath the dryer, I am able to ignore it by watching Rhonda. She is the only person I know of who can pick up Mister Benny without causing a disaster with Bernice. You would think she was picking up a newborn she's so gentle. She holds Mister Benny's head in her hand and looks down at him. "Now what're we gonna do today, Mister Benny? Same as usual?" Bernice smiles, transfixed on the monkey doll as if he might speak any minute. "Same thing!" She can't contain herself. "He wants the same thing!"

"I can handle that, we'll fix you right up," Rhonda keeps talking to the doll. While she leans Mister Benny back over the sink, Bernice takes hold of one dirty yellow monkey paw. "Just be still now, Mister Benny," Rhonda says, "this is some warm water, that's all. Let me know if it's too hot."

"It's fine. It's just fine with him." Bernice clasps her hands together over her chest.

"Bernice, I'm gonna dry Mister Benny's hair and then see what I can do with yours. Go have a seat in the shampoo chair." Rhonda walks over to me and feels my head. "God, that's been dry forever!" She switches off my vehicle and escorts me to the second chair. Bernice has leaned all the way back into the sink and fallen asleep, head dangling like it's about to be chopped off. That sometimes happens, and sometimes Rhonda lets her sleep, even if there is a line still waiting outside. Rhonda hurries to get me teased, shaped up, and sprayed before Bernice wakes up. My legs are starting to ache from my lower back all the way down the thighs and calves, like something is pinched in my spine. Rhonda helps me to my cane; I need it today. "Just tell her I went on back, honey, do you mind?" I say and keep moving.

When I pass Bernice's room, her son is inside, unwrapping a stick of chewing gum, waiting with his wife. He knows me, but he never calls me by name. Every time I see him I tell him the same thing. "Hello there, I'm Margaret Clayton. Bernice will be so glad to see you, I know."

"Is she in therapy? Or, I hope, a bath?" the wife says in a perky voice.

"No ma'am, she's still down having her hair done for Mother's Day. We all do, whether we're mothers or not. I think even some of the men do!"

"I imagine they'll be finished with her in a few minutes." The son glances at the wife while talking to me. "We have to go to a church thing later. That's the one thing about being a deacon that's changed my life, I can never be late." He lets out a wheezing laugh like I am supposed to be an insider on a joke. "You want some chewing gum?" he asks. "I can't stop chewing it. Better than cigarettes though, right?"

The wife doesn't acknowledge him at all. She moves things around on Bernice's dresser top, throwing tissues and greeting cards into the trash without looking at them.

"She'll be back. It doesn't take long," I say. "It never takes too long. Don't y'all want something to drink? She's got a refrigerator full of stuff."

The wife speaks this time. "I don't think so. We'll get something when we get to the car." She looks down at her watch.

"I'm gonna go get Mama. I'll be right back," the son says and takes off down the hall.

Alone with the wife, I can't decide whether to stay or go back to my room. "Are y'all taking Bernice out?"

"We're going to have lunch at the K&W, then come right back. She never eats much anyway. I think the cafeteria's better so she can take just what she wants and not waste."

"My nurse Lorraine told me the new Chinese restaurant was good. Have you been?"

"We don't like Chinese food. They use too much oil."

"Well I sure wouldn't want to get fat before the beauty contest." I strike a pose with a hand on one hip. She is expressionless. "Oh I'm teasing. I think it's wonderful that you young people are concerned about what you eat and your bodies and all. It's healthy. You all will probably live a lot longer than us."

The prospect of that does not seem to suit the wife very well, maybe because it's not much fun thinking about living forever while standing in a place that always smells faintly like urine. She picks up a wilted potted hydrangea and throws it in the garbage.

"Bernice loves to show pictures of her grandchildren. How old are they now?" I ask.

"Three and five," she says. "The oldest one just turned five."

"I have always loved that age. They're so curious. They'll talk about anything in the world. A friend of mine who used to teach kindergarten said it was like teaching college."

I think I might have broken the ice. She laughs. "Well I don't know about that, but my Christine is curious all right. Both of them are."

"Well I can't wait to meet them sometime. Bernice said they might come today."

"No, we decided we better let them stay home with the babysitter."

"Is one of them sick?" I ask.

"No, no. They're fine. I think sometimes they get depressed, you know, when they come here. They're little. They don't understand."

"You mean about Bernice?"

"No. Yes. Well in general you know. It's hard for them to see."

"She's their grandmother." The wife arches an eyebrow at the tone of my voice, and I can tell I've overstepped a boundary. "I'm sorry honey, it's none of my business."

She turns away from me to the sink and rinses her hands. "They're children. They love their grandmother, and she loves them. That's all that matters."

"Doesn't Mama look beautiful?" The son appears in the doorway with Bernice on his arm, and Mister Benny on hers, his yarn hair teased straight up and fluffy. "I told the girl that fixes hair I've never seen her look any prettier. Have you?"

I'm not sure to whom he is directing the question but I answer. "Bernice is always able to pull it together when she needs to, isn't that right?"

She crushes Mister Benny's head against her cheek. "We're going to the restaurant!" she squeals.

"You're going to need a sweater," the wife says. "You know you always get cold, even when everybody else is burning up."

The wife slides open the closet door, almost violently. Most of what is in there are housedresses and nightgowns with the tags still on them and bedroom shoes of every description in piles on the floor. There are two or three sweaters hanging, and beside them, a couple of dresses each for hot weather and cold. The son helps Bernice into the armchair that was intended for company and stands by the window, rocking from side to side with his hands in his pockets, jangling change or keys.

The wife buries her head in the closet. "I would give you this navy blue one, but it looks like something is spilled all over the front of it. It needs to go to the cleaners." She wads it up and throws it on the bed. "All these sweaters do. They all have an odor." She throws another pile on the bed.

"We'll take care of that, Mama," the son says. He has stopped jangling. The wife stares at him, somehow disappointed.

"This old red one is the only one that's even fitting to wear. We've got to go."

Bernice looks at me. "We're going to the restaurant! You come too, okay?"

"No, honey, Ann's going to be back to visit with me after while. She's showing a house. Y'all go on." I smile at the wife even though she isn't the one who invited me.

She hands the sweater to her husband. "Here Mama, let's get this on you so you'll be warm enough," he says. Bernice hesitates, then lays Mister Benny down on top of the pile of sweaters. It looks like a little nest made especially for him. He is resting peacefully.

The wife picks up her purse and waits in the doorway. "Are you all coming any time soon?"

The son sticks out his hand to shake. "Very nice to meet you. Or meet you again I guess," he wheezes a laugh. "You have a happy Mother's Day. Let's go to the car, Mama."

Bernice picks up Mister Benny from his bed, and the son almost forgets to take the pile of clothes until the wife gestures with her chin.

When she speaks this time, it is in a little girl's voice. "Now Miss

Bernice, you know you're not going to take Mister Benny to the restaurant. He'll be just fine right here, and he'll be right here when you
get back."

Bernice is silent. Her grip tightens on Mister Benny and she looks
at her son, who grins and starts the metallic jangling in his pocket
again with his free hand.

"Miss Bernice?" the wife continues. "If we don't go ahead, we're
not going to have time to have lunch. We have to get back to the
babysitter and then go to church."

The son starts to speak. "Greta . . ." he says, but she cuts him off.
"Don't even suggest it, Cameron. I can see it in your eyes and don't even
suggest it. It's Mother's Day, and I am not going to sit at a table in public
with that worn-out doll and pretend like that's all right. It's not."

Bernice says, "Mister Benny's going to the restaurant too, okay?"

"No. No, it is not okay. You can leave him for one hour, that's
all we'll be gone. One hour." The wife raises a finger to point at the
son, and several gold bracelets clank together against a large sparkling
wristwatch with a pink crocodile strap. "You have spoiled her. That's
what this is about and I don't know how many times I've told you.
She's spoiled."

The son leans into Bernice. "Mama, can you please leave Mister
Benny this once?"

Bernice looks at me. Her eyes are red and pleading. "He has to stay
with me."

"This is ridiculous." The wife turns to me. "Have you ever in your
life?"

"She's real tenderhearted. Maybe . . ." She doesn't let me finish, it's
clear she never intended to.

Cameron tries once more with Bernice, looking down at the floor
and shuffling again. "Mama, it won't be for long."

"No!" Bernice screams. "No, no, no, no!" She is slapping the air
with her hands, like waving smoke away.

The wife jumps in. "Stop making a scene. I mean it, Mrs. Stokes. That's enough, I mean it."

Bernice is sobbing. She staggers back and slumps in the chair.

"Should I go get Lorraine?" I ask.

The son puts a hand on Bernice's shoulder. "Mama, I think we're going to go on. You don't feel like going to a restaurant today. Just sit here and get some rest 'til you're feeling better. We're going to go on now. We'll come back though."

"I'll pull the car around." The wife reaches out an open palm for the keys, but he doesn't offer them.

Someone makes a gagging sound in the hall. From a distance, Lorraine calls out, "I need Alvin to clean this up, please. Mr. Evans has got sick all over creation."

"Good Lord," the wife hisses and turns on her heels.

"Bye-bye, Mama. I'll see you later, I promise." Cameron Stokes turns in the doorway back to me. "Y'all have a good Mother's Day. I'll see you again soon, okay Mama?" His jangle fades down the hall along with the sound of leather shoes on linoleum.

I sit down with Bernice. She lays Mister Benny's head in my lap while she massages his legs. "Sometimes they hurt," she says through tears. "I can't stand it when he's hurting. I'll rub them a little while, and he'll be all right."

CHAPTER TEN

RHONDA

The first time I did Mrs. Stokes's hair she didn't say a word, but the second time, a couple weeks later, she pulled out a wrinkled picture of someone in a deep burgundy cap and gown. She flashed it so quick that I couldn't see it clear at first. "His name's Wade. That's my boy Wade." Bernice held onto the creased and worn picture like she thought I might take it. She was showing it to me, but definitely not giving it to me. I wanted to tell her, "I was there. I heard him give a speech. I'm so sorry for you." But from the way she said what she did, he might still be alive in her mind, I couldn't tell. I said, "He looks like a real good guy," and let it go at that.

We all guessed in high school that Wade was his mama's favorite. He was everybody's favorite. He was smart and made all the grades and honors, but he was real nice, and I mean to anybody, not just the ones that everybody liked. Wade spoke to me every single time he saw me in the hall or outside. Didn't matter to him that we didn't have a thing in common. I was all the time trying to find a corner to smoke a cigarette, and shoot, I bet he never tasted tobacco in his life. I'd say "hey" back, take a puff off my cigarette, and blow smoke straight up in the air like a chimney, the way I still do when I'm feeling nervous or flirting.

We came from two different worlds. That much was drilled into me before I was old enough to start school. Mama and me lived with my Grandma in her house, the only house I remember. Grandma told us that somebody needed to teach me about the way of the world and it was going to have to be her because my mama was too sorry. She said, "You might as well get used to doing for other people, Rhonda, because that's how you're goin to survive in this world. That's what we do, what other people need done, and no use thinking you're different. You're not. Your fool Mama can't get that through her head, but I be damned if I'm not goin to get it through yours."

Mama got out of that house cause it's the only thing she could do to take care of herself. If she thought she coulda done that and take care of me too, she'd have took me with her. I know that. She didn't listen to Grandma; she did what she pleased, and I made up my mind to be like that too. At least I didn't *think* I was listening to her, but I was, and it's taken me all this time to know that I never did what I wanted to back then. I never could just listen to what my heart was saying and believe it. "Look before you leap" was one of Grandma's favorite things to say, and I got the idea that whatever I might want to do, that if I looked first, I'd see a huge bottomless black pit so deep that I'd know better than to leap. Ever.

When I was in high school, my best friend Tammy Moore got a white-and-black horse, not a field horse either, a regular riding horse. The man in Sanford who sold it to Tammy's daddy said her name was Wyndfield Girl, but we always called her plain Wendy. Actually her daddy got it because I think he liked the way she looked out in his pasture. He said she had been in rodeos, but none of us really believed that, including him. Mr. Moore said I was a natural. He said I could ride her a hell of a lot better than Tammy, like I could read Wendy's mind. I loved to ride that horse, I think I loved her more than Tammy did.

When you're a kid, sometimes things hit like lightning bolts, not everything has to be thought through forever. Think about movie stars. They're young and they get in their head they want to be an actress, and nothing, not their family or not having any money or anything else can stop them. They go after what they want no matter what, and it's like the rest of the world stops getting in their way and finally starts cooperating, going along with their plan, like the world's a trained circus.

I decided that if I could help Mr. Moore with Wendy, I would learn everything there was to know about horses, and then I could have a farm one day and raise them in a pasture with a wide-plank fence around it and a house sitting on a hill. I could sit out on the porch with a cup of coffee in the morning and look out at all my land and horses as far as I could see. It would be the kind of perfect square green pasture that you'd drive by in your car and say, "Have you ever seen a prettier farm in your life?" And that would be my farm and I would make a living on it, and besides my own horses, I would take care of other people's horses and teach children how to ride. When you can see something that clear, it's not right that you can't do something to get it.

The Moores moved the next winter, before the spring we graduated. They shut up the barn and put the whole farm up for sale. Tammy Moore cried her eyes out when Mr. Moore said he might need to sell Wendy since they didn't have as much land at the new place. She cried so much she got sick and stopped going to school, so he gave in, but I think he would have anyway because he was nice and would do anything in the world for his only daughter. I had my hopes up at first because they didn't go that far, just to Sampson County, but that might as well be Atlanta when you don't have a car. If I could have figured out a way, I would have gone over there and rode Wendy, groomed her and all, but Grandma said that this was exactly what she was talking about, wasting my time on something that I didn't have one bit of control over, and she said once I graduated I better be able to help with some money around there because she was getting too old to work double shifts waitressing. I listened to her. I had signed up for cosmetology a long time ago because the guidance counselor said it might be suited to me. As long as I went to class for three hours, three times a week, I could be on my way to getting a license. I would just need to do the rest of the course work at the community college and pass an exam. By the end of the next hellish Carolina summer, I was finished and licensed and cutting and teasing up hair at Evelyn's Beauty Shop on East Main Street. Grandma was as happy as she knew how to be, which wasn't much. At least there was some more money. The day I walked in with my state license, I don't know what I was expecting but I felt like showing it to her. Without looking up from her *TV Guide* she said, "About time we got some more money coming in here. Hope you weren't expecting a twenty-one gun salute."

The summer went slowly into fall like it almost always does here, and then finally winter, mild but not without a few cold snaps. Grandma had a stroke and then a second one, and it affected her walking and talking. Then she got sick with pneumonia, and even though it lingered, it looked like she might get better, but she died right about the time of the first spring dogwoods. I kept on working at Evelyn's. She'd always been nice to me, and the job had finally paid for me to buy a falling-apart used car. Johnny Greenan gave me a good deal at the Chevrolet place. We'd dated once or twice. I remember feeling like the whole thing was a big joke on me, finally having a way to get out. A car of my own. I could do exactly what my Mama did, leave Grandma, but the hell of it was I didn't need to because that bitch was dead and out of my life. Sometimes I wish she woulda lived at least a little while longer so I coulda done what I had thought about a thousand times. I would have loved to look in my rearview mirror and see her standing on the porch in a cloud of dirt while I pulled off down the driveway and onto the asphalt with everything I owned. Then I bet I'd know what Mama felt like.

A lot of people said, "Why don't you leave now, Rhonda? You

can sell that house and do anything you want to." I thought about it, I even got a Realtor to come and look at it, but that's as far as it went. I decided that's not what I wanted. That would have been giving up for good. Grandma wasn't the only thing in that house. Mama was in there too. And me—I was in that house, in the walls, in the floors, up underneath the porch. Everywhere where air could go in and out had some of me in it, and it was mine now to do exactly as I pleased. Most of the time, I stayed home.

We were real busy at the shop too. Close to Memorial Day, Evelyn told everybody that came in that she was sorry but she was going to have to close for high school graduation. She said she wanted to tell everybody early so they could have plenty of time to reschedule, even though the graduation wasn't until June 10.

"Why don't you put up a sign," Twiny Allen asked her, "so you don't have to think about it?"

"I don't know," Evelyn said, "I never have liked too many signs in a place of business," but the real reason was that unless she spoke the news personally, she wouldn't have the chance to tell everybody that her niece Becky had been picked out of the whole ninth grade to sing the graduation solo in front of the school.

It was fine with me cause I had started doing some work fixing up the house and I could have used a day off, that is until Evelyn asked me to go to graduation with her. I meant to tell her thank you but no, but before I could get it out of my mouth, the look on her face made me say, "That's sweet, Evelyn, I'd love to go with y'all." I would have never gone back to a graduation at my own school, I was barely out of there myself. I don't have nothing against it, I guess a lot of recent graduates go back because they still know other people or whatever, but it seems like they're usually more of the perfect cheerleader Honor Society I've-never-smelled-shit-in-my-life type. Turns out I knew almost everybody walking across the stage in caps and gowns, at least by sight. Hell, a lot of em would end up coming to me to get their hair done in a few years, after they went off somewhere to college and then came back home to where they started from in the first place.

It was no surprise to me when Wade Stokes stood up to make the valedictorian speech, introduced by the principal, Marty Howell. Mr. Howell and I had our own past because he was the one who had sentenced me to study hall every week until I got into cosmetology, which I think he sort of considered to be its own kind of punishment enough.

Mr. Howell cleared his throat and said, "Our school and entire community join together to wish Wade all the best as he goes off to Chapel Hill in the fall, but we're glad to have him around this summer as usual working at the swimming pool. So go on and put on a bathing suit because you might not get to see him again once he gets out there and starts changing the world."

Mr. Howell meant it to sound nice, but it was stupid to make a speech that ended with a dumb swimming pool, out of all the things he could have said. I'll never know for sure, but I coulda sworn by the way Wade had his lower lip pushed out just the tiniest bit that he didn't want to be up there. Evelyn's niece stood at the front edge of the stage to sing "You'll Never Walk Alone" after Wade got through talking. She was nervous at the beginning and her voice quivered. Evelyn started rolling the corners of her program, then clutching onto the armrests, but after a couple of lines, Becky settled down and sounded all right to me. Some people stood up at the end, Evelyn was one of the first ones, so I felt like I had to get up too.

"Rhonda, would you look?" Evelyn nudged me. "They could eat her up. I knew that would be a good song for her as soon as she told me."

"She did sound real pretty like she always does."

Evelyn leaned over into my ear. "I don't want to jinx anything, I'm afraid to say it, but I think she's going to be a professional. I'm already looking into getting her some training."

"I don't blame you, Evelyn, I would too."

Standing there clapping for the graduation solo, I could see Bernice Stokes way down front. I knew she was Wade's mama by the way she sat up so straight when he was talking. At the end of the ceremony, the families of the student big shots had to go up on stage for pictures. Wade shook a few hands and went straight to Bernice and gave her a big hug as soon as she reached the top step. He hugged her so hard she almost fell over and they both laughed their heads off. She had on a corsage of three little pink roses in a tight row, pinned right below her left shoulder. I liked that on her, I remember, because most of the mothers wore big old chrysanthemums with little ribbons in the school colors, burgundy and white.

Wade's older brother and their father waited at the bottom of the steps like they were impatient for Bernice to get out of the way so they could go up. The brother looked exactly like his father, even then, young as he was. I can see it still, every time he comes into Ridgecrest to visit Bernice. Evelyn's niece was having her picture made too, so we had to wait around. I don't know what anybody ever thought was gonna happen to all those pictures, there would only be one that ended up being in the newspaper, and that would prob'ly be of Mr. Howell giving a diploma to a person none of us even knew.

The day after Wade graduated, he started his summer job at the swimming pool to save up money, even though what I heard was that his scholarship paid for everything. I think he did it more because he wanted to, he got to see a lot of people down there at the pool, but not me. You had to pay to join it, not exactly a country club, but still expensive. I never went swimming anywhere but in the pond at Tammy Moore's farm, and once they moved, I didn't go there anymore because it made me sad to think about when we used to ride Wendy. A lot of girls went down to the pool to sit on a lounge chair without any plan of swimming. Wade never showed a whole lot of interest, and Evelyn said he thought he was too good with his big Chapel Hill scholarship to date a local girl.

I never saw him out with anybody, but I wouldn't have expected to because we woulda never gone anyplace with the same group of people. Wade was on his way to new things, bigger and better things, and I was trying to make something out of what I was left with here, a house and a job and being on my own. I stopped having my mail brought to the house after Grandma died. Evelyn's place was right down the street from the post office, and I liked walking down there and picking up my mail in person, even if a lot of it was junk. I always went at the end of the day during the week, and at lunchtime on Saturdays because it was only open a half day, and Evelyn's was usually packed with women getting their hair fixed for church. I walked into the post office as usual one weekend, dead on my feet from teasing hair, and thinking about going home to a cold beer and a sandwich later on. Wade was carrying a huge cardboard box. "You're late," he said, "I was expecting you to pick this up hours ago." The box was so big that he had to sort of peep around one corner of it to even see me. I didn't miss a beat. "I'm sorry sir but your secretary must not have told you that your appointment was canceled."

"To hell with her then, she's fired." He almost dropped the box trying to put it up on the counter.

"What you got in there, a dead body?"

"It weighs enough to be."

"Well if I hear there's been a murder, your secret's safe."

"I appreciate it. I need all the corroboration I can get."

"Damned if I know what that is, but if I've got it, you can have it."

The post office clerk interrupted. "That's going to be ten sixty, do you need a receipt?" Wade reached in his pocket and gave him the exact change. I went to open my mailbox. There were a couple of bills for me, and a *Progressive Farmer* magazine addressed to Grandma. I didn't have the energy to spend my time canceling all her mess; I guessed eventually everybody that needed to would figure out that there was no reply and would stop sending her stuff. There was also a thank-you note on pink paper from Evelyn's niece because I had given her a little bag of makeup and a lipstick as a present after she sang her solo. Evelyn made her write that note, I know it, but there's something I like about that kind of strictness. It makes a difference to people to be treated nice. When I came back around the corner of the lobby, Wade was standing at one of the desks, fighting with a ballpoint pen chained to the countertop.

"These things never write," he said. "I don't know why they put em out here."

"I've prob'ly got one in my pocketbook."

"That's all right. I was just trying to write something down so I wouldn't forget."

"I can't remember anything either," I said, and I don't know why I said it, because I've got one of the best memories of anybody I know. I remember birthdays, wedding anniversaries, hell, I remember what I ate for dinner a week ago. It's just what comes out of your mouth when you're young. You don't know why you say a lot of things, it seems like the way to keep the ball in the air, stay a part of something, interacting with another person, like floating a balloon, and when you're that age, it feels like the balloon could pop at any second. It's not until later that you realize that there ain't a balloon, there's only people trying to get through and feel like they're not all alone.

Wade held open the door. He almost knocked me down to get in front of me and then motioned me through with a sweep of his arm, like he was paving the way for royalty. That was the first time in my whole life anybody had done that. I'd been on a plenty of dates with guys my age, some older too, a couple soldiers from Fort Bragg. You would think with all that military discipline that they would know how to act but, at least with me, they forgot every bit of it when they had a few beers inside em. The only thing on their minds was how much trouble they could get into before their curfew at the base. Hey, I'm not complaining. I loved every minute that I was the center of attention, even if it didn't last but a few hours. If somebody had a car, and an idea of something fun, I was ready. But I remember thinking that day, "What are you up to, Wade Stokes?" He wasn't trying to flirt with me. I felt like he was being the most natural thing he could be, like he wasn't trying to do anything, just feeling good in his skin and not afraid to show it. We walked out on the sidewalk into the sun, a hot July Saturday. I was still fiddling inside my pocketbook for the pen that he had already said he didn't want. He reached out and put his hand on my shoulder, like a big brother.

"Come say 'hey' sometime if you're down by the pool. I'm there every day saving people from drowning. My secretary knows my schedule."

"I thought she was fired."

He started to walk away towards his car. "Guess I don't have the heart." He smiled.

"Good. Give her another chance." I wanted to think of something else to say, but nothing came out.

I feel like asking Bernice to show me that picture again sometime. I don't want to upset her though. She's real tenderhearted, that's what they say, Margaret does anyway. I don't talk to too many people here. I do my thing and leave, one day a week. Ada Everett don't give me the time of day unless she has to. She thinks I don't do nothing but hair and that I don't know anything else. That's all right with me, I don't have nothing to prove to her. I see plenty on my own. I see things the doctors don't. Some of the ones they send over here ain't worth two cents anyway. They treat coming to see these folks like going to the bathroom, that's how much time and attention they give to what they're doing. That's why I take my time doing hair, even if it takes all day and throws off the schedule. If it makes theses ladies feel like somebody's got some time they're not afraid to spend, then that's me trying to treat them as good as I can. I think Bernice knows it.

CHAPTER ELEVEN

LORRAINE

My first husband was a Palmer. Edward Gerard was his given name but I never knew him to be called anything but Scrape, and I don't have no idea why. He left three months after we were married. He had got me on the rebound, and when the first woman from Macon, Georgia, decided to show up again, that was the end of the time he had for me. My mama said she could have seen it all coming, and I reckon she could. Sometimes it's a lot easier to see something coming when it ain't coming at *you*. It's like this: when you're drivin the car, you can't be lookin at the map at the same time. First you've got to stop, look at where you want to go, then start up the engine again and head in that direction. I did not stop. I did not look.

When my second husband, Samuel Bullock, asked me to marry him, I threw the map away again and didn't look at the road signs. And there were lots of signs. Empty bottles, late nights with no explanation of where he was, then him coming in staggering and reeking. If I said something, and I usually did, we either started screaming at each other or he'd turn around and walk out, maybe not come back 'til morning, maybe not for two or three days. Mama asked if he hit me and I told her no, which was the truth. Whatever I have suffered in my life, that has not been part of it, and I thank the Lord for that because I don't know what I would have done, not then. I see how somebody well-meaning can say,

"He hit you? You leave now, girl, and don't look back." But I understand why when a woman is in the middle of it, the choice don't seem that clear, not right off anyway. I know there's shelters and numbers to call now, probably not enough, but they're there. But let a black woman call the police in North Carolina in the 1960s and tell em that her husband was about to beat her or already had. Well that's just niggers fightin and that's what niggers do, and if they came at all, it would only be cause they had to, and they wouldn't do nothing, everybody knew that, no use to even call, they wouldn't do a damn thing. Maybe it's different now, it seems like it is, but I don't know. I think people do the same things to each other they've always done.

A week after we got married, Samuel and me moved into a house that belonged to a Mr. Turlington, on a piece of his farm, in exchange for Samuel helping him in tobacco and cotton and whatever else needed doing. Mr. Turlington hired all the blacks he could and poor whites too to work in the fields come barning or picking time, but he needed one strong man to be his helper all the time. The tenant house was little. From the outside, it looked like it couldn't be but one room, but inside there was a little bedroom in the back, no hall, only a door connecting it to the main room, with a kitchen in one corner and a table with four chairs. The only other furniture was a flower patterned couch that Mr. Turlington's wife had told him to get out of her house or she was gon throw it away once she bought something new.

Mama came the day we moved in. "Your daddy would be sick if he was alive to see this. Living in a shack with a dirt farmer who ain't even farming his own land, and in the shape you're in? Are you happy with yourself now?" And I answered her, "I'm gon try to be," and I meant it. Three weeks later, I had myself a baby, a little boy, Thomas. Samuel was drunk the day he was born. I didn't see any road sign telling me which way I needed to go. I didn't see what I didn't look for.

It was a late August afternoon, Thomas wasn't but a few weeks old, and it had come a big rain. The air was so heavy with wet that you had to plow your way through it to walk around. We had us some flooding in places. Samuel was at home because it was too wet to go in the fields, and I told him I was gon take the truck and go to the store, and Mama said she would come help look after the baby.

Samuel said, "I don't need nobody's help to sit up in here and watch a baby sleep."

"Well she's comin anyway, so watch him 'til she gets here," I told him, and I went on to the Winn-Dixie.

I remember that store like it was this morning. I had already loaded up most of what I came for, but I was lookin real hard at the meat. We couldn't afford most of it, so I picked us out a big old broiler chicken. I had decided I was gon make us some chicken and rice cause I loved it ever since I was a little girl. In the next row over, I heard a woman's voice say, "Stop it now, Spencer, I'm not going to tell you again," and a little boy about three come runnin around the corner towards me fast as he could and fell down right beside my feet. He yelled out, cryin like he was about to die, so I picked him up, and his mother, a suntanned white woman in a short dress with blond hair in a ponytail came flying after him to where I was, next to the meat. "Thank you so much," she said, real polite. It surprised me how nice she was, and she took him out of my arms and put him up in the seat of her grocery cart. She smiled and shook her head. "You've got to watch them every minute, don't you?" I was thinking again wasn't she nice, when something hard rammed me in the stomach, hauled off and hit me like a log, that big and heavy. I put the chicken down. I knew something, a sudden dark thing. I left the cart in the middle of the aisle full of food and everything else and ran out to the parking lot, to the pickup. The white woman with the ponytail called, "Are you all right?" but I had done gone. One of the cashiers at the front looked at me like she thought I was stealin, but I reckon she saw my hands empty and didn't say nothing.

I pulled into my empty yard. Mama's car was not there. I decided, wished, that she had taken Thomas back to her house and Samuel had to go do something or other for Mr. Turlington, but I knew as soon as I thought it I was wrong about both of those things. Nobody can talk themselves out of the truth once they know it. Thomas was dead before anybody found him, suffocated, lying in his crib in our little bedroom in the back. Mama had got sidetracked and decided to stop on the way to buy some sweet potatoes from an old woman she knew up the road. When she pulled in at our house, Samuel was asleep in a chair on the porch, beer bottles on the floor like someone had scattered them looking for something. Whatever sound my baby tried to make, his daddy didn't hear. Whatever struggle my baby went through, his daddy didn't see or know nothing about. I wonder what my angel was doing while I was looking at chicken in a grocery store not five miles away. I wonder if he woke up coughing, strangled. I wonder if he was wheezing. I see him tryin to breathe, then not breathing, but tryin as hard as he could, his little lungs not having the strength. My baby Thomas tryin his best to stay alive with nobody to help him, not even his mama.

I didn't let Samuel touch me for near a year after that. I didn't care who he did touch or where he went to do it, long as it was out of my sight. I wasn't any wife to him, in the bed or anywhere else. When I finally did let him come close to me, I had April nine months later. I thought I could put the past in the past. I even tried to make myself feel something for my husband again, but that was hard to do when he couldn't give me nothing back. So I put all I had into April, raising her up the best I could do for her. She was my second chance. Whatever my Mama might have said about Samuel, and Scrape before him, she stood beside me every time, all the time. She looked after April every day while I worked a job and went to school. Samuel got to drinking so bad he couldn't hardly work, but Mr. Turlington felt sorry for me and thought a lot of April, so he kept paying him a little something to do whatever he could, which got to be less and less. Samuel was a young man but already turned old. I got tired of the fightin, it was almost every night, but after time, that was the only thing we did together. It was my habit until I couldn't do it no more.

CHAPTER TWELVE

APRIL

On the morning of my college graduation, like many of my classmates, the phone call of a parent or relative took the place of any need for an alarm clock. My particular alarm came at 7:30 A.M.

"We're here!" a voice squealed, followed by the more immediately recognizable voice of my mother. "Give me that phone!" I heard her say, with some banging around of the receiver, and then an effortful attempt at courtesy. "Are you asleep?" she asked demurely.

"Not anymore, Mama." I could hear Althea cheering "woo-hoo-hoo" in the background.

"Where are you?" I was inclined to whisper until I saw my roommate's bed empty. Janice had obviously spent the night at her boyfriend Brandon's, her usual home away from home. I was jealous of how much sex she had but was happy to have the room to myself most of the time. Not this morning. I was worried about her.

Althea grabbed the phone. "Honey, we're having breakfast down here on Hillsborough Street. We just had ordered and then your mama asked if we should call you and I said go on and call her she might want something to eat, it's gon be a big day for her too, so call, maybe she'll come down and meet us, and I told her I'd order her some coffee while she did, but then I decided I wanted to talk too so I picked up both of our pocketbooks and followed her and told the waiter not to bring us any coffee yet so it wouldn't get cold, and we'd be back at our booth in a minute." Althea came up for oxygen only briefly, then got to the point. "Come on down here, we'll wait for you if you want us to."

"I wish I could, Althea," I said although I didn't wish that at all, but Mama's insistence on manners from early childhood had obviously taken hold and stuck. "My car's broken down again, and I can't afford to spend another dime on it."

"That thing barely ran when you bought it."

"You are not allowed to say anything evil about that car, Althea. It's made for short trips."

"It's made for the junk pile. Here, talk to your mama." She relinquished the phone, and Mama's voice broke through the shuffling of changing hands.

"Go on back to sleep if you want to, baby. We can keep ourselves busy for a few hours. Althea wants to stop at Hudson Belk's."

"They're not gonna be open now, Mama."

"We're just sittin down to eat, we'll take our time."

"Why'd y'all come so early? I'm surprised you got Althea out of the bed."

"As long as I've waited for this day, child, you know I didn't sleep two hours. Althea knew better than to mess me up on your graduation. You rest. We'll pick you up about ten forty-five."

I hung up and yawned but found that I didn't want to go back to sleep. I didn't want to shower and dress yet either, so I lay in bed staring at the long crack in the ceiling that ran from the corner into the center of the room where it branched out like tributaries on the map of a river. I was lying so still that I wondered what it would be like to be in a coma where you were aware of everything but couldn't do or say anything. I had heard a story about a person who learned to use eye movements to communicate by "blinking" the alphabet with *A* being one blink, *B* two, all the way through. I started to blink my name but after sixteen blinks to get to *P,* I was too tired to do *R.* I might get an eyelid spasm or something and then I could lose control of my eyelid altogether and turn into one of those people who blinked all the time when they looked at you, like a nervous tic. I didn't think of myself as a nervous person, but Mama made it her habit to tell me that she was proud of me and she would be equally proud even if I didn't work so hard, so to please make sure that I didn't try to do too much. We already knew I would start UNC Med School, my first choice, in the fall, but I couldn't imagine being a doctor if I had a nervous tic in one of my eyes. I remember thinking that this was exactly how people lost their minds, obsessing on details, but what else does a person do on graduation morning? The big work is finished, if it weren't you wouldn't be there.

Uncharacteristically, I had stayed up all the previous night going to parties, the last count being either six or seven. Janice, my roommate, had appeared in the doorway at around 10 P.M. "You're coming, aren't you? Don't even try to tell me no, April, you said you'd come."

"I just came back to change clothes. I want to wear jeans." I had on a sheer skirt but I really didn't feel like wearing it all night even though it was hot out, a taste of the unbearable summer ahead. We had been out to dinner at a new place called the Cask of Amontillado. I guess the owners thought that naming a restaurant after an Edgar Allan Poe story seemed like a good idea in a college town, but I would have settled for better food and a less clever name. It was definitely more of a bar than a restaurant, but Janice wanted to go, so she rounded up the girls, no men allowed, and we headed out for "The Last Supper." That's what she called it, and I wondered whether life was really going to be so different the day after we put on caps and gowns. I had the vegetable lasagna and garlic bread. Guess it didn't matter that amontillado is Spanish. So much for the diet.

Janice persisted. "Well good, you're not backing out now. Hurry up." She dumped out her purse on the bed and started putting what she deemed essential for a round of house parties into a small designer backpack that she had gotten at an outlet mall off I-95.

"You act like I'm a wallflower." I defended myself. "Maybe that's because I actually look at my syllabus every once in a while?"

"Baby, if the shoe fits . . ." She continued rummaging through multiple lipsticks and hair accessories before picking the last two or three items that she could effectively wedge into the little pack once her wallet was tucked inside near the bottom. I put on jeans and some clog sandals that I knew Janice hated.

"You're wearing those hooves?"

"I only do it to spite you."

"Hey I'm looking out for you, girl. I'm just saying you're fishing with the wrong bait, that's all."

"I'm not fishing, Janice. I know that's hard for you to believe."

"Yeah, yeah, med school. I already know that tune, you don't need to sing it for me."

She fastened the backpack with so much effort that I wondered if she would actually be able to open it again without an explosion. "I wish I could focus like you do," she said.

"No you don't!" I snapped back, and both of us burst out laughing. Janice was an average student, which she was able to accomplish without studying at all, which seemed to be all right with her as well as her parents.

The first couple of stops were dead. Janice said it was still too early. More people would be coming out later. I saw Louis Yancey at the Omega Psi Phi party, the first time since we stopped dating after Spring Break.

"I was thinking about you," he said, but the look on his face made me think the words surprised even him.

"That's nice." I let it go. It hadn't been a bad break-up. More an inevitable one. We had both moved on I guess.

"I missed your help with Organic," he added. He was planning on going to dental school at Carolina once he graduated next year.

"I'm sure you did all right by yourself." I was gracious, thinking how true the words were. By yourself. By myself. I was going to be by myself for a while. I had decided that. I wanted to start off at Chapel Hill right, no baggage, no way.

"Are you gonna stay home this summer?" he continued. Was guilt really so powerful as to make him stay in this conversation, when even our body language mocked us by showing how awkward we felt? I've always envied those people who could stay friends with their exes. I've never been able to do it. Maybe my definition of friendship involves something I can't expect from a lover who is now someone else's lover.

"I'll be around," I answered, wishing immediately that I had thought of something else because that sounded like I might want him to call me, which I secretly did. "What about you?"

Janice appeared. "April, let's go. Shareen's giving us a ride to Brandon's. He's having a bunch of people over." She looked at Louis. "Come if you want to." She grabbed my hand and pulled me with her. She knew he wouldn't come; that's why she asked him.

Brandon met us at the door of his fourth-floor apartment with a half-empty bottle of Wild Turkey in his hand. Pretty expensive stuff for college, but according to Janice, he always seemed to have money in his pocket, and it never occurred to her to wonder where it came from. He didn't work. A campus job would have been beneath him, and for that I resented him, having spent my share of weekend time behind the checkout desk or shelving books at the library in exchange for part of my scholarship money.

"Hey baby, I thought you wasn't ever gonna get here!" He hugged her and I watched the arm with the bottle of swishing brown liquid wrap around her back. They kissed deeply. I wish I had stayed and talked to Louis. Janice would have never cast me as a third wheel on purpose, but I think sometimes people forget what it feels like when you're standing in a hallway, waiting to be invited inside, while two people, one of whom you came with, have their tongues down each other's throats. I pretended to look for something in my purse, wishing I hadn't just climbed four flights of stairs.

Inside, the music was loud. The living room was near dark and packed with bodies. One couple had pretty much taken over the sofa in a tangle of legs and arms. Brandon pulled Janice with him down the hall, presumably to the bedroom. I didn't know, I had never been here before, only heard about Janice's roller coaster of a relationship on a daily basis. Consequently, I felt like I knew the apartment, the setting for more middle-of-the night debriefings than I could count. I grabbed a glass of wine but didn't get to drink it because Tamyra Johnson who was in University Choir with me pulled me out to dance in a group. Tamyra was the best alto in choir, everybody said so, and she wanted to be a professional singer. I thought that if anybody could make it in show business, she ought to be able to. She ran to the stereo and stopped Mary J. Blige in the middle of a sentence. Tamyra turned to the whole room and screamed, "I feel the need for some old school, y'all!" I recognized the bass line—who wouldn't—it was "Fight the Power." Tamyra screamed, "All right now!" and threw her hands up in the air. I did the same. It felt good. I was graduating, and it felt good. She shouted at me over the noise of the crowd, "So are you excited?"

"Yes!" I yelled back. What else does a person say?

"Is your mama coming?"

"What do you think? She's bringing Althea, remember her?"

"She came to spring concert and never took off her sunglasses."

"That's her!" I was going to lose my voice if I kept trying to override the noise.

Tamyra did a twirl which cleared the people in her immediate vicinity and yelled out, "Hey, Althea's doin her thing. I have no problem with that."

"NOOO!" I recognized Janice's voice. Unmistakable. For everyone else, the cry blended in to the overall wildness. I heard Tamyra call out, "What's up?" but I was already headed down the hall. I could hear Janice crying in a pleading sort of way from one of the bedrooms. I opened the door without knocking. Janice's face was wet and smeared; her hands were over her mouth, and she pointed to the window, where Brandon, shirtless, was holding his dog, a boxer puppy, out by its neck, swinging it back and forth.

"What the hell, Janice?" I asked, shocked cold.

"He's scared, you idiot," Janice cried, stomping her feet. "Bring him back in!" The puppy whined, its eyes fearful.

"You think I'm out of control?" Brandon raged. "Does this look out of control to you? I'll show you who's in fuckin control!" He tightened his grip around the puppy's throat, making him yelp.

"Janice, let's go." I grabbed her hand. I wanted to remove her without even looking at Brandon.

"It's okay, April, I'm fine. He gets like this. I'm fine."

"It's not okay. I'm taking you out of here."

"Who the hell are you talkin to, bitch? This is between Janice and me. You need to get your ass out of my house, that's what you need to do."

"April, just go," Janice said.

"Janice, do you know what you're doing?"

"It's better if you go."

"You heard her, get the fuck out." Brandon sneered.

"I'm calling the police," I said.

"You do and I'll fuckin dropkick the dog."

"April, go, please. I'm begging you to go. I'll be fine. I'll see you at home."

I'm ashamed that I left her, I should have called the police anyway. Not that anything would have happened. By the time someone got there, Brandon would probably have been passed out, and Janice back out in the living room enjoying the party. She was used to it, that's what she said. He wasn't a bad guy, only when he had too much to drink, that's what she always said. She knew what I thought. That never stopped her.

I sat up in bed. It hadn't really hit me that I was actually graduating in a few hours until I heard Mama's voice on the phone, and even then it was like she was talking about someone else. I was going to have a diploma put into my hands before I knew it and be told what amounts to "Congratulations, you've done it, now go be an adult and make your life mean something, to yourself, your family, and your community." "Anything more than that is gravy," the chaplain had said at baccalaureate. Well, I was interested in gravy. I had worked too hard not to be. When they announced honors last week, I called Mama to tell her I was summa cum laude. First she asked, "Some of what?" but when I explained, she said she never in her life thought she would need to know Latin, but those particular words suited her fine.

The angle of the morning sun made a bright streak through the window, across the night table, now visibly very dusty, and onto the wall opposite. I heard sounds of first stirrings in the hall by my neighbors, also likely awakened by their own family alarms in whatever form. Shower spray blasted on tile, voices echoed in the cavernous bathroom. I didn't think about it at the time, but I would never wake up to that sound again in my life, not that it was necessarily something to be missed, much less mourned, but it occurred to me how quietly experience slips away unnoticed, camouflaged by its relative unimportance. Then at some point you step back and take a look, and what's in front of you is like a tangled wad of string, all the "unimportants" rolled together in a loose knot, to be recognized as your very own and cherished, or mistaken for trash and discarded. And if you're lucky, it hits you—that knot of strings, wound and intertwined, is your life, and savoring it is what you want to do. I think about my mother's work. She sees the biggest part of her job as helping to hold the threads of a life together, savoring anything at all that can be used to sew something lasting. Determinedly, she will stitch meaning into the fabric of a being, creating, for an old and lonely soul, a protective garment, for a time, against the chill of loss, forgetting, and being forgotten.

The door flew open, slamming against the particleboard armoire that served to hold whatever clothes a student deemed better than the wadded-up-in-a-drawer variety. Janice threw her backpack angrily on the bed, the force of which jolted the steel frame. "I told him he could fuck himself." She sneered as though I could enter without preface into her stream of consciousness, which in a way, I could.

I threw the covers off and put on a light bathrobe even though the May sunlight was already heating up the room. I cracked the window for some air and stood opposite her.

"Janice, you need to wake up."

"I know what you think, April, but it's not that. It's only sometimes it's like something snaps and he drinks too much and I don't know who the fuck he is when that happens, but it's not like it's all the time. He loves me."

"This is not about how he feels about you, Janice, this is about him having a problem."

"How do you know?" she retorted.

"What I know isn't the point. I want you to hear what I'm saying to you. Please." I picked up my cosmetic bag; I didn't know what else to say. The signs were embedded inside me like sensors before I was ever conscious of them, from when I was a child. There are the blurry memories of a towering man's voice and body—still, in my mind, I never see his face. There is no face, it's all sound, rage. It is my father, screaming at Mama, and when he had a "fit," as she called it, I was so afraid that I would hide in my room until it stopped, which usually wasn't until I heard a car start. That blessed sound meant it was over and I could come out and jump into bed, pretending to be asleep so

Mama wouldn't feel bad that I had heard all of it. She knew I wasn't asleep, and I knew that she knew, but the ritual saved us having to live through it again by talking about it and instead let us take in the quiet of temporary forgetfulness. A psychologist would say we should have addressed it and may well have been right, but at the time, we did what felt natural, protecting ourselves by licking our wounds privately rather than reopening them in the presence of one another. I believe that fortitude helped form me, perfectly or not.

I was five or six when my grandmother barreled into the yard in her old Oldsmobile station wagon—we didn't have a driveway. It was a hot summer morning because I was playing outside barefoot, and there was still dew on the ground, which made everything in the grass stick to my feet. Grandma kissed me on top of the head and marched straight into the house. Minutes later, she and Mama made several trips back to the car, loading it with mounds of suitcases, cardboard boxes, and bulging paper grocery bags.

"What are y'all doing?" I asked. My stomach had a knot in it.

Grandma said, "Y'all are coming for a long visit at my house, honey," and she stopped at Krispy Kreme and got us donuts on the way. They were good and warm, and Mama let me have two, knowing that I might feel sick afterwards from the heart-stopping combination of sugar and fried dough that for a child in North Carolina was like having heaven in your mouth. It wasn't long after that drive that Mama started wearing a nurse's uniform to work every day. We never went home again, and I never asked why. The intuition of a child holds more knowledge of what is real than adults ever imagine is the case.

Until I was twelve, I only heard about my father in bits and pieces, like a crossword puzzle that was never finished, a mix of cryptic clues paired with what were at best guessed-at answers. I saw him even less. He showed up at Grandma's from time to time, usually when she wasn't there if he could help it, but he ignored me and went straight for Mama. The sole consistency of those visits, deeply ingrained, was that they always ended with the same blur of rage in the kitchen that sent me running for the cool pine floor under my bed to hold my breath for the sound of his car leaving. The long-standing blur came to an end at the beginning of sixth grade. I came home from school and Mama was already home from work, which was strange in itself. She and Grandma were sitting in the living room together, and I could tell they were talking about something serious by the way they looked at me when I burst in the front door with my stack of books. I always carried a big stack of books. When people asked me why I had so many more than the other children my age I said, "I've got homework in all of em, what do you want me to do?" They always laughed and someone would say to Mama, "You got a smart one, Lorraine. Willful too. She's gon do just fine."

Instead of telling me to get started on my homework before dinner, Mama got up from the sofa and took the books from my arms. She tried to make a joke about how heavy they were and said if all that was in these books was going to have to fit into her little girl's head, they might have to clean out some of what was already in there. I didn't say anything because there's nothing worse for a child than when a grown-up is trying to pretend like everything's fine when it's clear that it's not. Mama piled the books on Grandma's low coffee table, my favorite place to sit on the floor and do my homework.

"April, I've got to tell you something and I don't know what you're gon feel, but I want to say that whatever you feel, that's all right."

"Yes ma'am?" I said.

She looked briefly at my grandmother, then back to me. "Your daddy's dead. He drove his car into a tree in the middle of the night."

I remember standing there and wondering if I was supposed to cry, but I waited for my eyes to start and they didn't. Then it bothered me that nothing happened. I was supposed to react. I replayed Mama's words in my mind and at the end of them, there was still a blank, like on a math test. I didn't know the right answer. Nothing came. Without moving, I said, "Can I have a snack?" Grandma jumped up on cue and went to the kitchen where she cut a piece of pound cake and poured a glass of milk. I took it back to her tiny second bedroom, the room that had become my room while she and Mama shared her bedroom, which still had two twin beds in it from when Granddaddy was alive. My room was also Grandma's sewing room, and she still had an old pedal sewing machine in addition to the newer Singer, which was the source of many of my clothes, and all of my dresses. I sat on the floor and ate sweet pound cake and waited for something to come into my head about my daddy and the only thing I could get to was the blur with no face and the shouting terrifying voice, and so I would take another bite of cake and let it fall apart in my mouth with a sip of cold milk, going back and forth with cake and milk, until it was gone and I stretched out on the bed in my clothes and fell asleep. I did not do my homework, I did not eat dinner, I slept all the way through the night. The next morning Mama told me we would drive to the funeral, she would take me. I asked her if we had to, and she said yes we did, that I might not feel like it right then, but there wouldn't be a chance to change my mind later. That day I would learn that you don't always leave people because you hate them, but instead because you cannot bear the burden of them. The agony of my daddy's living was my mother's slow dying, and she was not ready to die. She found it in herself to say no, not knowing exactly what the "no" even meant, but she knew that she couldn't do any more for the man she had loved and married. She couldn't watch her life and my childhood drain away slowly, dirty dishwater after the meal is long over.

Mama cried at the funeral, I did too, but I think it was more seeing her cry that got me upset. Grandma did not go. She had not hated my daddy, but she had not loved him either. She had therefore closed the chapter a long time ago and wasn't interested in reopening it. Soon after, we went back to what had become our life together, rather seamlessly. My daddy hadn't been part of it for years, he was less a part now. He was no longer someone whom, had I the desire, I could have sought out and found not more than fifty miles away. He was no more, and we went on.

I had the highest average in my grade, the first time a black girl or boy had ever had that distinction. Mama continued at the nursing home. It had become for her a fertile ground in which she planted an entirely new life, yielding more than she could have ever known ahead of time. Every night, or the ones when she got to eat supper at home, she told stories from her day at work, a little thing that one of her patients had done or said, a private moment shared with her because she had become an intimate by effect, a role that, it must be said, she treated like a royal appointment. Her stories were not a breach of that privacy, rather they were an invitation for us to enter into a way of looking at life, standing in the present with a view into the distance. Her work with old people changed her, and by effect, me, and I found myself looking at my own grandmother differently, the woman who had rescued us in a beat-up station wagon from a monster that I now am able to see as more sad than horrible.

Sometimes I sat at the table with Grandma and did nothing except look at her hands, thinking about everything they had touched in all her years of living. Cotton, tobacco leaves, babies, laundry and strong lye soap, then money in the cash register of the one-room store that Granddaddy ran in the country, less a store than a gathering place for black farm workers with no other place to come together except church one day a week. Until Granddaddy died, she had doled out Coca-Colas and hoop cheese and crackers to more people than she could count. She had handled fabric and thread and made quilts, blouses, dresses, pants, and one time in particular she tried to make a bathing suit for me but it was disastrous, by her own admission, and she never tried such a thing again. She defended her failure by telling me that people were not meant to linger in water anyway, it was for taking a bath and getting out of before you got sick. I also found myself listening to her voice, the changes in pitch when she recounted something that made her mad, or a piece of gossip from church, or a memory of something that happened to her and Granddaddy so long ago that the details would change every time she told the story. Sometimes she caught me staring at her and said, "What you lookin at, child, you make me nervous as a cat," but I think, without even recognizing it, she liked the attention. And I learned that attention is a prize in love, the first thing you give and the first thing to go when the new wears off.

The dorm's capacious bathroom had filled with steam by the time I had let the hot water spray pound my neck and shoulders for as long as I wanted. The hall was quieter. When I returned to the room, Janice was gone. On my pillow, she had written a note on a single sheet torn from a spiral composition book. Her handwriting was surprisingly beautiful for someone who didn't care much about anything to do with pen and paper.

Dear April, I DO hear you, and I will think about what you said, I promise. Thank you for listening (again). And Happy Graduation . . . to us both!!!

Love, J.

P.S. I borrowed your dark green earrings, OK?

Resilient as always, she was on to the next thing. I hoped I would see her later but knew it was unlikely with Brandon in the picture. Riffling through the few clothes I had not already packed, I searched for the coolest thing I could find to wear under the suffocating synthetic material of my graduation gown. I settled on a rust colored linen blouse and matching skirt. I had decided not to walk around campus in my cap and gown, but I wanted to put it on once in front of the mirror. The mortarboard fit, and surprisingly, I was ordained as

one of the extremely few people in the world who don't look idiotic
wearing one. Maybe it had to do with the size of my head, I don't
know. I stood looking in the mirror, feeling ready. I looked ready for
the next thing, med school and whatever else. My stomach growled.
I needed to eat something before the ceremony, or I'd have to wait
until after to go to lunch with Mama and Althea. I told her that I
didn't want her to spend a lot of money, that I'd be just as happy with
something simple. I meant it, but I knew even then that alongside
Mama's pride, my instinctive reserve would be negligible, especially
with Althea involved. She didn't have children of her own, and I was
hers by effect, especially on occasions when having a daughter was a
desirable accessory for her extremely busy life.

"Where do y'all have in mind, Mama?" I had asked. "You'll have
to make a reservation to go anywhere today because State is graduating too."

"You just don't worry about it," she answered. "It's gon be our
surprise."

I put on some earrings. I probably would have worn the ones Janice
took, but it didn't matter. Instead I chose some antique-finished silver
ones, and a silver chain with a cross that had belonged to Grandma,
the one thing she wore every day of her life. I rubbed my fingers over
the cross, it had tarnished some from years against my grandmother's
skin, sweating at work or at home, which was also mostly work. I
didn't feel particularly religious, but I had wanted that cross when she
died. I wanted to wear the strength of her years and the changes she
saw living them. I wanted her life to rub off on my skin and become
part of my body, not relegated to memory alone. I dropped the talis-
man inside my blouse and unzipped the gown, disrobing and throwing it over my arm. I decided to meet Mama and Althea downstairs
because if they came up to the room, Althea would have had more
than a few comments about the way we had decorated it, and of all
times, I didn't need to hear that on the day I was moving out. I was

leaving it forever anyway. Already I found myself caring about other things. Even if I couldn't name them, they were the real pieces of the future, poised to spring into my path, like a roomful of invited guests on the other side of a door, waiting to yell, "Surprise!" and rush in to celebrate an occasion with me, only me, at the center of it. I pushed open the heavy front door of the building and strolled into the brightness, out onto the perfectly watered and trimmed green lawn, the sort that should be a prerequisite for all college campuses. The smell of cut grass and flowering trees overwhelmed me as I shielded my eyes against the sun to see Mama and Althea walking toward me, cameras dangling.

"Hey!" Mama yelled. "We're late cause Althea was bound to try on a hat. I told her nobody was gon wear a hat to graduation, it wasn't like Easter Sunday."

Althea had obviously succeeded because she was holding a dark blue wide-brimmed beauty with a black satin ribbon on her head as she broke into a run. "Look at you, girl. Look at you!" she was half laughing, half crying. "It's your day, April!" The standard line she delivered was no less sincere for having been spoken to every honoree at every imaginable occasion, but seeing the two of them run across the Shaw University campus, it felt true, specifically for me. I held onto my mortarboard, for a minute I couldn't catch my breath, and then I broke into a run too, squealing my way into their outstretched arms.

CHAPTER THIRTEEN

RHONDA

The Grove Swim and Racquet Club has a long, curvy drive-way that runs down a hill through tall pine trees on both sides and then opens up into a wide space that looks like some-body decided by-God to build a swimming pool for their neigh-borhood and also by-God to dig up anything and everything in the way to make room for it. Besides a huge L-shaped swimming pool and a baby pool with a fountain in it, they also put in twelve tennis courts and a two-story brick building that looks to me like it oughta be a bank but has drink machines and wood benches outside. All my imagined pictures of how nice it must be were a whole lot prettier than how it really was once I was standing there looking at it for the first time. The Grove sure ain't a grove anymore.

I never told anybody I went to see Wade. I thought it was pretty brave of me just showing up, but then I also thought what the hell, if it's too weird, fuck it, I'll just leave. I'm all the time having to talk myself into stuff. If I only did what came natural, I woulda quit a long time ago.

The asphalt parking lot was full of cars that day, mostly brand-new ones, like shiny cellophane candy wrappers scattered in the sun. They said on TV it was gonna be ninety-three degrees by the middle of the afternoon but it already felt like twice that much to me, standing in cutoff shorts on blacktop that turned into a frying pan in summer. I guess everybody that didn't have to work for a living thought the pool was the only place to be on a Monday in August. I can't say I blame em.

A long red convertible wheeled into the lot close to where I was, so fast it sent pebbles and dirt flying. Some of em hit me in the legs, baby yellow jacket stings, like the driver was trying her best to tear up the pavement that her own club dues had paid for. That seemed like a dumb thing to me, but I really do wonder if maybe when you're rich you feel like you're bound to tear up something every once in a while just to remind yourself that you've got plenty of money to either fix it or buy something else. Believe me, there's lots of times I don't give a damn and don't mind if you know it, but I try to take care of what little bit of something I've got. Maybe one day I'll have some more and if I do, I hope I'll stay the same.

A fat lady was working hard to lift herself out of the red car, wearing a long kaftan sort of wraparound dress, big as a bedspread, with lime green and pink ferns and monkeys hanging by their tails printed top to bottom. She breathed hard and fanned herself once she was on her feet and steady. I kept my distance. I noticed she was wearing shoes with shells on top of them and kitten heels and I wondered if she might not be better off in a flip-flop. She lowered her wide round sunglasses and looked at me over her nose, but I reckon she decided she didn't know me and didn't need to, so she reached into the backseat, pulled out a tote bag full of magazines, and tucked a plastic bag of carrot sticks into it. Shit, I thought. I was positive I was the only one who either didn't belong or wasn't invited by a "belonger." The woman slammed her car door like she meant business, and I started to move my tail out of there, but she walked to the gate and inside, not paying me any more mind. So I stayed where I was, standing by the chain-link fence that went all the way around the pool, staring through little diamonds of wire. If I stared hard enough at the crisscrosses, everything else started to blur, but if I looked in the holes, the spaces between the wires, to what was on the other side, the fence went away. All those metal Xs started to look like nothing but a soft gray spiderweb floating at the edge of my eyeballs. I was playing, going back and forth, back and forth from plain to blurred 'til I thought I might give myself a headache messing with my eyes that way. I reckon I had been doing it for about twenty minutes when Wade blew the whistle hanging around his neck and yelled, "Adult swim!"

He stretched his arms up over his head like he was stiff from sitting a long time and glanced in my direction. "Hey!" he hollered out in a different voice, not his serious lifeguard yell, but a "I'll-be-damned" kind of voice, still loud enough to make a few women look up from their lounge chairs. Wade jumped down from the high lifeguard stand at the edge of the water, his chest and arms were all oiled up and his skin already dark brown even though the summer was only half over. He waved at me. I wished I hadn't come. Why did I come? Two girls in bikinis wrenched their heads around to see where he was going, spotted me, and when they saw him walking over, huddled into each other whispering. I oughta have known better than to come down here to the Money Pile, I thought. That's what Grandma called it, I can hear her. "You're exactly like your mama, too big for your britches. You got somethin to learn about the world, girl, mainly that it's theirs and not yours and never will be."

I waved back to him, really more of a half-assed wave, and started to leave on the little Yamaha cycle I had borrowed while my car was being fixed.

"Hey! Hold up!" he said, wiping his face with a faded blue towel that looked like it had seen better days, or too many chlorine summers. I got a lot better towels than that, I thought, and I use peroxide every day of my life. Hair chemicals are strong, and if you don't think so, look around you next time you're strolling through Wal-Mart.

A few adults, mostly older ones, were taking the pool away from a bunch of disappointed children who couldn't understand why they had to get out so a handful of ladies with wiggly rubber flower caps could dog paddle back and forth without ever getting their heads wet. I figured the girls near Wade's chair might go in the water too now that they were out of danger of being splashed or hit in the head with a beach ball, but I got real clear that getting wet was not in their plan, no matter how hot it got.

Wade put his hands on the fence in front of me. "Hey," he said again, "how you doin?" His face was inches from the chain links.

"Don't you have to stay up on your chair?" I asked. "What if somebody drowns?"

"I'm not the only one." Wade laughed and pointed back to a blond-haired heavyset guy over by the deep end with his nose covered in white. "I do the shallow, he does the deep, and with adult swim, the only one in the shallow is gonna be Mrs. Stockton doing her laps, steady as a heartbeat."

"What is that white stuff people put on their noses anyway? I've always wondered that," I said, even though I had never wondered it and didn't really care.

"Zinc oxide! Haven't you ever used zinc oxide? Mac's nose always burns and peels all summer, and he says the girls don't like it. I told him, 'Son, your nose isn't the reason you can't get a date.'" He laughed and I did too, not because it was that funny; I didn't even know who Max was. It just seemed like what you do when someone is being nice and laughs. You laugh back.

In the shallow end, a wrinkled woman in a royal blue one-piece with a white stripe on the angle stepped down the stairs into the water like she was in *Gone with the Wind*.

"She looks old to be swimming," I said.

"Shoot, Honey Stockton swims like a fish. She's eighty if she's a day, and she's down here every afternoon. Reads books in the shade. And I don't mean magazines either, she says she only reads the classics, all the books she didn't find time for when she was young. She won't go near that pool if there are children in it, but whenever I blow the whistle she's off like a shot."

I watched the woman still trying to make her way down the steps. "I don't know if I'd say 'like a shot.'" I laughed; he didn't. I felt stupid for being there, talking through a fence to a boy who wasn't any more interested in me than the man in the moon. I could tell. Girls can always tell.

"Do you want to come in?" he said, breaking the silence, thank God. "I can sign you in as my guest."

I guess it didn't occur to him that I didn't have on a bathing suit under my shorts.

"No thanks." I acted cool. "I gotta go, we're real busy at the beauty shop. There's a lot of weddings in summer. While the weather's good. Everybody's got to get their hair fixed, not just the bridal party."

"You do hair?" he asked, like he'd never laid eyes on a beautician before.

I know I turned red, I was embarrassed, but then I thought, "What the hell did he think I was, a doctor or lawyer?" I didn't answer him, which was a good thing because I was mad about being embarrassed, and I prob'ly woulda said something mean. Slow down, Rhonda, I told myself, the whole world ain't against you. Sometimes I have to be reminded of that, it's what comes with wanting to stand up for myself. Part of the territory, and it's a good thing I know it or I'd make myself some enemies without ever meaning to.

"I think that's great," Wade went on. "I always knew you had style, Rhonda, seeing you around school. Confident. You didn't know I knew your name did you?"

He must have seen I was shocked. We didn't know each other except to say "hey" once in a while.

"I just went and looked in an old yearbook at the class ahead of mine," he said. "Right there you were. I remember under your picture, where it says, 'Dreams.' Yours said: Horse Trainer."

I softened. "It's a dream that hasn't come true yet. Maybe, I don't know. I shoulda said 'Hair Trainer.' "

"It might be easier training horses," he said, and finally, we both laughed together. I'd never known any guys like him. So nice, for no reason other than he wanted to be. He was like a foreign country to me.

"Well I don't have to look in the yearbook to know you." I perked up. "Everybody knows you. The golden boy of all time, Wade Stokes."

"That's what you think?" His voice changed.

"That's what everybody says." I was trying to keep it light.

"But do you think that?"

"I know you're smart and goin to college on a scholarship and your family's got money, and you're probably gonna make a helluva lot more of it one day before long. And even if you don't you'll prob'ly have everything you ever want. Doesn't that about sum you up?"

"Maybe not," he said, looking down at his bare brown feet, and it's funny, right that second I knew we weren't flirting. Not that I ever really had thought we were but why else was I there except hoping he might be interested in me, in spite of believing, cause I'd been told to, that nobody like him would ever be interested in someone like me. He raked his hand through his wavy hair, curlier in the heat and humidity. It was longer than I remembered ever seeing it before.

Damn, Rhonda, I thought, can't you for once use a feather instead of a sledgehammer to make your point? "That sounded mean," I said. "I didn't mean for it to be mean. I'm sorry. I don't even know you."

I looked at the girls waiting near his chair, whispering less but still staring at us. He didn't belong to them any more than he did to me, and he never would. But I knew he liked me anyway. Not like a girlfriend. Just liking somebody because you like em.

"Why'd you tell me to come down here and see you that day at the post office?" I tried to change the subject.

"I wanted you to."

"Well I'm here."

He fiddled with the blue towel, finally wrapping it around his neck like a collar or a necklace. "I'm leaving, you know that. I probably won't come back, you figured that out too I think."

He snickered, not a funny laugh this time, but the way somebody does when he's about to say something that he's never thought of before, sort of like "the joke's on me." That kind of laugh. "Do you know I never broke a rule in my life?" he asked. "I mean I did stuff, but usually I'm busy doing everything exactly right. You're not like that, are you?"

"If you're sayin I'm not perfect, you're damn right about that."

"That's not what I mean. You don't try so hard. You don't care so much about everything."

"God almighty, you make it sound like something brave. Listen. Whatever I do, it's cause that's the only way I know to do. I ain't tryin to prove nothing to anybody, and I don't need a medal. I just keep goin."

"That's what I'm talking about. That's *exactly* what I'm talking about. I need the straight As and the prizes and all that. I don't even know when it happened, I've always been that way."

"Well you might oughta be thankful for that, you know? You get noticed. The only thing my grandma ever paid any attention to was my paycheck. I say there's a shitload of people to tell you what you can and can't do. I just gotta make sure the loudest voice I'm listenin to is Yours Truly."

He grinned. "I like that . . . Rhonda."

Mac blew the whistle from the other side of the pool. "All swim!" he screamed, and most of the old people came outta that pool like somebody had yelled, "Turd in the water!"

"I have to go back to my perch," Wade said. "I may have to save somebody anytime now."

"Hey Rhonda, come on in!" one of the girls squealed from an oversized nest of towels. I recognized her, older than Wade and me both, her name was Gwen something, a brunette with frizzy wild hair, while the girl beside her laughed with a loud snort and tied the straps of her friend's top to make it a little bit tighter and push her tits out against the fabric. I could help her with that hair, I thought and surprised myself by thinking something nice when they were enjoying the fact that I wasn't one of them.

Wade ignored it. "Come again, Rhonda," he said. "Bring your bathing suit next time." He raked his hands through his hair again and shook it out, it was still a little bit wet. I could see the old Wade was back now, whatever thick mud he had stepped in for those few minutes was gone now, dried up or washed off.

"Maybe I will," I answered, grabbing the fence and going up on my tiptoes. "Don't worry, you won't have to save me."

"You never know!" he yelled back, trotting away. With the sun in my eyes now, he faded out into a blur of blue pool water and lounge chairs and girls and towels and plastic bottles of lotion.

I brushed the damp hair off my forehead. I was burning up on that asphalt, they should have left it gravel, but then that fat lady in the red car woulda really had a kick-ass good time parking. A self-made tornado. I waited 'til Wade had climbed back up into his high chair, looking out over the world. He had to look out for all of em, that was his job. I wished I had asked him what he put down for *his* one big dream, and I didn't have a yearbook so I would never know. I wondered what somebody put down as a dream when they could do anything in the world. Did they even call it a dream anymore? I held onto the metal diamonds in the fence, still watching, until I noticed my hands, red from too many shampoos without gloves. Them and the fence were all I could see.

I didn't go back. I knew I wouldn't. It wasn't for me, not because I couldn't stand up to the beach towel girls. Hell, I've stood up to a lot worse than them. I got busy at the shop, summer ended. The pool people went back to whatever it was they did the rest of the year. I saw who I came to see, that's all. I guess I wanted proof. Wade Stokes was who I imagined he would be.

CHAPTER FOURTEEN

MARGARET

I t's too hot for a picnic. I'm positive that this must violate the Health Department's standards for what you can make old people do in rest homes. Just because it's the Fourth of July, some people may want to go sit out there and be eaten alive by flies while they're trying to gnaw on a hamburger bun, but not I. Lorraine said, "Don't worry, we'll be in the shade." Ordinarily I trust her about anything in the world, so why she is telling such a lie I have no idea because there *is* no shade at this time of day. When I look out the window, even the birds look hot to me; their back feathers shine like mirrors in the sun. All their movements are so fast and jerky, it's a wonder they don't have miniature heart attacks. Their hearts must be bigger than their brains or else they'd hide up in a cool longleaf pine.

I push the nurse button. I want to change my blouse if I've got to go out there and sit in Hades in honor of our country's freedom. Lorraine appears wearing an apron with bunches of grapes painted all over it. It says in cursive writing, *Le Bon Vin! Vive La France!* "What are you wearing that ridiculous thing for? Have you taken up gourmet cooking in addition to all manner of torture you inflict on your helpless victims?"

"I'm tryin to help get ready for the picnic. It's too much for the kitchen people by themselves."

"Are you really going to drag me out there in the middle of the day?"

"Yes I am because it'll do you good. You stay in here too much."

"Is that right? Well, while you're at it, why don't you go ahead and make reservations to Paris for the weekend?"

"You have got one smart mouth on you, woman. And you better be glad Jesus loves you and so do I, because if I didn't I'd put a pillow over your face and sit on it."

"I am not interested in your threats. I called you because I want to change my blouse. I will roast in this tight thing."

Lorraine pulls open the dresser drawer. She has to yank it because it's made out of particleboard with some kind of fake mahogany veneer on it. They will not let us have our own furniture in here, with the exception of one chair, so we are left with this kind of cheap mess that you couldn't even sell at a flea market.

"You usually freeze, all the time freezin," Lorraine says quietly while rummaging through the contents.

"If I were twenty years younger I'd sit out there naked if I thought I'd be more comfortable."

"That I'd just as soon not see." She hands me a light beige linen blouse. "Is this all right? I like it on you."

"When do we have to go?"

"The fire department's comin to set up chairs, so it's not gon be for another hour at least."

"Hey ho, how're y'all?" Bernice's head peers around the door frame. She steps inside on tiptoe like she's trying to prance but could topple over at any given moment. She is carrying a basket over her arm and points to it. "Mister Benny's taking a nap. Shhh."

"We'll keep our voices down, won't we, Lorraine?" I whisper.

"He's in a basket," Bernice whispers back. "Like Moses in a basket. It's not bulrushes though, that's in Egypt, and we are a long ways away from Egypt, I'll tell you that right now."

"Well good, he's in a safe place. We'll wake him up directly." I motion to her to bring the basket over to me. She sits on the edge of the bed, takes Mister Benny out, and places him beside my head. He smells like maple syrup. "Bernice, has Mister Benny been eating pancakes again?"

"He loves sweet things, both of us do. He fell in my plate but it was an accident. He loves the taste of syrup. I can always tell real from fake."

"Well I can't," Lorraine interjects. "April brought home some that somebody gave her from Vermont or somewhere up there. It all tastes the same to me."

There are two fire trucks, small ones, pulling into the field behind the building. My window looks out onto it and I'm tempted to try one more time to talk Lorraine into letting me watch the goings-on from here. My husband was a volunteer fireman for a few years, but he never got to ride in a truck as nice as these. Two men are setting up chairs. At least they're not the folding white ones like you see at a graveside. I would hate that. First of all, they're too little to be comfortable, and second, well put it this way, the second reason is such that when it comes to pass I won't have to worry about the first.

Bernice shoots up like a bottle rocket and is about to leave. "Let's go to the party now. It's a hamburger party. I used to throw parties in Raleigh. We're going to save us some seats out there. Mister Benny's little, you can sit with him."

Lorraine helps me lift up my arms, one at a time, to get them into the sleeves of the blouse. It hurts but I don't say anything. I know she knows it hurts, and she's trying not to raise them too far over my head. She knows that kind of arthritis pain can be too much. Some people don't know. Some folks here won't take a bath because the people that give them are too rough. It's not because they're senile and don't want to be clean; it's because it hurts, goddamn it. Just moving a body can hurt, which is something that no person can understand until it's too late for them to be sympathetic about it because they've left the ranks of the ignorant and joined the ranks of the suffering. I don't complain, except to Lorraine. She can take it. She wants me to tell her how I feel. Once the sleeves are on, the buttons down the front are easy. She starts to do it, but I push her hand away gently. I have to try it myself. And if it takes too long, Lorraine doesn't huff and puff, she waits, not smiling like "oh isn't that sweet." She doesn't saying anything at all, giving me time.

After she finishes up in the kitchen, she comes back for me. On her arm, I travel to the party outside. Everyone that's not bedridden approaches from all directions in various states of dress or lack thereof. One woman has on the same pajamas she wears every day, covered with penguins and white fur around the cuffs, sweltering though the day may be. Taken in all at once, it looks like a string of ghosts, ambling along so slowly that they appear to be floating.

Lorraine startles me by bending close to my ear once she has me settled in a folding chair. "What do you want on your hamburger?"

"I want it well done, Lorraine. And I mean done, I don't want any pink showing. It's not healthy. Just put a little bit of ketchup on it, nothing else. And some mayonnaise and onions, but not too much onion. I would take one tomato slice if they've got any that look anyhow, but not any of those thin pinkish-orange ones, I can't stand them. There ought to be some good tomatoes now."

"Later on I'll go back and get you something sweet. They haven't put out any dessert yet. It's too hot."

"I might have some banana pudding if they've got it, but make sure the vanilla wafers are soft or I'll pass. I've never had any as good as you brought me."

I see Lorraine beam. "That was my mama's recipe," she says. "I grew up on it near 'bout every Sunday of my life."

"I know that was some good eating," I add. "Come on back here and sit down with me when you get a plate."

Ada Everett, the queen bee, has stepped up onto a raised platform. She is waving her hands in the air, and she's got on more bracelets than Cleopatra, jangling like kitchen utensils. "Excuse me everybody, just a minute before y'all get started eating." Country music is blasting through two speakers that the fire department brought. I have never understood why the fire department has big outdoor stereo speakers but they do. In fact, I have found that this is true of most volunteer fire departments in North Carolina. They have access to loudspeakers. "Would you mind turning that music down?" Ada says when a fireman hands her a microphone. "Somebody please? Lorraine?" Ada has the slightest edge in her voice that I have come to wait for gleefully because it lets me know that she's on the verge of losing control. Control of what, I don't know. Us, I suppose. We're helpless all, but in our own way, uncontrollable I reckon.

Ada has managed to take charge of the whole group, which I do believe is her one mission in life, and which is exactly why the job of running this place is the best thing that could have ever happened to her. "I think we ought to say a blessing," she says in what I call her Splenda voice—it's got some sugar in it, but the end result is not the real thing. "But before that," she continues, "some folks asked me a few minutes ago if I would sing something that was appropriate for the Fourth of July. Of course I said I wasn't about to on short notice, but then I thought, maybe it's important for us all to take a minute to be patriotic, and think about the history of this country so we can be proud. Not that we're not already proud, but sometimes it's good to stop and think. That's what I always say."

"Oh my Lord, she's going to sing," I say out loud to nobody in particular.

She starts out a cappella, but she's pitched it too high, so it's in the sort of soprano voice that makes you sit up straight just because you feel like if you don't, something dreadful is going to happen to your spine. *Mine eyes have seen the glory of the coming of the Lord . . .*

I am aware that the "Battle Hymn" is historical and that a woman wrote it in the Civil War, but in my mind, putting religion into fighting music is like pouring kerosene on a fire that's already plenty hot. That kind of music is best confined to the sort of people who make landscape borders out of truck tires and have life-size crosses in their yards that light up at night.

Glory, Glory Hallelujah. His Truth is marching on. She repeats the last chorus and I get the sense she's going to go for a high note at the end, a premonition in which I am not disappointed. *His Truth—Is—Mar—ching—ON!*

Bernice, whom to this point, I have not seen, is standing by the barbecue grill, alternating between clapping wildly and whistling with two fingers in her mouth. She is holding Mister Benny under one arm, squeezing the monkey doll's head beyond recognition. She spots me and waves; I wave back and beckon her over. I have no idea where Lorraine is, but that's all right. I know she probably wants to talk to somebody besides me, somebody young who watches the same TV shows and goes shopping for shoes for their children on the weekends, someone who goes out to eat fish every Friday night. I don't expect anything of her. I know she cares about me. That ought to be enough for a person.

Ada is talking to two volunteer firemen who have walked over to congratulate her on her solo. I guess they wanted to hear something patriotic too, and she's the closest anybody could come to that around here. Independence Day doesn't ring too many bells for most of us.

Bernice is holding Mister Benny on her shoulders with his legs wrapped around her neck, like holding a small child to watch a parade. Unfortunately, there is no parade. She takes Mister Benny down and holds one of his worn monkey paws outstretched as she begins to walk from chair to chair, greeting people. Most everybody stops eating and says hello, pretending to have never met Mister Benny before, but a few, like Josephus Parker, whom I know because he owned the drugstore near me for close to twenty-five years, don't have any patience for Bernice. "Don't bring that doll around here, woman, I don't have any use for your foolishness!" he yells at the top of his lungs. Ada Everett stops talking to the firemen and whispers something to Lorraine. Josephus is not a happy man, but barking at Bernice is not gentlemanly, which in his day, would have meant something to him. Now he's given up on form altogether, which makes me wonder if this is what was underneath all the time. I have seen a lot of people suffering worse melancholy who can put on a face for someone who needs to see that face, for the sake of comfort or recognition, or to feel for a few minutes like we're all in this together and have something in common.

The truth is we don't have much in common except the fact that none of us is here by choice. I personally don't resent that anymore, except on bad days from time to time. On those days, it can be something as simple as seeing the same walls over and over, not remembering much about my own walls at home, that makes me mad.

"Look here at what I've got. I know you're gon be satisfied with this here." Lorraine is bending over me, holding out a huge bowl of banana pudding. She has scraped off most of the meringue and piled some extra vanilla wafer crust on top, exactly the way I love it.

"Bless your heart." I put the bowl in my lap because it's too heavy to hold with one hand while taking a plastic spoon in the other. "I know it's not going to be as good as your mama's though."

Bernice strolls over with Mister Benny on one arm and the other waving out to the side like she's in a beauty contest. I've become used to such changes of manner. She's gazing around the landscape like she's on the Biltmore Estate. "Hello there," she twitters, "we are so glad you could come today. Welcome." She obviously thinks this is her party, or maybe Mister Benny's.

"My name is Bernice Alton Stokes, and this is Mister Benny Stokes. I'm thrilled he could join me today."

"Yes honey, we've met on several occasions. Always a pleasure." I shake the paw that is offered me. She does a sort of flip with the hem of her dress, like she might be wearing a ball gown and is off to the next person. Josephus Parker has a mouthful of stringy coleslaw that he is chewing slowly to a near-liquid state. Maybe he shouldn't be eating that, it's hard on your stomach, I don't know, it's none of my business. Josephus gets up and precariously approaches the big metal cooker, made out of an old oil drum. He's going back for seconds, and he gets around just fine without a cane or anybody's help. The nurse on his hall is a pretty Filipino woman named Kiri or maybe Kari—it's a funny name, it sounds like an exotic bird when you say it out loud. Whenever she tries to help him walk, he shoos her off angrily. More power to him I reckon. Bernice has made her way around the seated crowd and over to the cooker. She has welcomed almost everyone in the spirit of a true hostess at a party that unfortunately has absolutely nothing to do with her.

"Hello there, how're y'all?" She sticks out Mister Benny's paw to Josephus Parker, but he's serving his plate at the condiment table and doesn't look up. Bernice starts to speak again. "I told you once," Josephus glares at her, eyes wide. "And I'm not going to tell you again, you crazy thing." He snatches Mister Benny and raises him over his head as best he can, like he's going to haul off and throw him. Bernice is stone silent, her mouth is open but nothing comes out. I am watching this scene, and it seems like things are moving slowly enough that I can stop them, there's space in between each action, each word. But I'm paralyzed. Mister Benny lands square in the barbecue. He's on fire, lying on top of the grill with sizzling beef patties all around him. Somebody yells for Ada Everett, I can't tell who. Kiri or Kari is trying to reach down into the deep cooker, but it's too hot and she can't find any tongs, primarily because one of the volunteer firemen is clacking them like a crab claw while talking away to Ada, presumably praising her vocal expertise. Her expression alters dramatically when she sees the commotion by the cooker.

"Bernice, leave him alone!" I shout when I see her reach toward the barbecue. I know she hasn't got enough sense not to stick her hand in there. I want to get up and slap Josephus Parker in the face, and if I could, I would. Lorraine grabs Bernice's arm and extinguishes Mister Benny with a spatula before lifting him out and handing him off to Kari. He is black and smoldering.

"We'll clean him up, darlin," Lorraine says, "he'll be all right." Lorraine is not a sentimental woman, but she can see that Bernice is on the edge of a cliff and is trying to avoid what might happen if she jumps.

"That's not him, take it away from me. That's not him," she screams at Kari. "He's burning. Reach in there and pull him out. Reach down in there!" Ada Everett is standing near her now, the crowd is silent at the sound of Bernice's cry.

"Bernice, that's enough," Ada says, putting a hand on her shoulder from behind.

Bernice snaps her head around, she has terror in her eyes. "Reach in there! You!"

"We have Mister Benny out, he's right here, Kari will clean him up." Ada is embarrassed in front of the firemen, who are stunned. One leans over to me and says, "They ought not to have crazy people in here with you all. There are places for them these days that are good, real good."

Bernice is struggling in Lorraine's strong arms. "Nobody knows him but me. Stop it. Nobody knows him. I know him. Get him out."

"Kari, go wash him off," Ada says. "And call Dr. Jordan, you'll have to have him paged. Get something to calm her down. Lorraine, you walk her back to her room if she'll go."

"She'll go with me." I'm startled how loud my voice sounds. "Let her come with me. Bernice, come on with me, we'll take care of it. You know how much Lorraine loves Mister Benny and she's not going to let anything happen to him. Now come on here, let's go rest. I need to rest, you come and help me get settled in like you do, hear?"

"Reach down in there and get him. Please, will you please?" Bernice is crying, softly now, more of a whimper. "Is he in there? He's little; he can't get out. Reach in there and get him out."

I can't do anything to help her. She's walking with me, but I'm not really doing anything. I wish I could look inside her and save her from everything that hurts her, the pain of a dead son, the mourning which had found its way into a vessel that could, for a time, seem to hold it. I want to scoop up her, and Mister Benny, and put them in my car and drive to Nags Head. That's what I want, to see the ocean again, and not look back. Not ever lay eyes on anybody here again. Lorraine can come too. She's scared of water, but I want her with me. And we'll call Ann once we get down there, at a fish camp eating some fried flounder with tartar sauce on it, and we'll tell her we're fine, and not to bother to come after us. And the waitress will come over and ask us if we want some more tea, and we'll say, "Yes, we sure would. What kind of pie do y'all have today?" Then she'll go and have a look at what's left. I know they'll have old-timey chocolate with meringue on top because they always do, and we'll sit there together as long as we want to, laughing and eating our chocolate pie.

CHAPTER FIFTEEN

RHONDA

I might have on too much makeup, I don't want to look like I'm trying too hard to cover up something there ain't no use hiding. I used to have some better fitting jeans too. I know how to go out at night, but in the daytime, I haven't had a lot of practice in a while. There's a million cars already here, I'm probably not gonna know but a handful of these people. I should have stayed home and taken my day off like most people and watched TV, gone to Kmart, maybe planted some petunias in the yard to give it some color.

Connie Donnell spots me as soon as I get out of the car and waves with both arms like she's signaling an airplane in for a landing. "Hey girl, we been waiting for you! Come on in!" I think it's strange she said "in" cause everybody's standing out in her yard, she couldn't fit all these people into her trailer if she wanted to. Connie glances behind her to a group of guys in a circle, looking serious like they might be solving the problems of the world with Budweiser and Marlboros. It's also strange she said, "we," cause she's standing next to a couple kissing each other that I've never seen before.

She looks over her shoulder again and hollers in a high voice that could curl hair, "Hey Mike, why don't you go get Rhonda a beer?"

A tall guy with thick blond hair and a goatee turns. "Am I the only one's got hands around here?"

"Yeah and I thought you had a few manners to go along with em but I guess I was wrong."

I interrupt. "I can wait on myself Connie. I been doin it a long time."

"I know that." She smiles and lowers her voice. "That's Mike, Rhonda. *The* Mike I told you about?"

My goal in coming to a pig pickin was to eat some good food and get a little tipsy. I shoulda known Connie would take it on herself to make things more complicated. She knew my luck in men lately and also that I was near giving up. So many assholes, too little time. I've been on a lot of dates, but only because I thought I ought to. Mike approaches with two dripping longnecks and touches one, icy cold, to the back of Connie's neck. "Shit!" she screams. "I'm gonna kill you!"

Mike jumps back, faking being scared, and bows from the waist, arms stretched out holding the bottles. "A brew for Your Highness. Or Highnesses, I oughta say." He winks.

"Now that's more like it." Connie recovers. "Mike, this is my friend Rhonda. We both used to do hair at Evelyn's before I saw the light. Rhonda still works down there." Connie drives a UPS truck now and preaches the glories of it like she was born again. I know she makes good money. She says she's saving up to haul off that trailer and build her a house.

"I guess that means I did not see the light, which would not be the first time, I promise you." I put out my hand. "Nice to meet you, Mike." His hand is soft like a woman's, not what I expected. I look at the ground. God, I hate these jeans I've got on.

Connie pats me on the shoulder and steps away from us. "I'm gonna let y'all get acquainted a little bit. I got a bunch of slaw and stuff in the house that I need to put out. We're fixin to eat soon." She breaks into a little trot towards the porch. She's running funny like she might have to pee.

Mike crosses his arms and stands with his legs spread apart like he's planting himself to keep from getting blown away by a tornado. "So," he says, "you been doin hair for a long time?"

"Only thing I've ever done. You could say it's my callin." I hear the sarcastic edge in my voice.

"Well I think it *is* a callin. Look around here and you'll see a few heads that look like they could use a come-to-Jesus moment."

"Too many permanents," I point out. "There's no goin back."

"Sorta like plastic surgery. The more you do, the more you need to do."

"What do you know about plastic surgery?"

"Not a damn thing. I don't know what I'm talkin about."

"I like a man who stands by what he says." I catch myself looking into his face. I like this guy, but I'll never let on to Connie that she was right in telling me I would. It's a nice open face. I don't love that goatee cause it seems like everybody's got one, but I like his face, especially his nose. It's hard to find a nose that is exactly the right size. I always have the feeling that it was the last thing God added to the face and then reached down into a grab bag and whatever came out got plopped on underneath the eyes whether it looks worth a damn or not. Some of em come out all right like Brad Pitt's, but most of em are off to begin with and get worse the older you get.

Connie yells from the porch. It's that shrieking voice again; she oughta work on that or either put it to use calling hogs. "Let's eat y'all! Come and get it 'fore I throw it out!" Somebody turns up the music; I guess the time for polite talk is over and now it's time to get rowdy before the sun goes down. Last time she threw a pig pickin and it lasted into the night, somebody called the police from down the street and said they could hear Alan Jackson like he was in their living room.

Mike looks at the long table on the other side of the yard, now loaded up with huge platters of barbecue, fried chicken, corn on the cob, and every kind of cake you might want. I wonder if this is the end of our conversation.

"Well it was nice meetin you, Mike," I say, so I can be the one to finish first.

"You not gonna eat?" Mike asks.

"Yeah I am, but I thought you might want to eat with your friends."

"I don't know none of those guys. I know Connie from work, that's all."

"Lord, don't start preachin the gospel of UPS to me, okay?"

"Hey it's a good job, she's glad to have it. We got a lot of women drivers now."

I soften. "I know, I'm glad for her." I feel like I'm about to ruin something sweet by pouring vinegar into it. I decide to change the subject.

"Can I tell you somethin and you won't think I'm weird?"

"I can't promise you what I'll think, but tell."

"Your nose is like Brad Pitt's."

Mike grins. "I thought you were goin to say somethin serious."

"His nose is serious to him."

"Is that good?"

"Hell yeah. Look what it's done for Brad."

"Good, cause I'm tryin my best here, and I need all the help I can get."

"You're doin fine." I feel a little embarrassed. He clinks his bottle against mine.

"Well then, thank you, Brad. I'll buy you a drink next time I'm in Beverly Hills." He takes a swig. "Don't hold your breath."

Connie is back now in full force. "Hey y'all, go on and fix you a plate. Some of these gluttons will eat everything out there and not think a thing of it." Mike leads me over to the table where I meet some of Connie's other friends. Now I'm wishing I had got here earlier, but it doesn't matter cause I promise myself to take everything one step at the time. Don't know what tomorrow's gonna bring. I'm gonna be myself for the rest of today. I might even make a few hair suggestions after I drink another beer or two. We get in line behind forty people or so, and he hands me a doubled up paper plate with a folded red-checkered napkin, along with a plastic knife and fork. "Thanks, I'm starvin to death," I tell him and help myself to a big serving spoon full of pulled pork barbecue, vinegary and peppery and a little bit smoky all at the same time. "I didn't know I was so hungry," I add because it seems like the thing to say and then I think how stupid it sounds.

"As soon as I saw you I knew you had an appetite," Mike says, following me in line and loading up his plate with everything Connie had fixed. "I've got one too."

We round the long table with plates piled up like mountains and take some iced tea from a big aluminum urn at one end. I'm staying all night, I decide, as long as it goes. As long as Mike has got two words to say. Turn it up, make it loud, bring it on. When the police come, I'll give em a beer.

CHAPTER SIXTEEN

LORRAINE

When I'm afraid, I choose to be the opposite. When I'm sad too, I choose the opposite. Same thing when I'm angry. Sometimes of course it don't work but lots of times it does. My reason is simple: because this is the day the Lord has made. I live with that thought in my mind and try to let everything else fall into place if it will.

I come to church because that's my habit. It's the only thing I have ever done on Sunday morning unless I'm working. Maybe I'm too superstitious to stop comin now, but I like to think I get something out of it, even if it's just one thing. The older I am, the more I like a good preacher, and when one's not good, I'm tempted to get up and walk out, not before saying, "Next time, do your homework before you come to school." We had a woman preacher from Durham visiting last Easter. She was finishing up at Duke Divinity School and she went to country churches if they needed somebody to fill in when the regular preacher was sick or gone on vacation. I liked that preacher. She stood up at the front and read scripture like she had thought hard about it. She took her time with the words. When she read Psalm 23, *The Lord is my shepherd, I shall not want,* I listened to it, which I usually don't do cause I've heard it so many times. *He restoreth my soul; my cup runneth over.*

When I glance down, I see the hands of an old woman, one

gettin old anyway. My hands tell the truth of how long I've been here. Today I'm holding a purse. Most days I'm holding the hand of someone who can't stand up by herself, or someone who's trying to get to the bathroom in time but can't make it. Or I'm holding a fork to put in a mouth gaping wide-open with no teeth. I'm holding a toothbrush or a comb or a washcloth or a diaper or a pillow or a glass of water or toilet paper. And after I finish, I tie what's left up in a plastic bag and carry it out with me to add to all the other trash bags from all the other rooms, and all the other nursing homes, hospital floors, and back bedrooms everywhere in the world where people need help to do the simplest things in life. We'll all get there sometime. *Surely goodness and mercy shall follow me all the days of my life.*

There's a notice in the service bulletin under the benediction. "The flowers on the altar today are in honor of Mrs. Bernice Stokes and Mrs. Margaret Clayton at Ridgecrest Nursing Center." I put em up there for no reason other than I felt like it, and they look mighty good if I do say so. I paid more than I meant to for them, but I'm glad I did. I went to the church office on Tuesday so Teresa Clark the secretary could print up my dedication. She looked at me funny when I gave her the names, even though she's only the typist and not a member of the church. "They're two of your nursing-home ladies? I don't guess you really call them patients, do you?" she said like she couldn't believe I would fix such a big bouquet for two demented old white women I clean up after. In her mind, the only thing that makes me any different from a maid is that I clean up in a rest home instead of somebody's house. It don't matter to her that I work with the RNs, take blood pressure, keep medical records, any of that. She thinks I'm like a slave in the big house, yes-ma'aming white people. Well yes, I do clean up. I clean up after anybody who's too old to do it for themselves and who doesn't have anybody else who can or will do it for them. I clean up after a lot of hours of loneliness when somebody deep down knows they haven't got much time left, and the little bit they do have is ticked off by daytime TV shows and holiday decorations in the cafeteria if they're lucky enough to be able to get down there and see them. I clean up after what's left of life. That's what I do, Teresa, while you sit at a machine in a nice dress and believe you have rose above what you call "service." Well I love serving. No, maybe that's not true, but I do love people, most of em. I can't help it. Even when they're as different from me as anybody could be, even when they don't make sense, because they are here, Teresa, and right now they are makin their way down the same path that I will have to walk one day. And you'll walk it too Teresa, whether you have on a nice dress or not and whether you have on lipstick or not. You might not even have enough mind left to know where you are. Her voice broke me out of my daydreaming. "Is that going to be all, Lorraine, or did you need something else?" She was pleasant enough; maybe I'm the one who made her a demon in my head. "No thank you, that's all I need, just wanted to take care of my ladies," I said and went on about my business.

I wish this service would hurry up and start. I saw some scuffling around the door to the choir loft, like they were gettin ready to come in but forgot something and got pulled back out into the hall. Somebody picked up the wrong music or needs a Kleenex or drink of water. I plan on taking the flowers to split with Margaret and Bernice tomorrow, they don't need to sit in here and die, that ain't nothin but waste. Miss Margaret needs cheering up. She's still as bossy as she ever was, and a know-it-all, but it's like she's fallin a step behind the clock. The light is dimming some, I expect nobody sees it but me. But I'm watching her, I'll keep a close eye on her because she needs somebody to call her back, help her hang on, or she's gon slip. First she's gon let go of the tiny little things, things that don't matter, and then they're gon start adding up, and the next thing you know, she won't be answering when you speak to her. Or she'll talk out of her head. I can't stop that working on her any more than I could on Bernice, or on me when my time comes, but I'll try to make sure she knows that I know what's goin on. I do dread the day when that woman stops tellin me what to do. I dread the day when she looks into my eyes and sees somebody else. She won't know me, or at least I won't be able to see that she does. Based on what I've seen, that's the day when we shouldn't keep our good-byes too far out of reach.

The choir is finally sitting. We're gon get out late today, that's for sure. I swear I can't get used to seein Althea up there in a robe. I never have thought she could sing nothin special, but ever since she had her last birthday, she says she's trying one new thing every year. I don't know if that means she will only do the thing for one year and then drop it, or if she's gon keep adding on, year after year. If so, she's gon die a busy woman. God bless her, she's sittin in the middle of the sopranos and her with a voice on the telephone that sounds like a man if you didn't know better. That's all right, Althea, go right on. You're not through yet and neither am I.

CHAPTER SEVENTEEN

Rhonda

I notice how Margaret crosses her legs in one of the dryer chairs. It looks like it's hard for her to do, but the way she's sitting makes me know what a pretty woman she was when she was young. "Rhonda honey, how are you?" she says. "Anything new since last week that you haven't already told us?"

She and Bernice like to come back down here lots of times when I'm closing up after a long day of doing God knows how many heads of hair. Some of em don't have any more than a few strands left, but they want it to be fixed and I understand that. I hope I've got some pride in how I look as long as I'm alive and got sense enough to do something about it.

Bernice is skimming through magazines without really looking at anything, just flipping pages. She likes to lick her index finger now and then to help her turn them, and she looks like a lady in an old movie every time she does it. Like she has all the time in the world and a bunch of servants running around and can read magazines whenever she wants to. Most of what I have in here are in shreds, mainly because I bring whatever ones Evelyn is gonna throw away at the salon, but at least there's something for people to do while they're waiting.

The three of us talk about the same things every time, the weather, what we had to eat that was good, do I know anybody they know who died, which I never do because I don't know anybody they know period, but I think when you're their age you feel like you've got to see who's still alive and who's not. We also try to keep track of any movie stars that have got married or divorced or had babies, and what's wrong with the way the country's being run. Those are the subjects, pretty much in that order, and they keep us pretty busy. I never exactly decided to keep my personal life personal, it just doesn't come up, not that there's so much to tell. It ain't a natural thing for me to talk about. I never talked to my grandma at all about my nights or weekends out, I wouldn't have if you'da put a gun to my head, and Mama was gone before I was old enough to want to do anything with a boy except run a race, which I usually won. But Margaret and Bernice won't leave me alone. That don't sound like a very nice way of putting it, I know. What I mean is that those two old women have gotten up under my skin. Maybe I'm still young enough that hanging around with me makes them feel young too.

I shake out a towel and start to fold it. "Well since you asked," I blurt out, "Yours Truly went out on a date." I surprise myself with how the words sound coming out of my mouth, like I'm a teenage babysitter teasing a couple of little girls I'm s'posed to be taking care of. I mighta known the two of them would be on me like crows in a cornfield. Margaret pinches Bernice on the arm in a real satisfied kind of way that makes her drop her magazine.

"Are you pickin a fight?" Bernice says. "Cause I'm strong. You can ask anybody around here."

"Honey, we're not fighting, we're talking," Margaret says. "Didn't you hear Rhonda? She's got a boyfriend."

"That's not what I said. I shoulda never brought this up." I shake out another towel so hard it pops.

Bernice claps her hands together. "Is it true love?" She sounds like she's the winner on a game show.

"Bernice, honestly," Margaret says. "Don't always go to the extreme with something." She gets up to get a Kleenex.

"Is he Prince Charming?" Bernice bats her eyes and crosses her arms at the wrist over her heart.

"I said I went on a date, y'all make it sound like it's the Second Coming."

"No, no, no, sweetheart, we're just excited is all," Margaret says. "It's not like you tell us news like this every week. What do you expect from a couple old ladies who think a kiss is a piece of chocolate?" She is pleased with her own joke. "Isn't that right, Bernice?" she adds, grinning back at her friend.

"Kiss me you fool!" Bernice cries out, fanning herself with an old magazine.

"I swear to God, y'all, don't start blabbin my business around here," I warn. "I'm tellin you cause I wanted to see what you think, but y'all need to be serious."

"Honey, we are serious," Margaret snaps. "When you're our age, keeping your eyes open is serious."

"What about Bernice?" I ask, knowing in my mind that she doesn't know the meaning of a secret, at least not anymore.

"Bernice isn't going to remember who went on a date, so even if she tells it, which she no doubt will, your identity will be spared, have no fear. Besides, the first person she's going to tell will probably be Alvin, and by the time she finishes it'll be so mixed up in a poker game that even he won't have any earthly idea what she's talking about."

"Okay then," I say. I can't help myself. I really am excited to give them the details. In fact, those two old things are the only people I even want to tell except for Connie.

"So?" Margaret says and sits back down, almost falling backwards in the chair with a soft plunk sound, and crosses her legs again, this time at the ankle, like a picture of the Queen of England, once she pushes the hair dryer out of the way. Bernice has her nose back in a magazine, *Progressive Farmer*, and I think, how the hell did that get in here?

"Aren't you going to tell us his name?" Margaret coos at me.

"Mike." I must be crazy. I sound like I've never been on a date before.

"Michael, row your boat ashore, Hallelujah!" Bernice sings at the top of her lungs, then busts out laughing.

"It's not Michael; well maybe it is, I don't know, but he goes by Mike. Just Mike."

"Uh-huh," Margaret says. "And what does Mike do?"

"He works for UPS. He's got a real good job."

"Good, good, so far so good." Margaret eggs me on.

"And . . . and that's kinda it."

"Where'd he take you?"

"Dinner under the stars I hope!" Bernice looks up from the *Progressive Farmer* where she is reading about, or at least looking at, giant pictures of boll weevils. "These right here are something terrible," she says, tapping a photo. "You've got a mess on your hands with these here. I know a lot about pests."

I focus more on Margaret, leaving Bernice to the crop bugs. I ain't proud of myself, but sometimes it's hard to keep throwing a ball to somebody who never catches it. "It was nice," I say. "An Italian kind of place with the littlest candleholders I've ever seen on the tables, and grapevines stenciled on the walls, you know, real elegant, and soft music, kinda classical I guess, violins and such. I didn't even think I liked classical, but I liked what they were playin. Anytime I ever hear classical music, it's all right when it's soft and pretty but then it'll surprise you with a loud blast that sounds like the end of the world. It's like whoever wrote it is tryin to scare you so bad you don't even know how loud to make your stereo cause if you overshoot it, you might go deaf."

"Do they have spaghetti?" Bernice never ceases to surprise me with what she takes in and what drifts on by. "I like spaghetti." She smiles. "But not SpaghettiOs, no ma'am, I do not." She turns to Margaret. "You love spaghetti, don't you?"

"Yes honey, I think pretty much everyone does, but I'm not sure that's what Rhonda had."

"Why not?" Bernice asks. "She went to Italy."

"No Bernice, a restaurant." I make an effort but decide to leave well enough alone. "We got fish," I say. "He asked if he could order somethin for me and I said sure, why not." I look at Bernice, who still is not satisfied about the Italy part. "But y'all, it doesn't even matter what you get cause they bring you spaghetti anyway."

"Ha!" Bernice yells.

"I told Mike, 'I can't eat all this. You'll have to haul me off in a trailer if I do.' He said, 'Rhonda, it's not a contest, just enjoy what you want.'"

Bernice cries out, "A beauty contest?"

"No, he meant eatin." I try to reel her in.

"I never heard tell of a eatin contest except at the state fair. Eat as many pies as you can, but you'll get sick if you don't mind!" Bernice is now howling. She has worked herself up into a full-out party.

Margaret is serious. "Rhonda, we don't need all the details. Let's talk about the important stuff. Is he kind? That's what I want to know. Do you think he is kind?"

I don't answer her right away cause as much as I've been thinking about him, I haven't ever had anybody come right out and put a question to me like that.

"I guess," I say. "I mean, I think he is, I don't know. But he did surprise me. When we got up to leave the restaurant, we passed a table with an older man and woman havin dinner by the window. She looked like she was tryin to carry on a conversation, he was diggin into a prime rib and not payin her any mind. You could tell she had got herself all fixed up to come out to dinner, and left up to him, they might as well be sittin at home in front of a TV eatin leftovers. I didn't know Mike had noticed until he walked over there as we were leavin and said, 'Excuse me, I'm sorry to interrupt y'all.' The man looked up, barely. Mike turned to the lady. 'I just had to stop and say I don't know what occasion y'all are celebratin but you look beautiful. Y'all are a real handsome couple.' I thought that woman's jaw was gonna drop. She turned bright red and fingered the pearls around her neck and said, 'Oh thank you. It's our anniversary. Forty years.' Her husband had gone back to sawin and chewin. 'That's a long time, isn't it?' she asked, like she couldn't hardly get her mind around it herself. 'Yes it is,' I said. Mike squeezed my hand. 'Y'all should be real proud,' he said and stood still for a minute, like maybe he was waitin for somethin from the man, who sat there dippin bread in a pool of bloody juice on his plate. Mike looked back to the wife. 'Anyway, sorry to bother y'all,' he said. 'Congratulations again.' He took my arm and we walked away. 'Thank you so much,' I heard the woman say, and then back to her husband, 'Wasn't that sweet, Raymond?' He didn't answer her."

"She ought to have told him to go to hell." Margaret sneers.

"She's mad now, she's hot as a firecracker!" Bernice cackles, looking at Margaret through a magazine that she has rolled up like a telescope.

"I'm not mad, I'm just telling the truth. I don't even know those people."

Bernice laughs. "She might get in a fight before supper!"

"Stop peeping at me through that tube, Bernice, you make me nervous." Margaret shifts in her chair, turning her whole body towards me. "Now, Rhonda. You're going out again I guess, aren't you?"

I'm trying to squeeze a big stack of folded towels into the only storage cabinet I have. "I don't know, he hasn't asked me yet."

"Oh, he's going to ask you," Margaret says, "I'll bet money on that."

I feel embarrassed cause she has come right out and said what I'm hoping but there's no way I woulda told. Bernice hasn't caught up with us just yet, but at least she has calmed down some. She points to Margaret like she's telling me a secret. "You get that girl right there mad, and you'll know somethin, I'll tell you that."

Margaret can see right through me. "Sweetheart, you really are worried."

"I've been goin out with friends mostly," I say. "Last time I went out with a stranger was a year ago. I was at the Y-Not Drop Inn, that's a bar pretty close to where I live. It's also got a little restaurant but nobody's hardly ever in there, everybody's all crowded into the bar part, especially on the weekends. I was there with my friend Connie, but she said she had gotten up real early for her route and was gonna head home, but did I want to stay. I said, 'Yeah I'm gonna finish my beer, go on.' It wasn't two seconds after she got off the stool that a guy sat down beside me.

"'I know you,' he said.

"I lit up a cigarette. 'From the movies?' I asked. A voice in my brain said real loud that I wasn't in the mood to be picked up. And believe me, if I was in the mood, nothin would stop me, so you know I must really not have been to blow him off like that. And he was good lookin too, in a stray dog kind of way.

"'I do know you,' he said. 'I can't remember your name, but I know you. From school.'

"'It's been a long time since I was in school,' I answered him. I really didn't want to be rushed through my beer. It was Friday night and I had spent all day with my hands in people's hair.'"

"You love hair, don't you?" Bernice interrupts, innocent as a five-year-old.

"Yes I do, but there can always be too much of a good thing," I say. "Anyway, turns out he had gone to college somewhere in the mountains and was working for a company that makes bike locks and I guess other locks too, but the bikes were the ones he talked about."

"What is there to say about a lock?" Margaret asks. "Either it locks or it doesn't. What else do you need to know?"

"I know, I know it's boring but some people might think what I do is boring too."

"I beg to differ," she says. "Under every head of hair is the head of a person. That's at least the potential for something interesting."

"Well he wasn't lyin. He was a year ahead of me, I found out later. Randy Roper. I didn't know him but I had seen him around. He played baseball. When he asked me didn't I want to get somethin to eat, I said, 'Not here. Have you ever seen anybody eat here?' We didn't go to a restaurant. I knew we weren't gonna eat as soon as I said 'not here.' He had a scar on his chest, told me he got it from the blade of a band saw that snapped off. Next morning, he left me lyin in bed at the Super8 and went to get coffee and didn't come back. So much for 'I-know-you' Mr. Randy Roper."

Margaret and Bernice sit staring at me, silent as two corpses. "Don't y'all feel sorry for me. I got what I wanted and so did he. Hey, I do what I need to do and I take what comes along with it."

"What did you get," Margaret says, "other than the obvious?"

I want to snap at her, it's like I hear my grandma in her voice, not that she said it mean, but I heard it that way. Judge and jury rolled up into one, that was Grandma. Instead, I feel the pressure start to build up behind my eyes, then tears. "I need Mike to be different."

Bernice picks up the whole stack of magazines she has piled on her lap and puts them on the floor. She gets up, slightly wobbly, and takes hold of my hands, still in the yellow rubber gloves that I use to clean sinks. She doesn't try to say anything, maybe somehow she knows it'll come out crazy, so she doesn't want to. Then she kisses me, on the mouth, and standing perfectly still, smiles the biggest smile you can think of before going back to her chair like absolutely nothing happened.

"You need to bring Mike around here, Rhonda," Margaret says. "When you feel ready to."

"He said he wants to come. He's heard me talk about y'all 'til I'm blue in the face and he wants to see y'all and everything else for himself. I said to him, 'Should I want to see where *you* work, cause I have to tell the truth, I don't really.' 'Darlin,' he said, 'anytime you want to see, just go stick your head in the truck, that's my place of business.'"

Margaret clears her throat. "I'm going to say something, sugar, and I assume you will bother to listen since you took the time to tell us that story in the first place."

"You're scarin me now."

"Rhonda." She pauses. "You deserve to be noticed. Not once or twice, always. Now that's a tall order, because when you stop acting like there's something worth noticing, then you can be sure everybody else will follow suit."

"We're just datin," I say.

Margaret goes on. "You want somebody to be different, you've got to be different. I myself didn't learn that. I spent a lot of time waiting for my husband to change, and I'm not so sure that he didn't actually try. That, my dear, was a pure waste of time. I don't know how much anybody changes, they just take on different forms at different times. Kind of like water. Sometimes it's liquid, sometimes it's ice, sometimes it's slush."

"I bought them slushies when they were little. Red, orange, grape, whatever they wanted at the 7-Eleven!" Bernice squeals. "If you drink em too fast, you'll get a headache. That's what I told them, and they listened." She seems real satisfied to have the last word.

"I'm listenin too," I say to both of em. "I am. Thank you."

"Anytime," Bernice says. "Have you got a bathroom?"

"You know exactly where it is." Margaret takes hold of Bernice's hand. "Down the hall. Come on, I'll go too. Let's get out of here so this girl can get on with her life. She's got a lot of fish still to fry."

I watch them teeter out and into the hall. It's so quiet that I can hear the fluorescent lights humming. I hate those lights cause they make the walls look fake. You can't see the real color of anything. But I don't want to turn them off. I don't want to close up. It's way past time for me to go, but if I leave too fast, I might forget something, and I don't want to have to come back to look for it.

CHAPTER EIGHTEEN

LORRAINE

By the time we pull into the parking lot, both of my passengers are sleepin like babies. Neither one of their families even knows Rhonda except by sight, so they had to sign release papers for me to bring them to the wedding. They're used to it, sometimes we'll take a van to the mall at Christmas, things like that, for any of em that are able. I like Rhonda all right even though I don't really know her that good except from helping people get to the salon when she's there.

When I volunteered to bring the ladies here today, Bernice's son asked me, "Do you have a car that'll run?"

I told him, "It gets me to and from work every day."

"Uh-huh. Okay," he said, like he was giving a test, then he added, "You know I'd take Mama myself, but my wife and I have plans we can't switch around, we got the kids and all."

"We'll be all right, don't worry yourself," I said as my way of lettin him know I didn't need or want to hear any explanations. We weren't going but ten miles down the road into the country. As for Margaret's daughter Ann, she'll be workin like she does every weekend showing houses, that's her busiest time. Standing with me in front of Ada Everett, I felt like she wanted to make a point. She said, "Lorraine, you know I trust you with Mama like I trust myself. If she wants to go, I want you to take her. Ada, are you going?"

"I can't leave here," Ada answered, handing over the form Ann needed to sign. "We've got a state inspection week after next. I wish I could, I think a lot of Rhonda."

Ann nodded. "I know Mama does too, even though she says she's hard on her head sometimes." She clicked down the hallway in expensive shoes. She needed to look good to sell houses. She spoke without turning back. "Bye Lorraine, I'll see you tomorrow." And I knew she would too cause I couldn't think of but maybe two or three times a year when she hadn't been down here at some point in the day. That was her way, everybody finds their own way here. Miss Margaret complains about her sometimes, but they all do. Loved ones get it the worst no matter what, but far as I know, that's life.

They tell me Rhonda hasn't known her fiancé but a few months. I expect she feels like she knows him pretty good to get married, and I hope for her sake she does. She wanted more than anything to have these two ladies come, Margaret barely able to walk some days, and Bernice with no tellin what's gon come out of her mouth at any time. Rhonda asked me if I thought their families would let em go and I told her I didn't think it would be a problem. Margaret wants to go to every wedding or funeral or baptism or any other service she can if somebody will take her. I've never in my life seen anybody so ready to go to get in the middle of somebody else's church service. "It's the rituals of life I'm interested in, Lorraine. Taking part in them is good for the soul." I say she's nosy, that's it. As for Bernice, she may or may not know she's at a wedding, you can't never tell. She loves Rhonda though and I think that's all right.

I turn off the ignition. "Y'all sleeping beauties gon wake up or you want me to go to the wedding and tell you about it later?"

Margaret stirs beside me and is the first one to say something. "Lord God, are we already here? That sun coming in the window puts me to sleep every time, I can't help it to save my life."

I don't realize Bernice is awake until she hollers from the backseat, "Is the bride here yet?"

"We thought you might fill in for her if she can't make it," Margaret says. She nudges me. It goes right over Bernice's head.

I get out and start the preparations of movin these ladies from car to church. I've parked as close as I can, but I still think I better take em one at the time, Bernice first cause she's a little bit easier to handle. She can still walk all right even though she's had one heart attack and they think she might have had a mild stroke too. She's fine if she don't get in a hurry, then she can't get her breath. I've got a walker for Margaret and a wheelchair in the trunk of the car cause I don't never know which one she might need and neither does she. When I ask her some days if she wants to take a walk, she says, "It depends on how long a trip you're planning." Today she's feelin all right. When I open the boot of the car, she snaps, "Don't start hauling out any of that artillery, Lorraine. I plan to walk into that church, but I want to hold onto your arm."

Bernice is at the door already. I told her to walk up the ramp to the side of the porch. There are only three shallow steps but she's not supposed to climb any stairs with her heart, and she knows I mean business. I learned a long time ago that the best way for me to help Bernice is to treat her like a bighearted, free-spirited child, and it's that much more important now that she's not well. "Bernice, wait there, we're all gon go in together." An usher opens the front door. He's a big man, probably at least 250 pounds, and has got a red face like it's sunburned in October and a reddish-blond bushy mustache. He claps his hands and rubs them together like he's gettin ready to roll dice. "Let me help y'all, take your time, they're not starting yet."

"Thank you, I 'preciate it," I say, coming up the ramp real slow with Miss Margaret. I can see from the way he takes Bernice's arm that he's got a grandmother who loves him. Margaret sees it too. "That's a sweet boy right there," she says.

"You feelin all right?" I ask her when we get to the top of the walkway.

"If I'm not you'll be the first to know."

"I don't doubt that."

I take three programs and we follow the big usher down the aisle. Bernice is waving to some people, and I know she don't know one soul at this wedding. Most of em are waving back like they think they're s'posed to know who in the world she is. I hope he don't put us too close to the front cause I might have to take one of the ladies out if they need to go to the bathroom, and I need to figure out soon where exactly it might be. We get ourselves situated on a long pew with nobody else on it even though the rest of the little church looks like it's full. I put myself between Margaret and Bernice so I can do whatever I need to for either one of em. A side door opens up front and a girl and two boys come out, all of em in their thirties or somewhere around there, a few years younger than Rhonda by what I can tell.

"Is the bride here yet?" Bernice asks me again. "I sure do want to meet her."

Margaret leans out around me. "Honey, it's Rhonda. She fixes your hair." Then Margaret starts to read her program out loud, and she doesn't know how loud her voice is. "Stairway . . . to . . . Heaven," she says, like she's making an announcement. "That's a song?" She turns to me and I tell her yes, and I know it is, but maybe I'm thinking of the wrong one cause I never heard it at a wedding.

Bernice sticks her head out around me to Margaret. "I'm going to get a hairdo. You want one too?" she says. "Later on," Margaret says. I like the way she talks to Bernice real matter-of-fact. I learn a lot from her.

The wedding party is gathering in the back of the church, people around us are turning and whispering to each other. There are a lot of people crammed into these pews. I hear a woman's high voice from

the back, as loud as if she was standing beside us. I can't make out all
of what she says, but I hear real clear: "She works with Rhonda, and
Rhonda wants em all here. You got a problem?" I know I've heard
that voice before. There's some scuffling around in the bridesmaids,
a lot of activity. I can see they've got on peach-colored dresses with
wide white ribbons around the waist.

The sound of a sharp crack rises above the rumbling, sounds like
skin on skin to me. Margaret says, "Somebody got slapped back there,
Lorraine. I heard it, didn't you hear her yell?" There's still music playing but it don't cover the noise. Bernice turns all the way around and
sounds shocked. "She's crying!" she tries to whisper but it's way too
loud to be a whisper. The people around us look like they want to
ignore what's goin on even though you'd have to be deaf not to know
there was a fight back in that vestibule. I feel like I'm gon die if I don't
turn and see for myself. The usher who took us in is holding onto a
tall girl with long hair and moves her off to one side. Her makeup is
smeared all over her face. Somebody says, "Okay, Connie! Shhh!" and
the first pair of the wedding party is ready to start walking in. The
music changes and it's a little bit livelier, I know it from the radio. My
program says, "You Are the Wind Beneath My Wigs" but somebody
has gone through and crossed out the last word with a blue marker
and wrote in "Wings" on top of it. That mistake had to be a joke on
Rhonda; if not, then God does have more of a sense of humor than
I give Him credit for. The first couple starts down the aisle, followed
by four or five more. The congregation is smiling the same as all
wedding guests do, but they look as uncomfortable as a spell of bad
indigestion.

The tall girl who was crying is the last bridesmaid out, drooping
on the arm of the big usher. She looks like she had time to wipe off
her face but her eyes are still red. Margaret has forgotten the fight and
already moved on to the next thing in her mind. You can't never tell
about somebody old, sometimes they'll hang onto the littlest thing

that doesn't matter and can't let it go for nothing, then something that might seem big to most people, they don't care about it over a minute or two. She taps my hand and says, "I'm surprised to see that color on bridesmaids in October, I don't care if it *is* warm." She clucks her tongue. "Bless her heart, that's what she wanted and that's what she got." I'm glad to be in between the two of them because side by side they could get on a roll about something. The usher who brought us in smiles my way when he passes while the tall girl looks straight ahead with a smirk on her face.

Now that everybody's up front who's supposed to be there, I recognize Rhonda's friend Connie, she delivers packages to the nursing home once in a while. Rhonda told me it was her best friend and asked wasn't it something that we were on her delivery route out of all the UPS drivers in the county? Connie nods at me and the ladies like she's saying, "Don't you worry, I took care of the problem," and I realize she's the one who slapped that tall girl, and at the same time that I'm in the middle of a roomful of white faces. I know this story all too well, but whenever I forget, something like this happens to remind me that there's no end to it. I've been angry before, every black person has been, but now I feel less angry than I do like a pretty balloon has popped in front of my face. I am here with my two friends, they are here because I brought em, and they want to be here. That's the only reason I don't get up and leave.

I thank God when "Here Comes the Bride" starts. It's the most familiar thing to me so far at this wedding and it has got to mean we're gettin close to the reason we're here. I tell Margaret and Bernice they don't have to stand up if they don't feel like it, but they both surprise me and get on their feet by holding onto the pew in front of us and pulling up. I'm grateful they can. Rising up when you're weak makes a person stronger. By standing, they're saying that Rhonda matters and they matter too. I feel better when I think about how showing respect to one person makes every person worth more. Standing in this crowd makes the ladies as much a part of life as anybody else. Bernice jabs me hard on the shoulder with a bony finger. "Here comes the bride!" She can barely stand it she's so excited. Holding on, I rise up too.

CHAPTER NINETEEN

MARGARET

My mouth is cotton. The oversized red numbers on the digital alarm clock beside my bed read 9:42 P.M. The colon between the 9 and the 42 flashes all the time, marking the seconds, which could make me lose my mind if I stare at it. I have got to have something to drink, and I don't want water. I don't know who's on duty at this time of night but it won't be Lorraine, and she's the only one who'll bring me Co-Cola because it has caffeine in it. I'll have to take my chances and ring the buzzer. The only other light in the room besides the alarm clock is an electric jack-o'-lantern plugged in on top of my bookshelf. I don't know where it came from, I guess Ann brought it, although plug-in plastic is not usually her style. I know they wouldn't let us have a real pumpkin because it would start to rot and bugs would get in it, and it's probably against the law to have a real candle inside. This one's eyes are upside down triangles with upturned eyebrows like he's surprised. I don't care if it's plastic; I like it. I like the glow.

"Yes ma'am?" There's a young woman with jet-black hair at the door. "Did you want something?"

"Are you a nurse?"

"No ma'am I'm not. Do you need a nurse?" She is not smiling.

"No ma'am, I need a Co-Cola if you could spare one, please. I'm about to thirst to death."

She walks away. "I'll be back," she says.

I look back at the jack-o'-lantern. I'm going to call him Ole Jim. When we were little, Callie and I loved ghost stories. I think what we really loved is that Mother could make up tales that were as good as any you could read in a book. She used to tell one about a man named Ole Jim, who lost his mind and threw two children, brother and sister, down a well where they drowned on Halloween night. Mother said Ole Jim's soul was punished by roaming the earth until he could hold a little child's hand and say he was sorry. She told us if we were ever lying in bed and got a chill out of nowhere, that was Ole Jim trying to snuggle up beside us and say he was sorry. That might sound like a scary thing to say to a child, but Callie and I ate it up like sugar. Mother had a hundred stories she learned from her grandmother, who had a touch of Lumbee Indian in her. Mother may not have believed in ghosts, but she definitely allowed for things in this world that cannot be explained by anyone. That, combined with the fact that she taught Sunday school every week of her life that I remember, made her a most interesting minister's wife. She called herself religious, but she didn't have any problem also saying that she didn't think it was possible to know everything there was to know about God from the Bible or a church or a preacher.

The girl with the black hair is back. She looks like she could be part Indian herself, her cheeks are so high and proud. Her hair is shiny in the fluorescent hall light.

"I've got a Sprite here for you. Can you drink it by yourself?"

"Have you got a straw?" I ask. She's already gone.

I take a good long sip of Sprite even though it's not what I asked for. It burns the back of my throat a little, but in that lovely way an ice-cold drink does when you're parched. I feel the TV remote under my left hip and retrieve it. I'm wide-awake, might as well see if anything is on.

"Boo!"

I look at the doorway and no one is there.

A single hand reaches around the door like a claw, and I hear a wicked laugh. "Boo!" again. Bernice is looking in now, pointing at me and laughing. "I got you!" she says. "I scared you!"

"What do you want in the middle of the night?"

"You've got the TV on. Are you having a pajama party?"

"I'm having insomnia," I say, thankfully feeling a little tired again already.

"Let's watch TV." She pulls up the visitor chair. It makes a scraping sound on the floor that makes me cringe slightly. Before sitting down, she snatches one of the blankets off my bed. "You don't need two, do you?" she says, "You don't look cold."

She takes the remote and starts clicking. She flies past CNN, MTV, and the Food Network, which I have loved ever since being in here where nothing tastes like anything you've had before in your life, and I don't mean that as a compliment. She lingers for a moment on a nature program about snakes but keeps going until she lands on a black-and-white movie with Vincent Price. "This is scary like Halloween. Let's be scared, okay?" She is trying to edge up into the bed with me, and I let her.

"Trick or Treat's coming," she continued. "We're gonna have to get some candy."

"Well you're not going to find a thing in here. All I've got is peanut brittle somebody brought, and please tell me who in here has the teeth for peanut brittle."

"Trick or Treat is his favorite day because he loves sweets."

"Are we going to watch this or not, Bernice?"

"He didn't want to dress up at all but I said he couldn't go to people's doors without a costume."

I am accustomed to Bernice not making sense, but I feel annoyed,

I can't help it. "Stop talking and moving around before one of us falls out of the bed," I tell her.

"You can dress up like a monkey if you want to but that's not very scary, sweetheart. How about a green goblin with a big hook nose?"

"Who?" I ask tersely.

"Why are you acting like you don't know my boy when you've met him a hundred times?"

"You're talking about Cameron's children? I'm sure they're long in bed by now." She practically disregards me.

"No, Cameron's too old for Trick or Treat. He won't go. Don't make him, his daddy said."

A woman screams on TV. A wax museum figure has just reached out and tried to strangle her. It is blood-curdling. I take the remote from Bernice and turn the volume down. It occurs to me that Vincent Price looked dead even when he was alive. He is young in this movie but he still looks like a corpse. I feel sorry for him. I wonder if he ever got married.

Bernice continues. "He told me he wanted to be a monkey because he thinks they're nice and I told him that some monkeys are not that nice, but he said the ones he likes are nice and he wanted to be one. I have never been one to sew very well but I learned that Halloween by trial and error."

"Bernice, are you telling a story?" I ask. She could have seen an article in a magazine for all I know and I personally have always felt that she was taking in a lot more than any of us think.

"I'm telling it exactly as it happened. Wade knew what he wanted to wear and he stuck to it."

"Wade?" I've never heard her say his name out loud. I probably wouldn't even know if it weren't for Rhonda. Bernice is not acting like Bernice. I'm wondering if I should call the black-haired girl or a nurse to come down here. Bernice is trying to talk about something important and there's nobody here. They ought to call Cameron.

Bernice turns the volume back up. Vincent Price is standing in the dark except for a few candles. You would have to be an idiot not to know that he is the murderer. As far as I know, he's always the murderer.

"Bernice, I want to call a nurse. Will you tell me some more about Wade? I think somebody needs to come down here."

"That's the end of the story. I made his monkey outfit, and right before he walked out the door, he decided to carry a bunch of bananas with him, and whenever he rang the bell, he yelled 'trick or treat' with a mouthful of mashed-up banana, holding the uneaten part up in the face of whoever answered just in case they might not know he was a monkey. He was so cute you could eat him, and he got more candy than anybody else. Maybe people were tired of scary things and they liked the change."

I ring the buzzer. What's going on in her head right now? Is she trying to break through or does she even know what she's saying? What does it feel like when all the stories inside you dry up and the only thing you can talk about is what's in front of you in the moment, without the comfort of your own memories or intelligence? That's how she lives every day, but she is telling me this now and I believe she knows that she's telling me.

Mathilda, the pill nurse, doesn't know how to speak except to shout. "What are you doing in that bed, Bernice? Don't you know we have insurance to think about around here? Get out before one of you falls out and breaks your neck!"

"Mathilda, this is important. Bernice is talking about her deceased son, and I think you should call Cameron and tell him. Or maybe a doctor."

"When is Bernice not talking?"

"I know. This is not the same. She's talking about her life."

"I am not about to disturb her son and family, much less the doctor on call at this hour. I don't see any substantial change to report."

If I could throw something and knock that know-nothing red-headed hog square in the mouth I would do it with every ounce of strength I have and not even ask God's forgiveness for it. That's how mad she makes me.

Bernice has taken the peanut brittle off my nightstand and is biting down on it with her molars but not having much success. I take the candy away from her.

"Tell her what you told me, honey. Tell Mathilda."

Bernice looks at me, then slowly at the scowling face in the doorway. "I told her about Wade and the Trick or Treat when he dressed up like a monkey. I made the costume like a chimpanzee, but he said that would not do because he wanted to have a tail and chimpanzees did not have tails. 'Don't you know that, Mother?' he said, frowning. He couldn't believe I might not know my monkeys."

Mathilda's expression has not warmed at all. "She is having a delusion about her dead son, Mrs. Clayton, no more and no less. It happens in cases of dementia. There's nothing to worry about. Bernice, come with me to your room and I'll give you something to help you sleep."

"No thank you, dear." Bernice smiles. "We've already ordered." She turns to me and I see in her eyes that it's gone, the light, the flicker of an old light. "I guess we'll have to save room for dessert!" She takes another slab of rock-hard peanut brittle. The police are taking Vincent Price away. He does not look as though he even realizes what's happening to him, a real loony. Mathilda turns the TV off without asking and helps Bernice down from my bed and onto her feet, then escorts her into the hall, and shuts off the light with a sweep of her hand, not looking back at me. Ole Jim is staring his crazy-man murderer smile across the room. He looks like he wants to tell me something. I want to remember everything that's ever happened to me, all that I have done, and every person I've known. I want to be able to call every name, recall every joke, keep secrets. I have to try. It's easier to let all of it slide down the bank and float away on the river's current. If I lose something, anything at all, there'll be no one who can help me find it. It will have been washed away, gone.

CHAPTER TWENTY

RHONDA

I told Mike to go on and go fishing. It's Sunday, I'm taking the day off, and I want to spend this morning writing thank-you notes. Connie's coming over and we're gonna go to either Pizza Hut or the cafeteria, whatever she's in the mood for. It don't matter to me, I told her let's do something that's fast and easy. It's not like we got so many wedding presents that it's gonna take me all day, but I want to take my time and do these right. I want to say something I really mean instead of the same words over and over. I owe it to Margaret Clayton for teaching me how to write a proper thank-you note while I was shampooing her hair. She told me first you're supposed to say a general thank-you like "thank you so much for your thoughtful gift," then you mention something specific about whatever it is you're being thankful for so they know you paid attention, like "I especially like the blue because it will fit so perfectly in my dining room," then finally you say something about the future, "I look forward to seeing you again soon," or "I hope you have lovely holidays," something like that.

At the end of Margaret's lesson, Bernice stood up and put her hand over her heart and said, "Why don't you write, 'Thank you so much, you'll never know how much this means to me. I do so love you.'"

Margaret said, "She's been watching old black-and-white movies. I believe I'd try to think of something else."

I feel like I'm already behind. I haven't had the chance to get everything back together since the honeymoon. Mike took me to Cozumel for a week. It wasn't a surprise, we planned the whole thing together. Connie had already been there and she told me it was her favorite vacation she ever had. Plenty of sun, margaritas on the beach, and real cheap. It didn't rain a drop the whole time we were there so we basically lived on the beach, going back and forth to the pool bar. I went parasailing too, which was a hoot because I couldn't understand the teachers, if that's what you call them.

Mike said, "Honey, what were you expectin? I told you to learn a little Spanish before we came."

They gave me a lot of instructions while they were strapping me in on the beach, four little men all talking at the same time. "Hold here, señora. Raise up arms, señora. Let go with your feet, señora." Any time one of them said something that sounded like a question, I nodded and said, "Gracias" because I didn't want them to think I wasn't listening. With no warning, the boat motor fired up and started pulling, tightening on the rope and I had to run because it was pulling me across the sand with the parachute blown up behind. Those Mexican guys were talking and pointing the whole time, but by that point I was in take-off mode and not thinking about anything else. Mike cupped his hands and yelled over the sound of the motor, "You know what to do, right? Do you know what you're supposed to do?" I didn't know there was anything *to* do and I figured he was messing with me, but he sounded sort of concerned, so I wondered if there might be something I should be concerned about.

As the motor got louder, I left the ground and my legs were dangling in the air. I was surprised at how not scared I was. It was like being a big old seagull, gliding over sand and water, looking down at tiny moving things. When I thought we were far enough out for my liking, I tried to get their attention, "Hey y'all! Hey!!" They were so far down I prob'ly sounded like a bird. Finally we took a real wide turn and started heading back in. "This is more like it," I thought. I liked being where I could see land getting closer instead of further away. I could also see Mike the size of an ant in bright red surfer shorts. I waved real wild with one arm because I wanted to hold on with the other one even if I was strapped in. Somebody blew a high shrill whistle, off in the distance. I didn't think much of it, but they kept blowing like there was a fire. I was waving to Mike, but then everybody on the beach, Mike and all the Mexican guys, were waving at me, but not waving like when you're saying hi. And I'm thinking, "Why is that idiot down there blowin a whistle like he's directin traffic?" We got close enough in that I thought we oughta be going down, but the boat engine revved up again and we turned back out into the ocean. I yelled, "Hey, where the hell are y'all goin?" like it did any good to yell and me a mile up in the air hanging on a string. The three guys on the boat all made the same gesture like they were pulling something in the air, then they pointed up at me. It took a couple of rounds of charades to get me to notice a canvas web belt hanging by my right shoulder. It had a bright fluorescent orange loop tied into it that made it seem like something you were supposed to notice, so I grabbed it and pulled. Nothing happened that I could tell, but they clapped and cheered down on the boat. I figured I'd keep pulling as long as they weren't going crazy or blowing whistles, which they didn't do, so we came in for a landing, real soft. Connie laughed 'til she about peed because she couldn't believe I didn't know you had to pull on the rope to help bring the parasail back down. "Didn't you listen to a word they said?" She fanned herself with a napkin. I told her I didn't have any plans to do it again, so she was wasting her breath on me.

I asked her if she had a good time at the wedding, but she confessed that she couldn't talk about it without saying something about the fight. Lynn Barber had made a comment that she didn't know who that colored woman was with those two old ladies, and did anybody know why she was here. Connie already didn't like the tone she asked in and said yes she most certainly did know, and that the black woman was a nurse that worked with Rhonda and what did it matter to Lynn anyway? Lynn said, "Since when are you in the NAACP?" and Connie hauled off and slapped her.

Connie said, "Rhonda, I would have told you that day, but I didn't see any sense in messin up your wedding. That ain't a thing but ignorance."

"It's okay. I don't know what I would have done if I'da heard it. Maybe I wouldn't have hit her though."

"Hey, it's not like I go around beatin up bridesmaids," Connie said.

"I know, your heart's in the right place. It's your hands I worry about."

Connie had always been known to stand up for herself or anybody else she thought was getting the short end of the stick. Honestly, I think that's why they hired her right off at UPS when most of the drivers were men. They saw she had a backbone. Connie's favorite quote was "R-E-S-P-E-C-T. Find out what it means to me," only she acted like it was from the Bible instead of Aretha Franklin.

At first I decide not to write Lynn Barber a thank-you note at all, but I change my mind and keep it real short.

Dear Lynn, thank you for being a part of my wedding. I hope the day was special for you.

Sincerely, Rhonda

They always say, "If you can't say something nice, don't say nothing at all." But there's more to it than that. Margaret Clayton also taught me that if you don't have something nice to say, you *can* still say something, it's all in the wording. Hell, I felt like the day prob'ly *was* special for Lynn; after all, she got smacked in the face.

I have to save my thank-you note to Margaret and Bernice. I don't know what to say, but I want it to be exactly right. The two of them brought me a present early when they came to get their hair done for the ceremony. Together they handed me something flat and square, wrapped in real elegant silver paper with purple ribbon. I told them I wished they hadn't bought anything.

Margaret said, "Honey, calm down, you haven't seen what it is yet."

"It's a picture!" Bernice yelled.

"Well there you go," Margaret added. "There's nothing like a surprise."

Inside the box was a framed photo of the three of us that Lorraine took, all of us wearing Santa Claus hats in the salon. "My God, I was just gettin to know y'all," I said. "Look how nervous I am!"

Margaret answered, "Honey, you look fine. I, on the other hand, am quite sure I didn't want to have that ridiculous hat on my head. That was some of Lorraine's doing, left over from the Christmas party."

"They have a Christmas party every year!" Bernice added. Margaret patted her arm. "And I know you love it sweetheart, so I'm going to keep my mouth shut."

I couldn't wait to show Connie. She asked if I was gonna put it out with my Christmas decorations.

"Hell, those women mean a whole lot more to me than Christmas," I said. "I'm leaving it out all the time. I still can't believe they came."

"Why not?" Connie said. "You're one of the most regular things in their lives."

"Maybe," I said.

Connie kept on. "It's what you do, Rhonda. You take care of em every time you wash their hair and tell em they look nice. Everybody needs takin care of. That's why I never was a good beautician; I didn't care enough about makin other women look good."

Before the wedding, Bernice had brought in a picture from a magazine of a girl with blond dreadlocks and said she wanted her hair done like that for a change. "I like that girl's hair. It's like rope," she said. I talked her out of it by telling her that if I did that I wouldn't be able to shampoo her hair the way she liked. I'm sure Cameron Stokes would have loved to see his mother with four-inch-long dreadlocks. Lorraine put their wedding clothes together for them. I could tell she took the time to pick out the dressiest things they had in their closets. Both of them had on suits, Bernice with a high-neck silk blouse and a big gold brooch and Margaret with a bow that tied at the neck and strands of pearls peeking out underneath it. When Mike and me turned around to face the congregation after it was over, my eyes went straight to them. They were the first faces I looked for. Bernice waved and blew a kiss. Mike waved back.

Margaret made it to the head of the receiving line awful fast for someone whose legs are not always dependable. She let go of Lorraine's arm and grabbed Mike's hand in both of hers. "Now listen to me. You take care of this girl here. We'll be watching you, son."

Bernice added, "We love her so very much," and she did a curtsy that made her trip over her own feet.

Mike kept her from falling, and Margaret quietly turned and told Lorraine to please put Bernice's television on something besides the BBC.

It's hard to say "thank you" when you're not sure what you're thanking somebody for. I might write one line about the picture, but that don't begin to tell it. I guess one thing I want them to know is that they're the ones who've been taking care of me. Maybe only once a week, but faithful. I wish that word didn't sound so religious. Faith to me is putting my heart where my hope is. I don't have no doubt what Margaret Clayton and Bernice Stokes hope for me. I feel it every time I see em. I believe I can be happy, which is more than I was brought up to wish for. That's progress, and I'm not one to sit around and wait.

CHAPTER TWENTY-ONE

MARGARET

Escaping was not my idea in the first place, I'll swear with my hand on the Bible, something I have never done except the one time in my life I had to go to a court of law, and that was only because my maid Desiree shot her husband in the leg with a pistol. I'm not saying I didn't *want* to get out, I mean I didn't actually plot it. Where did we really think we were going to end up anyway without being tracked down? It would have to have been a hell of a lot further away than downtown Raleigh, I'll tell you that. We'd have had to make it to a secluded beach in Mexico or somewhere, and that truly would have been a feat because the only thing I can say in Spanish is "burrito" and Bernice, well, need I say more?

All that being the case, it was still worth every minute, even listening to my daughter Ann tell everybody in creation and me personally about a hundred times that she was so beside herself with worry that she got a migraine headache and had to go to bed sick for two days. Poor thing couldn't swallow a thing but soda crackers and ginger ale. I'm sorry for her trouble, but she's never been someplace like this that she couldn't get out of if she wanted to.

I do not want anybody's pity. I've lived a long time on this earth and I've worn myself out in pleasure and in pain, and that's enough. And I've never been sick to speak of except for the flu or a urinary infection sometimes, that's it. I know my time's coming sooner or later, we all do, but the kicker of it is, right here I sit, old as Methuselah, and most of the time I feel pretty damn good. The only time I'm a little bit out of sorts is when I eat something greasy, and that's something that's not going to change. I was raised on fried chicken, pork barbecue, and hot-as-fire sausage, and I have absolutely no intention of changing my diet now as long I can persuade Ann to smuggle contraband in here.

As with most great escapes, timing was everything. I had woken up from my nap and was about to switch on the television but dropped the remote. It would ordinarily have to stay there until someone else picked it up. I don't think I'm able to reach that far over the side of the bed without it looking like attempted suicide.

"Don't get up, don't get up," Bernice cried, walking in from the hallway. "We'll get it for you, darlin." The "we" meant herself and the stuffed animal she was carrying. I hadn't yet gotten used to the fact that she no longer carried Mister Benny. It had definitely taken some time for her to get over his being burned up, but she was back to her old self now, and at her side waking or sleeping was her new friend, a bright red, white, and blue stuffed bulldog with no eyes. I had often asked Bernice if her friend had a name, but I finally gave up when all she said was, "You don't know her. Her people are from Virginia." I guess she figured if she never told anybody that bulldog's name, she'd never risk the same fate as befell Mister Benny, who in my opinion was probably enjoying his eternal rest at this very moment at the bottom of the county landfill.

Bernice put the remote on the table beside my bed, almost knocking over a water pitcher and my glass of ice. "Thank you Bernice, bless your heart. Otherwise, that thing would have to stay down there 'til dooms-day or a nurse walks by, and I don't know which one will come first."

"I like helping you, Margaret." Bernice smiled her usual toothy grin. "I'll help you every day. You're my neighbor."

"I am, sugar. You have no idea how much I appreciate that."

"I want to do something." She leaned in real close, and I got a little nervous that her upper plate of dentures was so loose it would fall out of her mouth and onto my lap. "I want to leave here tonight. Both of us."

I stared directly into her eyes and said, "We're here together and we'll do all right, but don't start thinking about getting out. It doesn't lead to anything."

I was probably more blunt with her than I ought to have been, but I had to tell myself that same thing every now and again when I had a real good day, walking and eating and digesting. I might start wondering if I could sleep in my own bed again. I knew better. I knew better, and it didn't matter if it made me mad or not.

"We can go, we can go right now, I've got my own money," Bernice continued, as serious as I'd ever heard her.

"Bernice, you do not have any money, go to bed."

She promptly reached down inside the bosom of her nightgown and pulled out a wad of green, all crumpled up in a roll.

"One, two, three, four, five, six . . ." She kept counting all the way up to ten twenty-dollar bills as she laid them down beside me on the blanket. I cranked myself up in the bed. No doubt about it, she had stashed away a nice little bankroll. The most I'd ever been able to keep tucked away was fifty dollars—that's what Ann gave me to keep here "for emergencies" as she called them. I have no idea what kind of emergency she thinks happens here except one where an ambulance comes to get you, but I don't argue. I like having a little cash around me.

I lowered my voice. "Where in God's name did this come from? Get over there and close that door."

Bernice peeked out into the hallway, pulled my door to, and scampered back in. The only sound was a quick "whish, whish" of her slide-on scuffs dragging across the linoleum floor.

I picked the money up off the bed and handed it back. "I don't know where you got this, but if you stole it, you're going to be in more trouble than anybody who ever lived."

Bernice held her ground as usual. "It's my money, all mine. Won it. You ask Alvin."

"Alvin?"

"Poker playing. Ask Alvin. I won it. We play in the middle of the night. He's supposed to be washing floors, but he bets money. I got ten bills right here. Just like the Ten Commandments. All the thou shalt nots. I memorized them. I won this money. It's all mine. Always save for a rainy day. I hid it good too. But don't hide your light under a bushel—that's in the Bible. Did you know that?"

I was accustomed to Bernice's forays out of the sane world, but I had no idea what she was talking about. I knew she used to have money once upon a time, but I also knew that she didn't have a cent of it to herself anymore.

"Bernice, tell me where we're going to go when we can't even go to the parking lot? You take your money and put it wherever you got it from and go to bed."

She leaned in again. "I'll show you. It's a trick I saw Alvin do."

"Bernice . . ." I started to reiterate my objection, waiting for something sensible to come so I could say it and be done with it. Instead a crystal-clear picture dropped down in front of my eyes. It was the next morning and there was a bowl of cornflakes in front of me, and a local Baptist youth choir was at the door of my room in matching red T-shirts singing something like, "God is my Rock—rock on, God." An epiphany of sorts.

"Let's do it." I grabbed both her shoulders. "Right now, before I think another thing about it. Reach down there and undo this bed rail."

Sometimes things make more sense the more you think about them, and sometimes they make less, and it often doesn't have to do with anything except the way you're feeling in that exact minute. Right then, Bernice's plan sounded like the most sensible thing in the world.

It was like she knew she needed my brain, which is no great shakes, believe me, but she figured in her own special Bernice way that we'd make a good team. Don't ever rule out how somebody's mind might be working, even when it looks like it's not working at all.

"Get ready to go, let's go, get ready," Bernice said, scurrying back into the hall and to her room.

"Don't worry about me. You give me five minutes."

I managed to struggle into pants and a sports jacket, the same things I had taken off earlier. That's the kind of outfit I liked for traveling because it was comfortable to sit in. Then I got my cane, just in case, and cracked open the door to take a look at the nurses' station. There was a big clock hanging in the hallway with light-up numbers. Nine o'clock. Everybody went home after feeding us dinner and cleaning up except the janitors and a couple of nurses on duty. One was sitting at the desk flipping through a clipboard. I thought her name was Gina, and I did not have a good feeling about her. I had seen her stand right there when a buzzer was going off in somebody's room and instead of checking to see what was wrong, she'd take her time talking to Alvin or another one of the cleaners about the best way to grow tomatoes. With all the halls sticking out from the nurses' station like points on a star, trying to go anywhere except to the other end of our own hall meant we would have to pass right by her.

Bernice reappeared, gesturing wildly. "Come on! Come on!"

"Lead on," I answered and pulled the door closed behind me as I stepped into the hall. The rail along the side of the wall made it easy for me to walk at a good clip. Gina looked up when we approached the desk. Before she could say anything, I told her I had a leg cramp and that I really didn't want to have to take any pain medicine so Bernice was walking with me.

"It's late," Gina said. I waited for her to say something more, but she didn't, simply went back to shuffling papers.

"I can't wait to close my eyes," I said loud enough so she could hear, and we strolled leisurely around the desk.

When we got to the end of the hall opposite ours, Bernice reached down for something under one of the linoleum tiles. "This is my trick. Alvin does it so the door won't lock. He smokes cigarettes outside. It's my trick now," she said and stuck the found object, a bent nail, into the crack of the door, enough to keep it from closing all the way.

"Bernice, you win the prize. You and your friend . . ." I stopped. "Don't you think it's about time you told me her name?" I pointed at the eyeless bulldog crushed under her arm.

She smiled and said, "You don't know her. She's from Virginia. You tell me a name."

Without even thinking, I said, "Well being that she's patriotic colors and all, why don't you call her Betsy Ross?" I knew Betsy Ross was not from Virginia, but I also knew Bernice didn't know that, and I had no idea where she got the idea of Virginia anyway.

"Betsy Ross! Betsy Ross is the boss!" Bernice was delighted.

The air outside was fresh, just a little chilly, exactly the way I liked night air to be. I wanted to stand right where I was and do nothing but breathe, take it all in, but Bernice had hold of my arm and tugged me along. We walked past picnic tables at the edge of the parking lot and down the driveway toward the road. The trail of white cigarette butts on the ground told me that Alvin was not the only one doing the door trick.

Cars passed in both directions, and directly across the road was a gas station and an Ace Hardware store, both closed, on either side of an all-night Tastee-Freez. It was Shangri-La as far as I was concerned because from my own window I couldn't see one thing except a water tower and a trailer park at the edge of somebody's dirt field.

"Bernice sweetheart, I guess the Tastee-Freez has got our name on it. What do you think?"

Nobody looked up when we walked in, not that there were more than a handful of people, just a couple of teenagers with their faces about two inches from each other, and a bearlike man wearing a base-ball cap sitting in a booth eating a hamburger in big bites, like a cow chewing cud. The lights were enough to blind a person—I have always despised bright lights in a room where somebody's trying to eat.

Bernice walked directly up to the counter where a girl with thick black lines painted around her eyes and what looked like a fish hook hanging out of her nose said flatly, "Help you?"

"Y'all have banana splits?" Bernice stood up on her tiptoes and leaned in like she was saying magic words and then plopped Betsy Ross on the counter in front of the girl.

"Let me help you, Bernice," I intervened. The girl's expression told me what she was thinking, staring at the red-white-and-blue bulldog. "God, this is one crazy old bitch. Why on my shift?"

I picked up the dog and said, "I know Gardner Jr.'s going to be one happy boy when he gets this back." I took a stab at making Betsy sound like she belonged to somebody other than an eighty-year-old woman. "Make it two banana splits, please," I continued, gently pull-ing Bernice away from the counter with me toward a booth and out of suspicion's line of fire.

"Lots of nuts!" Bernice waved her hand to the girl, and I thought to myself, "You're not kidding."

We took a booth across a narrow aisle from the hamburger man, who looked like a truck driver to me—he had that "I stay up all night and drive" look about him. I went to the self-serve area and brought back two cups of ice water, and when I sat down again, he looked at me rather suddenly, " 'Scuse me, could you pass me that bottle of ketchup? Mine's run out." He pointed at a little tray of condiments on our table.

"Yes sir, I can." I reached over to him without getting up.

"Thank you. I 'preciate it. I have to have ketchup on my hamburger. I like ketchup on every kind of meat, you name it, steak, chicken, pork chops. I like it on fish too. Shrimp, oysters, every kind of meat."

"I know what you mean, sometimes you need a little flavor." I smiled. Bernice smiled too but didn't say anything, thank the Lord. She was bouncing Betsy Ross in her lap like a baby she was trying to burp.

"Y'all out walkin at night?" he asked.

I thought for sure we'd been found out. "Pardon me?"

"Nothin. I didn't see any headlights pull in out there, and then y'all come on in. None of my business."

"No, no, that's all right." I nodded toward Bernice. "My friend lives down the road, and I'm keeping her company. She used to have a car, but somebody stole it right out from under her carport. Have you ever in your life?" I have no idea why in the world I added in a car theft, it came out of my mouth, but sometimes I think the more unbelievable something sounds, the more people believe it.

"Number three—two banana splits!" the zombie girl called from the counter, and I fished in my pocket for the little scrap of paper she gave me when I paid.

"Keep your seat," our new neighbor said, "I'll get it." He returned smiling, satisfied with his good deed. "Here you go," he said. "I wish I could eat somethin like this but I been tryin to cut back when I can. Doctor told me my cholesterol and blood pressure both are too high up."

"Son, when you get to be our age, you just sort of say, 'damn the torpedoes' about that kind of thing. I know it's valuable information for some people, but I can barely think about things I need to, much less about what's in everything I put in my mouth."

"Is that right?" He smiled even bigger.

"Yes sir, it is. When it's my time, I will go willingly. Dr. Shiraka says I have the blood pressure of a teenager, and I say well then if I drop dead tomorrow I guess that's one more girl cut down in her prime, ain't that right, Bernice?"

Bernice's head popped up with a mouthful of strawberry sauce and whipped cream. "Right," she answered. She was already so busy mashing up ice cream, bananas, and nuts into a soup that she looked at me like she had no idea who was even talking to her. That's what I call being focused on what you're doing.

"Yes ma'am, well that's wonderful to know you're doin so good." He sat back down on the edge of the booth closest to Bernice and me. "Tell you what, y'all ladies want me to run you back down the road home?"

"Excuse me?" I said.

"I've got a truck right there, haven't I?" he said kindly, pointing toward the plate glass windows which made me feel like we were in a fish tank bathed in neon light. "I'm goin on into Raleigh but I'll be glad to drop you."

Now I know all about strangers in a Tastee-Freez turning out to be ax murderers or kidnappers; I watch more than enough television. But once in a while I think it's bound to be all right to trust your instincts. I sure couldn't picture Bernice and me as candidates for some big ransom, and he seemed like a nice enough man. It had been a long time since anybody whatsoever other than Bernice or Lorraine brought me anything of their own free will, just to be nice, the way he brought us over our ice cream. I saw the girl at the counter talk to him like she knew him, so he must have been pretty regular there, not like somebody drifting through.

"What would you say if I told you we wanted to go to Raleigh?" I tried the words on for size.

"I used to live in Raleigh, North Carolina!" Bernice cried out, sucking on a maraschino cherry with the stem hanging out of her mouth.

I turned to her. "Yes you did, sugar, the one and only." I turned back to my unsuspecting chauffeur-in-waiting.

"What in the world business do y'all ladies have in Raleigh at nighttime?"

"Same as anybody else." I realized I sounded defensive. "Bernice wants to see the Capitol building—she hasn't been in years—and I'm going to the Art Museum. We thought we'd either try to find somebody to take us or rent a car in the morning, but we weren't looking forward to that part. You could just leave us off at the Hilton, and don't worry one minute, we can pay every bit of our own way. We always have and always will."

Something changed in his face. I could tell he was not about to touch us with a ten-foot pole.

"I'll just drop y'all at home," he answered.

He knew that I knew we had been found out. I squared my jaw and started over. "All right, here it is—plain as I know how to make it, son. We're not supposed to be here, you figured that out without my help. No disrespect intended, but where we *are* supposed to be is no concern of yours—that is unless you're blood kin, which you clearly are not. And the truth is, whether we want to or not, we will go back to where we're supposed to be, it's just a matter of when."

I looked to Bernice, then sporting a chocolate mustache, for a response that she didn't offer, so I continued. "What happens between now and the time some responsible citizen or family member fetches us remains to be seen. You can either let us ride with you for one precious hour of your time and know that you're protecting us from whatever mess we might get into on our own, or you can leave us here with our Banana Barge Specials and go on about your business, in which case we're still not where we're supposed to be, and we're still not going back until somebody makes us."

Bernice chimed in, "We're not going."

"Thank you, honey," I said.

We waited for him to reply to what I thought was a very convincing line of reasoning on my part. We didn't have to wait long. "I don't think so, ladies."

I pushed. "I don't know what you're worried about. We're the ones who've got something to worry about. You could walk right out of here, call the police, and tell them there's two old ladies in the Tastee-Freez who somebody's gonna be looking for if they aren't already."

"I wouldn't do that. Hey, what y'all do is none of my business."

"Exactly," I shot back. "That's exactly right."

I saw something register in his eyes. "You oughta be a lawyer or somethin, you know that? You sure can talk."

"Is that a yes? You're going there anyway."

"I don't know. Okay." He put on his Windbreaker. We followed, but not too close. I wanted us to leave exactly the way we came in, by ourselves. Bernice stopped in front of the raccoon-eyed girl behind the counter and said, "You make a good banana split. Big too. You do good work in ice cream. You can make yourself some good money in ice cream."

I heard the Raccoon whisper, "Go to hell."

I ignored it. "Thank you very much! Good night!" I said, pushing open the door with Bernice's help, and we were back in the parking lot. Our friend had already started the truck and pulled it around so we wouldn't have to walk any further than necessary. It's gotten to the point that I can't walk in anything except a shoe with almost no heel, and there I was wearing church shoes, so I was thankful. We got up into the cab with some help. We were awkward like dead weight, so it must have felt like trying to haul two pianos up through a second-story window.

As soon as we were on the road, I started not feeling good. Bernice knew even without my saying anything because she said, "You look sick. Are you gonna vomit?" Leave it to her to cut right to the meat of something. "No ma'am I am not," I said determinedly, but I wasn't so sure. Maybe it was the excitement of doing something, I don't know. I didn't care. After riding a while with my eyes closed I felt better, and soon our friend was helping us down from the truck. He handed me his phone number. "No thank you," I said, "I appreciate it, but your commitment to Bernice and me is hereby finished, sir. We are indebted to you for your kindness."

"You sure?" he stuck his head out of the rolled down window. I nodded to reiterate. "Well, y'all stay out of trouble. Adios then," and he drove away, probably to another Tastee-Freez eventually, in another dark town.

The lobby of the Raleigh Hilton had undergone a major renovation since the last time I was there, but that had been so long ago I'm not sure they had electricity. I guess change is good, everybody always says it is, but you never really know which changes will end up being good and which ones will later be called mistakes. The decor of the Hilton definitely fell into the "mistake" category. One whole end of the lobby was a glassed-in open atrium thing with flowery bamboo sofas and so many plants hanging from the ceiling that it looked like the Amazon had come to North Carolina. It was way too humid, so I pulled off my jacket and noticed Bernice fanning herself with her pocketbook. I guess it never occurred to anybody that it would be like a greenhouse with all those plants, even at night, unless they ran the air conditioner all year long.

We paused by the door and Bernice whispered, "Are we gonna stay all night?"

"We most certainly are." I was indignant in case anybody could overhear. "Aren't we simply two ladies in search of accommodation? Just have a seat somewhere over there in Costa Rica. Betsy Ross will love being around all those trees."

I walked on thick turquoise carpet to the front desk. A young man there was reading a magazine. He was very suntanned as though he'd been in Florida on vacation and was wearing a lot of silver rings. The lobby was empty; it was after eleven. Raleigh had never been a night owl kind of place, and that didn't bother me. I had never stayed up all night anyway except for a couple of New Year's Eves in Atlanta.

As soon as the boy at the desk spotted me, he snapped to attention.

"Good evening, my name is Andrew, how can I assist you?" He had big white teeth and blue eyes the color of the sky. I wanted to hug him he was so cute.

"Ma'am?" He was waiting.

"Yes, yes you can. May we have a room please, my friend and I?"

"Are we holding a reservation for you?" He jangled a silver bracelet on one wrist.

"We don't have one; we're here spur of the moment. I think that's the best way to travel, don't you?"

"I hope I have something left." He rolled his eyes like he was letting me in on a secret. "There's a marching band convention through the weekend. Regional Finals."

"How about that." I raised my eyebrows, turning to Bernice to get her attention, but all I could see was her head bobbing in and out of all those trees and vines under glass.

My movie star Andrew looked up from a blue computer screen. "I do have one room with a king if you don't mind sleeping together. I mean sharing. Sorry." He jangled the bracelet around his face, flustered.

"We'll take it; that'll be just fine."

I took the room keys from the counter and turned around to catch Bernice with black dirt all over her blouse, holding a handful of exotic plants, all ripped up by the roots. "You've got to weed out a garden or it won't grow!" she yelled. I got to her as fast as I could. "Give me those!" I crammed everything she had collected behind some species of potted palm, pulling her with me to the elevator, dirt and all.

What I heard through the wall in the middle of the night sounded like "Love Me Tender," done up-beat style on the trombone, but whoever was playing kept messing up and going back to the beginning to start over, which was enough to drive anybody insane. I'm not a musician, but I do not believe "Love Me Tender" is a hard song to play, and on the third or fourth butchering, I gave up and got out of bed. Bernice was sound asleep; I knew from experience that she could snore through a tornado. Betsy Ross lay crushed under her neck. They both looked peaceful as cherubs. I thought if I could get a swallow of something to drink I might be able to get to sleep too. I missed Lorraine. She made sure there was a whole Co-Cola on my bed table every night, not a glass of sour cranberry juice like some of those other girls brought.

My neighbor finally switched songs. Elvis is not made for the trombone. I've confessed that I was never a musician, but whoever thought they were going to win a marching band contest by playing Elvis was even less of one. I tried to picture a clever band director somewhere up in Illinois or Ohio thinking, "We'll have those North Carolina judges right where we want em if we do an Elvis medley." I could have told them they would stand a lot better chance with "Stars and Stripes Forever" and anybody knows how overused that old thing is. At least it was *meant* to be played by a band. Sometimes you can change what a thing is meant for, but more times you can't, no matter what you do. The trick is knowing the difference. Think about what I'm saying the next time you hear a marching band try to play "Moon River."

I tried to settle into a stiff wing chair by the window and turned on the TV with the volume way down. Bernice was lying still as a log. I put my head back and watched a woman say straight into the camera that she had had sex with her mother, father, and son, but she didn't know it because she was drunk so much of the time. I am not a big drinker, but on those few occasions when I have imbibed, I can tell you one thing. I don't care how drunk you are, you know if you're in bed with your mother. Whenever I watch these shows, Lorraine says, "Why do you watch this mess? Where do they find these people?" and I tell her they must not be very hard to find because there's no shortage of them. The woman on TV droned on about her sex life. Her voice got steadily softer and lower until it started to sound like a man. I stopped trying to listen. Then there were more voices, all talking at the same time but not saying words. The beginnings of daylight made me squint. I woke up, my neck aching, still in the chair.

"Bernice," I said. My voice was hoarse from sleep. Sunlight was pouring through the thin shiny curtains. "Bernice honey, get up. I'm calling Ann to come get us. Wake up."

She had the sheet pulled up so it almost covered her head, with Betsy Ross tossed to one side. I wanted to go over and give her a little shake, but I had to work out my arthritis some before I could do anything as bold as take a step. "You can't hide all day, Bernice. Get up from there. We're going home now. You know we've got to go home, sugar." I was mildly disgusted by how cheerful I sounded first thing in the morning.

Once I got to her, I did the one thing I knew would get some action out of my partner in crime. I snatched Betsy Ross, knowing that I was the only person in the world besides Rhonda who could do so without causing Armageddon. She was still. I pulled down the sheet from her head.

"Not now, Bernice." That's what came out. "Not now." No one heard.

I waited for Ann in the lobby, planting myself on a wicker love seat in the middle of the glassed-in rainforest, surrounded by boys and girls in green and gold uniforms with big white plumes on their hats. Shining gold and silver metal gleamed on everything from tubas to flutes all over the room.

Don't believe it the next time somebody tells you they've seen a peaceful smile on the face of a dead person. They're liars. What you see is *nothing*. I needed that woman. I still do.

I sank down deeper into the chair cushion and felt genuinely tired for the first time. I closed my eyes lightly. I could see the two of us, Bernice and me, inching our way across the parking lot in the dark like drunk snails. We found our freedom at a Tastee-Freez. For a few hours, we got to be like people who come and go and eat and sleep when they want to. I remember holding Bernice's arm, feeling like a wildcat. She was beside herself, pointing at the oversized pictures of ice cream creations. "I don't want any pineapple sauce, just strawberry," she said. "Lots of strawberry."

"We can have anything we want," I told her.

"One—two—three—four!" a voice pierced my ears, startling me back to the present. I opened my eyes, for a moment I panicked. I thought the Hilton was having a fire drill. Then snare drums rolled, a high pitched whistle blew, and the "Stars and Stripes Forever" blared full throttle. Thunder sounded in my head, and I looked around me. Horns of all shapes and sizes protruded from red faces of children blowing with all the wind God gave them. There must have been sixty, seventy, eighty. I lowered my shoulders and leaned my head back a second time. Bernice was there again, still there, ice cream dripping from her chin. I felt Betsy Ross in my lap, she was staring up at me, eyeless. If somebody had asked me in that moment what joy was, I would have had to say John Philip Sousa in a tropical garden in downtown Raleigh. If there's a God, and I have always believed so, those children won a trophy that day. It should have been the biggest trophy in the whole state of North Carolina. To hell with Elvis.

"Mama? Mama are you all right?" I heard Ann call out over the sound of the brass. I didn't see her immediately, but I could smell her perfume and hear her jewelry clanking behind me. She appeared in front of my face. "I'm so sorry, Mama. I don't know what to say, I'm torn up. Let's go home."

She pulled me to my feet. "What did you say?" I yelled as loud as I could. Ann guided me gently with her arm around my waist. I almost ran into a chair and stopped to look at a chubby girl with pigtails wearing a green and gold uniform, standing by herself in between two hibiscus plants. She was playing the Sousa piccolo solo with all of her heart in it. "Mama, we need to go," Ann comforted me, and then to herself, "I've never heard such a racket in my life inside a building." I went with her unbegrudgingly, she was there to help me, but I glanced back at the piccolo player. I needed to see her again. Bright morning rays poured through the glass over her head and made her whole body shine. The music played on. I think she had wings.

CHAPTER TWENTY-TWO

RHONDA

I'll wash her hair and rinse it real good before I tease it. I'm not gonna tease it too much though cause she didn't like that. She mashed her hair down with her hands every time I tried to do anything with it to make it look fuller. I've got to put on a sweater before I can do anything. I'm freezing in this basement. I know they have to keep it this way, but I can't concentrate. I'm trying to get her situated so I can work on her better, but her head don't move much at all. I remembered to bring a little lavender eye pillow that I got out of a catalog. It said it was for relaxing and feeling rejuvenated, but I tried it and found out I'd just as soon smoke a cigarette. I'm gonna put it over her eyes, real gentle. I don't want to look at her eyes; I'm scared they might open up part way. They put what they call eye caps under her lids to help keep em closed, that's what Paul Gaines told me and he works here so he oughta know. Still, he said changes are happening all the time in a dead body. I wish he hadn't called her a dead body just because he's used to messing with dead people all the time. She's Bernice to me. Bernice.

I had to ask her people if I could fix her hair, and they said yes, it would be one less thing they had to think about. Bernice's son never did look me in the face the whole time I was talking to him, just stared down at the floor. I think he'd been drinking.

I know that look, eyes red around the rims. His wife did come into the salon later, looking all around sort of like she was thinking about buying the place. "Are you the lady that asked to style Mrs. Stokes's hair?" She raised her eyebrows high and perky.

"I'm Rhonda."

"Rhonda. I wanted to tell you that will be fine with us, and thank you very much." She looked down at her watch and walked out before I said a word. I can't decide if she was rude or nervous, probably both. But this is between Bernice and me. I wanted to say my good-bye the same way I said hello to her for the first time, raking my hands through her soft hair. I don't need to be friends with her family. Family can be overrated anyway, at least the one you're born with.

All my growing up years I stayed as far away from my grandma as I could. She told me more times than I can count that I didn't look or act like a girl, much less like a lady. She was always on me for something. I used to close myself in my room while she took her nap in the afternoon in front of the TV watching her programs. By myself, I made up all kinda hairdos for my dolls, trying to copy out of my mama's magazines, and I would put homemade dresses on em too. Mama couldn't buy much with what she made being a secretary, but she knew I loved to work on dolls, so she would get me one for my birthday every year. Sometimes a baby, sometimes a grown woman doll. She bought me a black doll one time, and I liked it even though Grandma didn't and told us so. Mama didn't care. She handed me that doll and said, "The world is a big place, Rhonda, with lots of people in it."

I played dolls every day as soon as I could run in the door from school and throw my books down. When Mama came in, she brought a glass of milk and something sweet to my room. I loved that because it was like being waited on when you're sick or in a restaurant. Lots of times she stayed and watched from the doorway.

"I ought to let you work on me sometime, sugar, I think you've got talent. Don't ever waste talent," she'd say. Then she'd kiss me on top of my head, and I could smell her powder. I loved that smell, like clouds, if you could catch one and hold it.

I was twelve when she left. It was in May cause it was the night of my birthday. I was in bed but not asleep, and I heard yelling in the front of the house. That wasn't anything unusual—Mama and Grandma fought almost every night. Sometimes it was only a couple of mean sentences, thrown like spears at a target; other times it might last a whole hour, broken up by short snatches of silence. I always thought the silence was them thinking up the next hateful thing they could say to each other. On this night the sound was coming from outside, and that was different, because they usually did their fighting in the living room or kitchen, and it ended by one of them storming off and slamming a door to her bedroom.

I got up and looked out the window in time to see Mama spinning out of the driveway in her old Buick with dirt flying everywhere. I screamed out after her even though the window was shut tight, then ran outside in my nightgown and jumped off the porch, falling on the ground, still yelling. By that time she was nothing but a big dust cloud. It was like Grandma had practiced for this moment. She grabbed me by the shoulder and said it was no time to cry, that my time to be a child had ended, and now was the time to put away childish things. Then she took my hand and walked me to my room. I thought she was going to tuck me back in bed and ask me to say my prayers even though I had already said them once. Instead, she told me to stand to one side. "Witness the beginning of becoming a grown-up woman," she said, and she gathered up all my dolls and their little clothes and shoes and tiny pocketbooks that Mama bought, hauled them into the kitchen, and threw them in the trash with fish bones and eggshells and other mashed-up garbage. I cried, "Grandma, don't!" but she turned and pointed a finger directly at my nose, "You're grown up now and I dare you to fish them dolls out. Let the past be in the past." I hid everything I cared about from her from that day on. I tried not to talk to her at all except to answer her questions, which got to be fewer the older she got and the less time I spent at home with her. Far as I'm concerned, she lost me the same night she lost Mama, but I doubt she ever knew it, not that she would have cared much. I can't to this day tell you what she cared about. I can't think of anything.

I've tried my best, but I'm gonna have to cut this tangle out of Bernice's hair. I know she don't feel me pulling on it, but I can't stand the thought of yanking on her hair just because she can't feel it. She used to drive me crazy saying, "Be careful not to pull Mister Benny's hair, Rhonda. He's sensitive. He can feel everything, you might not know it, but he can." I prob'ly snapped something back at her. I hope I didn't, I think I was pretty patient most of the time without having to try too hard. I washed Mister Benny's few strands of yarn hair many a time, and then that bulldog's after that. Childish things, that's what they were, the stuffed animals of an old woman. I don't know how to feel except soft for somebody like that. She always acted like she liked me. That meant something to me. She would try to stay and keep talking after she got her hair fixed, even if I was working on somebody else. I always liked when she stayed. I don't think I told her.

In the last month she was alive, Grandma had to go to the hospital twice before the one time when she would never come back out. The last time the ambulance took her, I went to see her lying in the hospital bed, bloated and gray-skinned. It's strange what you think about when you see somebody sick in the hospital. My first thought was that I must look really old without makeup. And then that I didn't want nothing from Grandma except for one thing and I hadn't never asked for it, I guess because it never crossed my mind that she might tell me the thing I wanted to know.

"Grandma," I started, "why did Mama leave us on my birthday?" She looked up and breathed out a sigh like a puff of air when you pick up something too heavy and finally get to put it down. She was laboring to get words out.

"She left because she couldn't be a mother to you. Lord knows that would have ruined her plans, so she left the job to me."

Grandma died the next afternoon. I was at work, Evelyn answered the phone and handed it to me, but I knew what the call was about from the way she avoided looking at me. I did not cry, I did not get mad, I didn't do anything different from what I usually do. I have no doubt that Grandma will spend her meanness on whoever she meets on the other side, and she better hope it's not Jesus right away, because even he'll have none of her, I'm goddamn sure of that.

Connie asked me if I hated her so much then why did I fix her hair before she was buried? I couldn't answer her then and still can't. It wasn't to make peace with her or anything holy sounding like that. It might have been pure spite—I could treat her like a doll that couldn't feel anything. A lot of people said they were touched that I wanted to fix her hair for the last time. The funeral home lady who stood at the door made a point to tell everybody who came in for the viewing. She liked letting them in on some insider information which is probably something that a funeral director doesn't get to do very often. I don't even remember what I made Grandma's hair look like, and that's one thing I never forget. I have a photo album inside my head of everybody's hair I've ever fixed. I can tell you the length, the color, permanent or not, everything. I know exactly what they all look like. It's like turning the pages of a book. But Grandma's hair was like plastic straw that's in the bottom of a Easter basket, so there wasn't much I coulda done even if my heart was in it. Bernice's hair is a whole lot nicer. Whenever I had her head over the sink getting ready to shampoo her, I told her I could run my hands through her hair all day long. It's the same now, fine and soft, like feathers. She's an angel with feathers, lying on a metal table. Touching her, I think of Wade's long hair in his lifeguard summer, the last time I saw him. I wonder if this is what his hair felt like. He came from her, this lady who couldn't say two things in a row that made sense. But she was his mother, she raised him, and that was lodged forever inside her, even if she couldn't remember it all the time. I'm resting with my hands in her hair, feeling the warm soapy water and the softness. I'll be gentle on her head, even now. It's like taking care of him too, a boy who thought he had to take care of the whole world.

The door behind me sounds like a jail cell opening, a hollow metal ringing out. "'Scuse me Rhonda, are you 'bout finished in here?" asks Paul, in a maroon jacket and matching tie.

"I'm gettin there," I answer. I want him to go away. This ain't none of his business.

"We need to dress her for the viewing, so if you can hurry up some, that will make my life easier."

"I'll tell you when I'm through." I don't look up from what I'm doing.

Paul sees from the look on my face that he needs to give me some space, and he points to a phone on the wall. "Call me. Push star-three and it'll ring upstairs." He closes the metal door behind him and I can hear his feet clomping back up the steps, up to the main floor, where there's prob'ly another service going on for somebody else. They're good at making you feel like you're the only one who's died, when on any given day there's got to be three or four deaths going on.

He can wait. Bernice is going to look her best, I don't care if it takes me the rest of the afternoon. People are going to cluck-cluck about how sad it was that her mind went, and how the last few years couldn't have meant much to her anyway. But they're gonna say how good she looks, they won't be able to help themselves because I'm goin to make her look better dead than some of them look alive. They'll stroll by and tap each other on the arm and whisper about it, but I won't be there to hear what they say. This is my viewing right here.

I'm goin home and make some eggs and ham and then I'm gonna take myself a good bath. I'll be at the funeral, but I don't want to be here in the middle of a crowd of talking people at a funeral home.

At Grandma's viewing, her face looked like somebody had put a hot fireball in her mouth and forgot to take it out. She looked like she wanted to scream and spit out that fiery thing but couldn't do anything, so instead her pain and fury stayed trapped in her lips and the skin around her mouth. All her cruel years were pursed into one expression.

I don't miss her at all. I'm still changing the house, prob'ly will be for a long time. It don't take much cause I can do a lot of the work myself. Last week I painted the kitchen orange. Mike likes it. He says I've got a great sense of style. Bright hot orange makes me think of a sunny day and a place where you can sit outside and drink iced tea. That's my dream now. Sitting somewhere pretty with a wet glass of tea in my hand, full of lemon and sugar, and reading a magazine with my legs crossed. I take it all in, everything there is to see, hear, and smell. People look at me funny cause I'm sitting in the sun drinking tea instead of running around like they are between houses, offices, churches, day cares, and everything else. I take a long swallow of my tea, swing my leg, and smile when they go by, that's all.

One day Mike wants to make my old bedroom into a exercise room. I'll never use it, but he thinks he will, so I said, "Go for it." I'm glad he wants to stay in shape and look good, especially since he's not going to do it sitting on his tail all day long in a UPS truck. I told him that first I wanted him to help me build a little house outside, in the back. And once we get it built, we're goin to hook up heat and air-conditioning and fix the inside real nice, and one day that's gonna be where I cut hair, called Rhonda's Style for Today. That's what the sign will say, and under the name, "Tuesdays–Saturdays. Call for an appointment, or just drop in."

Paul told me not to spray Bernice's hair but I'm goin to anyway.

She's goin to have to be moved around by God knows who. Paul said hairspray could be flammable and that they have their own that they like to use. I know better than anybody what good hairspray is and nobody's goin to be smoking a cigarette around her face. I'm gonna spray her head just like I sprayed it every week since I've known her. This is one head that's goin to stay looking exactly like it does right now. I lift up the pillow I put over her eyes. They're all the way closed like they're s'posed to be. I trace my finger along one of her eyebrows. She's all right now.

CHAPTER TWENTY-THREE

MARGARET

If it's good luck when it rains on someone's wedding day, what kind of luck is it when it rains on a funeral? I dreaded getting out of bed as soon as I looked out the window. Ann came by yesterday afternoon to ask me if I wanted to sit with the family at the funeral home viewing. She said Bernice would have wanted me to. I know damn well what Bernice would have wanted, but I didn't go. I didn't have the energy, and Bernice would understand that too. There were lots of days she led me around holding onto her arm for dear life when I had a weak spell.

Now here we are, they're going to start in a few minutes. The choir is walking in, robed in green, followed by a preacher that I do not recognize as any of the ones who came to visit Bernice. I do not feel comforted by this place, neither the building nor the people in it. It's a sanctuary, it's supposed to make one feel safe. Instead I'm staring straight ahead at a casket, looking at something that's going to happen to me and everyone else in here. A promise of salvation may offer comfort, but it is no preventive medicine. What's going to happen is going to happen, and then we are no more of this earth.

I'm sitting on the second row with Ann. I am wearing a light gray suit and that's exactly how I feel. I am noncommittal, not about Bernice, but about all this ceremony and the scripted talk about dying that goes along with it. Even if heaven is an actual place, a real noun of a place, I can't say for sure that I want to go. Crystal rivers and streets of gold are nothing but old gospel song lyrics in my mind. If there's a mansion awaiting me, I'd rather have a short tour with a Realtor before I have to move in. I'd a whole lot rather think that heaven would turn all my senses upside down. What's liquid here is solid there. And maybe the way people see is not with eyes. Maybe they don't see at all. I sound like Lorraine talking now. She has all the imagination that a person needs to have faith. She believes like nobody else I ever knew. Still, whatever it's like there, I do know that I'm about ready to hang it up here. I'm not thinking about Bernice. I'm sitting here dressed up, going through my own life as though it's an oversized filing cabinet, and I might find a lost document that will tell me something I never knew. I'd settle to find anything that might help me know what's coming, if I've got more ahead of me.

It's too hot in this room. I look up at the ceiling and I remember a time sitting in my car with the windows rolled up, just this hot. It is summer and there has been a hard rain, I can tell by looking around at the ground, but it has not cooled the temperature one bit. I would like to roll the windows down and let some air in, but they're electric and I don't have the car keys because my husband Charles has gone inside to buy some cigarettes. He doesn't smoke since he had a heart attack. They're for me. I'm going to give them up too, but not yet, not in this picture. I'm holding a potted peace lily in my lap. It's heavy but the porcelain pot is cool on my thighs. A big blue bow decorates the base of it. We are going to the VA hospital. I was scared to put the lily in the backseat of the Plymouth because once you turn off the highway it's bumpy and I was afraid it would turn over. Not that Charles is a bad driver. He has driven us to the Chesapeake Bay and the Blue Ridge Mountains and a few times down to Florida.

I stare at the chandelier above my head. This is a pretty church. There's no telling how long it's been since Bernice has been here, maybe since Wade got killed. I'm glad they didn't do it at the funeral home. A funeral home is a place for death only, while a church building at least gets to witness every stage of life. It's the same as the difference between one slice and the whole pie. The chandelier is all reflection of light. It hurts my eyes a little, but I don't want to look away.

I can see us walking down a hall with faint green walls at the VA hospital. There is a hard tile floor that has seen many a mop to rectify many a disaster. We are visiting Papa Clayton, Charles's father. He has been bedridden for two years because of having lost his legs to diabetes. Papa Clayton refuses artificial limbs and will not be put in a wheelchair. I am bringing him a potted peace lily. I do not know why. There are way too many young men in this hospital. All of them are back from Vietnam, most missing body parts, and some missing their right minds. I am bringing Papa Clayton a peace lily and I don't have the slightest idea why. It must be Father's Day.

The choir and soloist sit down after singing "The Old Rugged Cross." I wonder who chose that hymn; it's the national anthem of funerals, at least Southern ones. More people would like hymns if they weren't depressing. That one sounds to me like one long moan. It's sad enough to be sitting here without having to hear that. Bernice wouldn't have liked it at all. Maybe I'm the only one here who knows that. One time she pulled Lorraine into my room and said she wanted us to be witnesses, and when I asked "To what?" she said, "Funeral Wishes." Lorraine said she didn't want to talk about a funeral in the middle of the day, but Bernice would not be diverted. She insisted that she be buried in long sleeves, and that Mister Benny should have the same. That was before his untimely demise of course, when I guess she still assumed they would depart this earth as a team. And she said the only hymn that she would allow to be sung would be "Amazing Grace." And there would be no other religious singing, and no organ music of any kind whatsoever. She would prefer a country song if it could be fit into the program. And she wanted a flute to play because she said she wanted to hear something that sounded like butterflies, that's what she liked to think leaving this earth was like, a butterfly leaving a flower. She asked if we needed to write it down, and I told her, no, I believe she'd made a good enough impression. I knew she wouldn't remember any of it in ten minutes anyway. Lorraine said, "I already told y'all once, I ain't studyin this," and walked out of the room.

The preacher is going on now, earnest seeming enough. If I had been paying attention I would have probably heard him say, "Friends and family of dear Bernice Stokes." That's a reasonable way to start a funeral. Cameron and Greta Stokes and their two children are opposite me in the pew across the aisle. I wave to the little ones, who wave back even though they have no idea who I am. That's how children are. Wave at them, and they wave back. Greta stares straight ahead. She is wearing a hat. She is trying to look like the idea of what she thinks a well-bred Southern wife of a man who has lost his mother looks like. Bernice's son brings a handkerchief to his eyes, then his nose, in one continuous gesture. He is sweating. It seems to me that he's been sweating every time I've ever seen him.

I am digging in my purse, which I am aware has always been a distracting and very time-consuming habit of mine, but I feel like I will die if I don't find a mint or piece of hard candy, my throat is so dry. There is a woman standing behind the pulpit now with a fountain of curly blond hair and very pale skin except for a red inflamed area at the nape of her neck, reading from the Bible. I don't recognize what she's reading. I'm not sure it's from the Bible; I must have misunderstood. It sounds more like poetry, and something makes me think I heard it in a movie. Could be; Bernice loved old movies. Hell, half the time she thought she was in one. Aside from that, all she wanted to do was talk. The talk got progressively nonsensical and childlike as time went on, but so do most things the more you dwell on them, so it never bothered me. Bernice was only being Bernice.

The morning after she passed away, Rhonda closed the beauty shop and came to me to ask if I thought Bernice's family would mind if she did her hair for the funeral. I said, "Rhonda, that is so lovely, I know Bernice would have loved it, but she would also probably insist that you did Betsy Ross's hair too." There wasn't as much hair on the bulldog as there had been on Mister Benny, but she had always obliged Bernice by putting a little shampoo on the short hair and around the ears.

"You're talkin about that bulldog? Since when does it have a name?"

"Since I suggested it, and don't ask me why I did."

"Well are they gonna bury her with Betsy Ross then?" Rhonda asked in all sincerity.

Thinking of the daughter-in-law, I answered quickly, "No. No, I don't think so."

"Well that's not right. People get buried with all kind of things pushed in down by their feet. My great uncle got buried with a fishin pole."

"Is that right?"

"Yes it is, and the funeral home was glad to do it too. The man there said one time he buried a lady with a saxophone."

"Well as I said, that's not going to happen. Actually, I think Bernice would want you to have old Betsy, you took such good care of her every week. And may the Stars and Stripes forever wave."

"You don't think her family might want her? Maybe for the grandchildren?"

"Rhonda. Honey. I believe you have met Greta Stokes and so I think you already know the answer to that question. Consider yourself lucky, Bernice used to keep whiskey up inside Mister Benny until she got caught. No telling what you might find. I'm sure she got herself a regular stash winning poker games with Alvin and the rest of them. You and Mike might be able to have yourselves a full-blown cocktail party."

Rhonda laughed, but I could see she wasn't through crying yet. As it turned out, Greta Stokes couldn't have cared less what arrangements were made. She didn't go with her husband to pick out the casket or flowers. She went to Hudson Belk and bought a new outfit for Bernice to be buried in. "Something appropriate," she said, because "there is not a thing fitting to wear to a dog fight in that closet of hers, not to mention that everything is stained with God-knows-what and wadded up like trash."

I feel tired. I hear the door open in the back of the sanctuary, and I turn as discreetly as I can. Lorraine is standing in the aisle, scanning the congregation. The usher tries to hand her a service bulletin but she slips quickly past him and situates herself on the end of a back pew. It's not like her to be late, I had wanted her to sit with me and Ann, but I swear I don't know how she does everything she does anyway. At least she made it. She nods when she sees me looking at her, and I feel like I can rest. She had to be here, and now she is. I cup my hand to Ann's ear and whisper, "Lorraine." That's all I need to say. I want to lie down, but I'm not sleepy. Lorraine gave me a second cup of coffee this morning even though she's supposed to keep a watch on my caffeine. I need to move around or something. I can't concentrate.

The preacher is standing again, saying some thank-yous on behalf of the family. There's an awful lot of noise up there, can't anyone else hear it? The organ is playing, but what's coming out isn't organ music. The sound at the front is louder now, it's deafening. The organist is smiling, but what I hear is Hank Williams singing "Why Don't You Love Me Like You Used to Do?" The preacher does not notice. How can he not notice? The choir is sitting still, no one is moving. The bottom half of the casket is cracked open. I cough and I see a leg. Bernice has kicked open the casket lid. I'm too old to be here. I need to lie down. Bernice is sitting up now, she's laughing, sort of dancing in the casket with her arms over her head. "Now that's what I like," she cries out. "You can give me Hank any day of the week.

He makes me feel sad and happy and wild all at the same time. That's what a funeral needs to be. This is me. This is what I like!" She is out of the casket now, straightening the bottom of her dress. I turn to my daughter Ann to say something. She sees nothing. She is listening intently to the preacher whose mouth is moving, even though no words are coming out. I start to stand up. Ann turns and puts her hand on my arm. "Do you need to go out?" she whispers. She means, "Do you need to go to the bathroom?" because that is what she always assumes when I try to leave any room. A skinny usher with two white carnations on his jacket stares at me. I can tell from his face that he thinks I may be feeling ill, dying, as far as he knows. I settle back down. I will not draw attention to myself. I'm obviously not well. This is my damn medication. I'm going to kill Lorraine. She is supposed to watch Mathilda. She's giving me too much, I know it. I've always known it. I've become so used to pill-taking that I don't even know what's me and what's a chemical reaction. I'm going to hide. I take the church bulletin from the pew in front of me and hold it close to my face. People probably think I'm upset. I am.

"I don't like this dress, you know that, don't you?" Bernice has picked me out of the congregation. "You were supposed to be in charge of what I'm to be buried in, so please explain to me why I have this thing on?"

The preacher is going right on preaching, and here she comes, walking straight down the aisle as pretty as you please. She's coming toward me; there's nothing I can do about it. I try not to look up at her but she keeps on talking. "I have never liked powdery blue, or any powdery color for that matter. They look like the kind of pajamas that sick people wear. In case you haven't noticed, I'm not sick." Why is she speaking this way? Why is she speaking at all, and she's clear as a bell. This is another Bernice. No. This is my medication. I am definitely going to kill Lorraine as soon as I get my hands on her.

People are watching the casket be carried down the aisle. "Nobody's in it!" I almost say out loud but catch myself. Bernice is standing over me. I will not speak. I will not talk to her. Absolutely not. I will not speak. This is exactly how old people lose their minds. This is it and it's happening to me right now. Why will she not go away? I'm going to force her back into that casket. I fix my eyes on her like a target. I brought her out and now I'm going to put her back where she's supposed to be. She won't look back at me. She's swaying down the aisle, and now Hank is singing "If You Love Me Half as Much as I Love You."

People are standing up and filing out after the casket. My daughter Ann reaches for my hand. I pull away. Bernice has me blocked in. Ann looks at me askew but stays with me. She probably thinks I want a few more minutes before we go to the graveside. Bernice touches Ann's shoulder but she doesn't notice. Undiscouraged, Bernice speaks to her anyway, nodding my way. "Honey, I know she's always driven you a little crazy, but she's a good girl, you need to remember that when you lose your patience with her."

I refuse to acknowledge her. "Do you hear me or am I talking to a brick wall?" I stare straight ahead. I will not give into voices; this is where it all starts. The slipping away into senility. The one thing I have had is my mind and I will not let it go. This is how it begins, and I will not accept it. I will not participate. Her voice doesn't exist to me. She leans down close to my face. "You go ahead and sit there. I've got all day. I've got my mind made up to talk to you and I've got all the time in the world."

Bernice walks up to the woman who sang "The Old Rugged Cross." "I've never seen this woman before in my life. Do you know her? I was hoping Ole Hank would sing 'Hey Good Lookin'.' I have always loved that song. There aren't enough young people here. I know a lot of young people. Where are they? Where's Rhonda?" She is momentarily distracted by someone she recognizes and points him out to me. "That man is a deacon in this church and has had an affair with the organist, who also happens to be the preacher's wife, for going on ten years. He thinks no one knows but everyone knows, including the preacher." She continues, as though for my personal edification. "And the lady behind you, Leola Matthews, has never missed a funeral for the thirty years I've known her. One time she told me that she's even gone to funerals when she's on vacation. She picks out the obituaries in the local newspaper and then shows up on time. I told her years ago I thought it was the most morbid thing I'd ever heard tell of, but she told me that on the contrary it certainly is not. She said it always makes her feel grateful. I can understand that."

Bernice continues surveying the room. "Too many black dresses and other assorted outfits here. I thought I said a long time ago, 'God forbid everyone wear black to my funeral.' I want some red. I've always adored red. I'm tired of what passes as tradition to keep us from thinking about what we like, or to make us feel guilty for being different. I do hate this sick blue dress they've got me in. I don't know why you let them do this." She glares my way.

"I didn't."

"What?" Ann whispers, placing a hand over mine.

I say nothing, shake my head slightly, and retrieve my hand.

Ann excuses herself to give me some privacy, while other friends and relatives file by. Bernice steps out into the aisle in front of her son and daughter-in-law. "I feel sorry for him. He has lost the desire to be curious about anything. That is his worst fault. Greta's not the problem. She's sad in her own way, sad, you know?"

There is only one person left in the room besides me. She is sitting in a back corner, and just when I decide that she's too far away for me to see well enough to identify, I recognize Rhonda. Bernice's voice lowers to a whisper. "Do you know she did my hair? She was always so kind to me. You probably thought I was senile and gone. But I insisted. I wouldn't leave you alone. You were alive. You were the most alive thing I saw around me in that place. Not scared to give life a go as long as we could. We did all right, didn't we?"

I am burning. "What do you want?" I shout. An usher clears his throat behind me in the vestibule. He has heard me, wonders if something is wrong, and is letting me know that he's back there, ready to help or to intervene at the right moment, just give him the signal.

"Why are you talking like this?" I shock myself as I hear the words fall off my tongue. "You have never talked this way."

"You mean lucid?" She laughs. "I don't really know. It just happened, like what's in my mind is no longer being blown around like a hurricane. I feel settled inside, and when I open my mouth I know what's coming out."

"You are dead." I lower my voice.

"Well at least I'm here," she says.

"Mama, I'm sorry to bother you, but you've got to get in the car. It's here at the front and they're ready to go." Ann is standing beside me.

"I'm coming." I get up.

"Good. Come on. It's going to pour as sure as day." Ann walks out. Rhonda is leaving now too, dabbing her eyes with a wadded Kleenex.

"Bernice, I am not going to talk to you." I start down the aisle toward the foyer. I am fleeing, but I am not afraid. I am not losing my mind. I am not losing control of myself. "I am finished talking," I tell her again.

"Suit yourself, sweetheart," she says. "I can talk to you whenever I want to."

I am walking away telling myself that I will not remember this once I sleep for a while.

Bernice follows me. "Can't I tell you one more thing?"

"You can tell me why you're walking around talking."

"Actually, I can't tell you that because I don't understand it myself." Bernice smiles. "But I want you to know something if you don't already. Life is choosing whom and what you love. Everything else follows."

She is gone from sight. "Thank you," she whispers, her voice lingering.

I stop and turn around, raising my cane toward the empty front of the sanctuary. "Thank me? I didn't keep you from dying. I didn't keep you from losing your mind either. Who's supposed to sit with me now? Who's going to get me out of a chair? Not you. I'm tired of going from one day to the next with a bottle of Tylenol."

The organist is playing "Amazing Grace." She is frowning at the sheet music in front of her. At the foot of the porch steps, Ann has the car door open, and the same skinny usher is holding an umbrella. We have to go to the grave.

CHAPTER TWENTY-FOUR

RHONDA

The stationery is thick like cloth and expensive-looking, even though it's frayed at the corners from being handled too much. I never bought stationery myself 'til I got married, but I can tell when something is nice. I think I got that from my Mama; she told me I had a good eye. Some of the pages have stains, some of the words are smeared. A thin navy blue line runs all the way around the edge of each piece of paper with "Bernice A. Stokes" printed at the top in the kind of curly letters that no real person could ever do, they're so perfect. Grandma all the time told me my writing looked a nest of copperheads whenever I tried to show her my homework. I was stupid to look for some kind of compliment from her, but that's the way you are when you're young; you don't know no better. "Is that why you go to school?" she said. "I stopped goin when I was thirteen years old and I can write better than that," then she hoisted herself out of her chair and turned the TV up as loud as it would go.

"Could you please tell me why we have been summoned down here? You've already fixed my hair once today, unless you took advantage of my failing brain and lied about it." Margaret is standing in the door on a walker with Lorraine steadying her.

Lorraine adds, "I had to drag her, Rhonda. I told her you said it was important. I think that's the only reason she came. Too jealous I might know somethin she don't."

Margaret rattles her way in and sits down. "And to think all this time, Lorraine, I've been foolish enough to think you tell me everything you know."

"Woman, your head ain't big enough to hold all I know," Lorraine follows.

"Let's turn our attention to Rhonda if you think that's possible. I'll deal with you on my own time."

"It's gon be dinnertime soon, Rhonda," Lorraine says. That's her way of letting me know that we might only have Miss Margaret's patience for a short while. Patience goes and comes when a person gets old, I've learned that much. You gotta go with the flow.

"Oh look, isn't that a sight?" Margaret points to the wall shelf behind me.

Once I had inherited Bernice's bulldog, I decided she oughta park herself in full view in the salon. I even made a little sign with magic marker that said, "Miss Betsy Ross." I don't know if the real Betsy Ross was single or married, but I wrote it how I liked. Bernice would have loved it, I know, and if anybody wants to say something about it, the hell with em.

Margaret is thrilled. "Perched up there on display like she's in a museum! That's wonderful, Rhonda, we'll see her every time we come in here."

"Yeah." They're still waiting for the reason I called them. "That's what I wanted to tell y'all," I say. "I knew I wanted to sit her out somewhere, so I decided to wash her off a little bit first and when I started trying to unzip her, I felt something crumply up in there."

"I told you!" Margaret cries. "What did that rascal do?"

"She had some letters," I said, but Margaret is cracking up before I can finish telling.

"Lord have mercy! Who in the world wrote letters to Bernice? I can't imagine *her* writing much more than her name, can you, Lorraine?"

"I don't know," Lorraine says. From what I can tell, Lorraine is somebody who tries to never jump to conclusions, maybe because she's seen too many things not turn out like they ought to, working in this place every day.

I pick up where I left off. "I didn't want to read em by myself," I say. "I thought maybe I shouldn't be reading em at all."

Margaret doesn't like what she thinks is nonsense. "You make it sound like a mystery, Rhonda. What in the devil are they, some old Christmas cards or something she stuck up in there?"

"I'm tryin to tell y'all." It's my turn to be impatient now, and I sound that way. "She wrote a bunch of letters to Wade." I hold up the bundle of folded paper and shake it in front of them.

Margaret looks awful suspicious. I think she's wondering why if such a thing exists, she didn't either know about them or find them before me. She isn't acting jealous, more curious.

Lorraine is the one to break the silence. "Y'all were a whole lot closer to Bernice than me, but I tell you one thing. If she hid those letters, she knew exactly what she was doin. There ain't no way to prove it, but you'll never tell me different. I don't care how out of her mind she got."

"The question is, y'all . . ." I say, "should I give them to her other son, what's his name?"

"Cameron?" Margaret asks. "Good Lord, if she had wanted him and his wife to have those, do you think she would have hid them in Betsy Ross? She might not have known much, Rhonda, but she knew that if those two ever had the first chance, that dog would be in the Dumpster before they got out of the parking lot."

"That's a fact." Lorraine nods to Margaret.

"Go on then and read them." Margaret pushes me. "This is about as private as we're going to get."

"Wait a minute." Lorraine gets up and closes the door, not that I'm expecting anybody.

"I guess I felt like I needed permission, you know? I didn't want to be the only one," I say. I unfold an extra chair that I keep in case of overflow and sit close to them so they can hear.

Dear Wade . . .

My voice shakes some, but I swallow and start over.

Dear Wade,
I thought I'd be hungry but I'm not. There's so much food left over from last night when we had visitation here. Everyone is worrying I might not eat. I don't feel like it, but I'll eat, they needn't worry. If anyone finds this letter they will say I'm depressed. I haven't taken off my clothes from the funeral even though it's been over for two hours. I can't change clothes because after I take off this dress, I don't know what I'll put on. What does a person put on after they come home from their child's funeral? I feel like I could decide anything except when to take off these clothes.

"Bless her heart," Lorraine says. Margaret's face is flat and gray as a piece of slate. I don't know if it's pain or shock.

I expect they've spread the flowers and wreaths all over the fresh dirt by now. I want to see that tomorrow, first thing. It's supposed to be sunny all day, and I'm going to take some pictures of those flowers, Wade. There were so many beautiful arrangements, some of them from people that hadn't seen you since you were little. They all remembered you though, they said. They told me things they remembered.
After much pleading on my part, Cameron and Greta finally agreed to leave me alone in my house. They wanted me to spend the night with them, but that's not where I want to be right now. I need to be in my house. I had to promise them I'd answer the phone if it rang because

they'd call to check on me. They were smart to make that deal because you always did laugh at me for not answering the phone. You liked saying that what most of the world thought of as a lifeline was a terrible inconvenience for me, and you were right.

I don't want to talk to Cameron. I need time on my own. I have always loved your brother, but I've never been able to talk to him. I think you knew that. I wish I could, but just because he came from me doesn't mean I have anything in common with him. I looked at him today beside me in the pew, staring at the ceiling above where you were, and the first thing I thought was that I have never known one real feeling he harbors. About anything.

When he was little, six or seven, on the first day of Little League, he all of a sudden didn't want to go up to bat. Your daddy kept saying, "Go on, Cam, this is the fun part. You might hit a home run." Cam loved to catch the ball, playing outfield, but nothing your daddy said mattered; he still didn't want to bat. I walked up to him at the dugout, something that was frowned upon by the coach as you can imagine, but I did it anyway. I leaned down and whispered close to his face so no one else could hear. "Are you afraid of something, honey?" and I knew he was. "The ball is gonna hit me," he barely got the words out, starting to cry with embarrassment. "That's not going to happen, sweetheart. Nobody's aiming the ball at you." And he narrowed his eyes at me and snarled, "Something that's not aimed at you can hit you anyway." I told him he was right, and I went back and told the coach he was not going to bat, and Cam and your daddy and I went to the car. I might have saved him from Little League but I never saved him from being afraid. I will admit to you that I don't have much patience for fear, no matter that it was my own son. It was like he was born with it, and you were born totally without it, and I can't understand for all my life what I did to make you that way. I don't think I ever tried to save you from anything. I hope that was all right. I hope one day I'll know it was all right.

I'm not finished writing all I want to but I'm going to stop. It's *probably best to stop. Right now I'm going to eat something and go to bed. There are three dishes of pork chops in the refrigerator, which makes me think that the Women's Circle list must have gotten mixed up somehow because they usually have it sorted out to a fare-thee-well so that nothing is duplicated when there's a funeral. My job is always to bring a cake. Have you ever wondered how cake got to be the thing that people bring to make something special?*

I'm going to go see your flowers tomorrow. I promise you that one thing. I'll tell Cam to come pick me up. Good night, my sweet youngest.

I love you with everything I am,

Your Mother

Margaret's face has changed now, it's more drawn out around the mouth and chin. "I would like to have some water, please," she says.

Lorraine gets up without answering and takes a paper cup from the stack I keep on the counter. Their constant poking at each other has stopped, I don't reckon it can hold up.

"There's more," I say. "Do you want to hear more?" They don't answer me with words. I take it as a sign to go on. Lorraine hands Margaret tap water from the sink and sits back down. I take the next folded sheet from the little pile in my lap.

Dear Wade,
I told myself I was not going to write another letter, but then I decided that it's nobody's business except mine, so here I sit. It's finally spring, daffodils and tulips are coming up in the yard. Remember how we used to take handfuls of bulbs and throw them out among the trees and then put them in the ground wherever they landed? I still do that. I like the recklessness of it. I like to be surprised by what comes up where. We've got all different kinds of daffodils, yellow ones, then some white ones, and some that have a yellow buttercup on white petals. I wish I could put some on your grave, but you know how daffodils

are, they only last a day or two. That's how they are, beautiful but short-lived.

I feel more tired the last few weeks. I haven't been talking to anybody except Cam and I never remember what we talk about an hour after. Maybe it's not interesting, I don't know, but I feel like I'm not there some of the time. I can speak my thoughts the most clearly with you, it helps me to write them out. I can see what I think and I can put my words together slowly. I don't have to perform sentences for anyone else but you.

I hope you are resting. "Eternal Rest" is written on the headstone of the man beside yours. Edward S. Boone. He was a colonel in the army in WWII. Eternal rest makes me uneasy inside, as a concept I mean. I like rest, but as fuel for activity; I want things to happen. If you really are at rest, I don't know how to picture you, so I made up an image in my mind. You are sitting in your daddy's chair like when you would come for Sunday dinner, and you're reading with a pen in one hand, marking in the book like you have ever since you learned to read. I used to try to stop you from marking up all your books, but you said how else were you supposed to be able to find what's important? I like looking at you in the lamplight, marking important things. That's the way I will think of you tonight. Find everything that's worth remembering and share it all with me in the morning. Sweet dreams, darling son.

My love always,
Your Mother

P.S. As I already said, I didn't put daffodils on the grave. Last time I went, a girl I've never seen before had a big armful of magnolia branches that she was scattering around your headstone. Cameron asked me if I knew her and I said no, so he started to get out of the car and say something. I told him to be still, leave her alone. I like those leaves, they're green and shiny, and they'll stay that way for a long time.

"I don't think I can read any more right now," I say. I feel disoriented the way you do if you get on one of those spinning rides on the midway, the kind where you're pinned up against the inside of a big wheel and then the floor drops out from under you. And even though you know it's not really gone and it will raise up again to meet your feet, you can't help but wonder what might happen if you started sliding down the wall and couldn't get back up and the ride didn't stop.

Lorraine can see through me. "Don't think she didn't know, honey. There's ways of knowin that we don't know nothin about."

I start to refold the letters, about to put them away.

Margaret reaches out a trembling, heavy veined hand. "Give them to me, sweetheart," she says, her voice softer than I've ever heard her. She stares at the wrinkled note paper then starts to read, so slow that it's like she's making it up as she goes.

Dear Wade,

I am angry today. I can't put my finger on any one thing but I feel like I'd like to pick up a precious object and shatter it. It's raining and that always makes me feel depressed, but I'm not mad at the weather. Ordinarily I would make a full pot of coffee and sit down to read a magazine or do some sewing. These drops are louder than usual, and bigger. They sound like a million tiny hammers, relentless, driving, harsh. I imagine pins falling from the sky and landing on my skin, one by one. At first there is only a light stinging prick, but then I begin to hurt all over, the combined effect of miniature stabbings.

Nighttime is the hardest. Every night I like to eat a big bowl of ice cream, chocolate, vanilla, and strawberry. Neapolitan. That's the one thing I do like clockwork and I haven't gained a pound. When you were old enough to open the freezer by yourself, you used to love to eat all the strawberry. Later on someone would take out the carton and find a big hole beside the forlorn chocolate and vanilla. More than once your daddy said, "Somebody that you never thought about might want some strawberry, Wade, and there won't be one dab left." He didn't really care, it was more what he felt like he ought to say, and next time you looked in the outside freezer there would be a new carton of Neapolitan right next to the one with the missing strawberry. I don't know why he didn't just buy you a whole carton of strawberry ice cream, but I'm not sure you would have served yourself from it even if he had. I think there was part of you that liked digging the strawberry out and flatly rejecting the chocolate and vanilla. You wanted anybody who looked to know exactly what you thought of those other flavors. You were leaving your mark.

I have stopped driving altogether now, so I have to depend on your brother and Greta to buy my groceries. I could still drive if I wanted to, but I don't care about it anymore as long as somebody will take me. Usually that means Greta because Cameron works too hard. "I never saw anybody eat so much ice cream," Greta says every time I ask her to get me some. Last week she added, "There aren't many places I can find old-fashioned Neapolitan, Mrs. Stokes. You might want to try branching out in your flavors sometime." I will never tell her how many cartons I've thrown in the garbage with only the strawberry eaten out. I feel like eating some right now. I hope you are too, Wade honey. You just go on and eat your favorite, I'll clean up whatever you don't want.

Make sure you sleep enough, sweetheart. I myself have had a terrible time with sleep. Seems like I want to stay up all night long.

Loving you forever,

Mother

P.S. I have saved your toys, so you will recognize them all.

Margaret motions to Lorraine and hands her the last letter, like passing a torch. She's done as much as she can do, somebody else has to carry it the rest of the way. Lorraine squints, holding the page at arm's length, she's been saying she ought to get herself some glasses. Her voice sounds strong after Margaret's.

Dear Benjamin Wade,

If I have to leave here I want you with me. Cameron says I'm mov-
ing to a more comfortable place. I like where we are. I don't want to go
somewhere I've never been. I won't know where anything is. I won't
know where the bathroom is, or towels. I won't know where the food is. I
told him I am comfortable, but comfortable is not what he means. Greta
is whispering to him all the time. I don't have any neighbors and she
thinks I ought to have. I can't take all your toys, some of them will have
to stay here if he makes us go. Don't cry, Benny Wade. You're not going
to end up with a bunch of strangers, I'll personally see to it. I thought
you could help me. I can't think straight. I can't finish what's on my
mind. It's all nerves. My daddy was a nervous man. Don't stray too far.
Please, I am begging you now. My child, my baby. Maybe I can keep
one eye on you all the time, I don't mind.

A strange muffled sound comes out of Lorraine, and I picture a
sort of small wounded animal wrestling itself free from a trap. "Take
it, Rhonda." She hands the paper back and gets up from her chair.
Margaret's eyes are closed. She does not open them with Lorraine's
stirring. I look at the crumpled sheet. The last words are blurred but
stand out anyway; they're all alone. I'm looking for an ending that's
not on the page.

I can't

I love

She didn't manage to sign her name.

CHAPTER TWENTY-FIVE

LORRAINE

I don't usually pray out loud, matter of fact I don't like to, sounds too much like a preacher, but maybe if I do tonight my mind won't wander so bad. I been talking to you a long time, so if you been listenin even half of that time then you know me good as anybody, and I mean all of me. It says in the Bible you know us better than we know ourselves, that's what I was taught. And I was raised on "He's Got the Whole World in His Hands" which I think is sayin close to the same thing. So here's my question: What if you don't care near as much about our lives as we think you do? I'm not talkin about our souls or even our bodies, I'm talkin about regular old things one day to the next. I do believe in you being good in a general kind of way, but the older I get, the more I can't imagine you getting personally involved with all the mess we ask for to try to be happy or free or even holy. I know some people who pray for something just about as crazy as what they ought to eat for dinner. Now me, I can't believe it matters a hill of beans to you if I find a parking place or not. And I don't think you're studyin whether or not I get a raise just because I think I ought to.

I think, why should I pray for something I ain't even gon remember in a few months and yet expect you to focus on it right this minute and serve up some kind of answer that satisfies me? So I ain't gon be prayin anytime soon for you to take the corn

off my little toe or to make my flowers grow. And I ain't sayin that
other people shouldn't pray for those things if that's the burden that's
been placed on their heart and it just won't go away. All I'm sayin is
the things I want answers to are a whole lot bigger than that, and if my
life so far tells me anything, then you ain't gon be givin those answers
anytime soon.

I sat right there in the beauty shop and heard what Bernice Stokes
wrote to a dead boy, her heart so broke that it started to break her
mind too. I know as good as anybody we find a way through our pain
however we can, my own baby died before he got a chance to crawl.
But I ain't somebody who believes you *cause* suffering, like feeding a
child castor oil, to make us better people long as we can swallow it
and keep it down without vomiting. If I did think that, I would never
walk into a church again. You might be distant but you can't be that
cruel. Things happen to us, that's it, some of em we make happen
ourselves. But it's hard on us to live our hurts over and over. If you
want to shed some light on that one, I will sure try to keep my eyes
open. I get tired of hearing God's will this-and-that, it was meant to
be this-and-that. The universe is tellin me this-and-that. Sounds to
me like a fortune-teller talkin. If that's the way life works, all it would
take to figure everything out is a bunch of people smart enough to
connect the dots. Like somebody who can figure out a puzzle just by
starin at it long enough.

I can believe you're present with us, I don't know why but that's
never been a hard one for me. Especially when I look at babies. And
trees. But I wonder what in the world prayer would turn into if we
didn't have anything to ask for. I don't know how much faith I have,
but I do have a mind, and I ain't ready to give up on my questions. So
as soon as I say, "there's a God and I'm sure of it," then what comes out
of that? As far as I can tell, not a whole lot you can put your finger on
and hold it there. Faith don't move in straight lines, at least not mine.
I think maybe it has got to eat itself up and wear itself out every now

and then. I've had to learn to do without understanding, I learn it every day at work when I see somebody at the end of their life, some a lot worse off than others. I've had to learn to do without answers because there ain't enough of em to even count. What I think and what I like and don't like ain't much more than specks on glass, they just get in the way of being able to see good, that's all. If I can learn to love what I *don't* know as much as what I do, then I might be able to do without everything under the sun needin to have a name, and maybe I could make room for what don't have a name.

That's all the prayin I feel like I can do right now. If Jacob could fight all night with an angel and still get a blessing, then I think you can handle me speakin my mind for five minutes. I know it don't bother you, me askin the same questions all the time. Just give me sense enough to see whatever you show me. That's what I pray. That's all I pray. And I know I will again so you might as well be ready for me. Until then, bless me however I need it. And everybody else who needs a blessing. I will try to be grateful, I ought to at least be able to do that. Amen.

CHAPTER TWENTY-SIX

APRIL

We live in a country where politicians talk as much about God and sin as preachers do. I have spent my life in church and as far as I can tell there are really only two unforgivable sins. Killing, stealing, lust, greed, gluttony—none of them are on the list. In our pitiful need to absolve each other and be absolved of anything that serves our purposes, those particular wrongs are at best temporary stains, like chocolate on a white blouse. The only exceptions for which we turn our heads, offer no understanding, and willingly excommunicate all offenders are sickness and aging. We can tolerate neither so we do our best to obliterate both. Poverty could also be on that list, although at least money and resources can remedy that. But as Mama always says, "I don't care who you are, Sick and Old are comin to see you whether you invite em or not." Being a doctor is a way for me to check myself, to remind myself that my salvation does not lie in miracles or Jesus' atonement as much as it does in my conscious, active choice to embrace the marginalized and try to love them, which, for me, is nothing short of Sisyphean. When I feel I've begun to rise to the challenge, the boulder of new responsibility rolls back over the top of me, dragging me with it, straight down to the bottom of their needs, where I start over again, with, for a time, a redefined if unnamed sense of humility.

In the fall of my third year of medical school at Chapel Hill, my mother came to spend Thanksgiving Day. She had arranged for weeks to be off work and also that her cousin Melvin check out the insides of her ancient Impala to verify that it was up to the trek. Mama had it all planned, she would drive into Raleigh and have Melvin give the car the once over, she would spend the night there with him and his wife Mary Alice, then she would get up early on Thanksgiving morning and drive to Chapel Hill. The whole drive was less than a couple hours, but when I asked Mama why she didn't want to come on to my apartment the night before, she said, "April, you know I don't like a long drive, I need to break it up. Don't you be studyin me anyway, you put that turkey in at the crack of dawn like I told you and I'll take care of the rest when I get there." The authoritative sound of Mama's voice warmed me, which was comforting, given what I wanted to say to her when she arrived. I had had plenty of opportunities over the last few weeks, but I hadn't wanted to say it over the phone.

Mama's car pulled into the parking lot the next morning before I had finished a cup of coffee, much less showered. My roommates were still asleep, tired from a late night of dancing the night before, kicking off the holiday weekend which would be our last chance to do anything but study until the end of the term. At Mama's insistence I had invited them to stay for her Thanksgiving dinner, to which, surprisingly, they had agreed. Notwithstanding the fact that students of any kind are usually starving, my roommates were both rich by our standards and also from big northern cities, and I had assumed that the idea of my mama driving up from the North Carolina Sandhills to bring Thanksgiving to her daughter would strike them as provincial beyond words. I was wrong. They were as excited as if they had been invited to the Dean's house.

"Anybody here?" Mama had already opened the door without knocking. I didn't mind. It would never occur to her that she might intrude on anything. She spends her days and nights looking in on people who sometimes couldn't verbally invite her to come into their rooms if their lives depended on it. She has become a priestess of instinct, a religion all its own and one deserving of the utmost respect.

"Come in, Mama. Corey and Jasmine are still asleep I think."

"That's all right. Put on some shoes, child, and come on to the car with me. I've got a load out there and it's gon rain or miss a good chance."

I started for the door, and Mama evaluated my thin sweater and pajama bottoms. "Girl, you're gon freeze, but I ain't gon tell a grown woman what to put on."

"Let's hurry and I'll be fine." I physically maneuvered her out the door. Mama's car was piled with Tupperware, Teflon, aluminum, and every other kind of food container imaginable. "Mama, you brought too much," I said.

"Hush and carry these pans inside. The Lord has blessed me with a daughter who's gon be a doctor, least I can do is make sure y'all don't go hungry."

"We'll never eat all this."

"Hush and go on." Mama had piled a stack of four pans onto my outstretched arms and I turned to go up the outdoor stairs to the second floor apartment.

"Keep em level now," she called behind me. The car door slammed and she followed with a huge picnic basket in one hand and a cardboard box of glass serving bowls balanced on the other arm.

I had had the good sense to clear the kitchen counter of the coffee pot, toaster, blender, and microwave, which Mama refused to use for anything except making popcorn, because she thought it was the most clever way to do it. We unpacked containers and lifted the covers off pots and pans to make sure everything had survived the treacherous journey from Raleigh. Four glass bowls held field peas, sweet corn, butterbeans, and greens. A large flat rectangular pan contained dressing, which neither my Mama nor anybody she knew would even think of cooking inside the bird, so it was a separate and unrelated dish. Another pan contained sliced honey baked ham, covered in foil, and in another, moist sourdough ready to be patted out into biscuits and put into a hot 500-degree oven for a few minutes, then smothered in butter and molasses, or her homemade fig preserves. Mama said the secret to making biscuits was a hot, hot oven for a short time. There were also two pies, pecan and sweet potato, and a coconut cake, which was her specialty because it was so moist that it sort of rolled around in your mouth without falling apart. You didn't want to chew and you didn't want to swallow, you wanted to taste the butter, coconut, cream, and vanilla, until finally they melted away and you were dying to raise your fork for another bite.

"I was goin to fry a chicken," she said, "but I don't like chicken sittin overnight unless you're gon eat it for a cold snack, then it's all right."

"When did you have time to do all this when you had to work yesterday?"

"Most of it last night at Melvin and Mary Alice's, they're old and they don't care if I come in and take over their kitchen once in a while. I left them enough to have a Thanksgiving feast today, but they don't eat nothing much, like little birds, both of em. Do Corey and Jasmine like fried chicken?"

"I don't know. We don't need any more food, Mama."

"I don't eat much fried food anymore either. It's the one thing I can think of I don't like about modern medicine, when they told us we couldn't eat anything fried. A piece of chicken or fish fried right, I mean by somebody who knows what they're doin, is the best thing you've ever put in your mouth, and anybody who says different ain't tasted what I have."

"Good morning, you must be April's mother." Jasmine, already showered and dressed, reached out her hand to Mama. I could tell by the way Mama's eyes widened that she didn't expect Jasmine to be black. Two black women doctors might be more than her pride could hold. I had purposely not told her so I could witness this moment, my mother's own experience-formed, hard-understood world changing in front of her eyes. Mama excitedly grabbed Jasmine's hand with both of hers and pulled her off balance. It was clear she liked her on sight. Mama's work had given her a keen sense of sizing people up, regardless of what was on the surface. Once when I asked her how she kept her sanity being in that nursing home every day, she said in a serious whisper, "Honey, if all I saw was what's right on top, they would all look the same to me. All of em old and can't do nothin, some can't even talk. No, you got to look harder than that."

Jasmine laughed as she regained her footing, and Mama spoke in a low baritone. "I hope we didn't wake y'all up banging around up in here." She looked at me in a pretend-mad way like it was my fault.

"No, no, we were all up late," Jasmine replied. "You should know how much we've been looking forward to today. Is there anything I can do to help?"

"Not one thing, child," Mama answered before I had a chance.

"Thanks, Jas," I added. "Just relax. We might go for a walk after we get everything ready to go."

Mama jumped in. "Oh it's ready. All we got to do is heat up some of these here pans and we can eat whenever y'all want to."

"I'm gonna wake up Corey." Jasmine sounded determined. "He's slept long enough." She picked up her coffee mug and walked down the hall barefoot. We could hear her knock lightly on Corey's door.

"She ought not to wake him up, April. Not on account of me."

"She's not on account of you, Mama. But let's give them both some privacy 'til they're up and going. We can take a quick walk to stretch our legs and then come on back and finish putting together dinner."

The walk from the med school to what I call the pretty part of campus is far, so I decided to drive, telling Mama I needed to get some milk anyway. "Who's gon be open on Thanksgiving, April? This ain't Raleigh."

"I know, Mama. All the more reason that there'll be a store open, students are always running out of something, holiday or not."

I parked on Franklin Street near the post office. "Have you been there before?" Mama pointed from her window to the Morehead Planetarium across the street.

"Not since a field trip in third grade. But I remember it very well. Someone threw up when the galaxy started spinning and they had to turn on all the lights."

"I sure would like to go there one time before I die."

"First of all, when are you dying, and second, why do you want to go to a planetarium?"

"Because I would like to look up in that dome and see how they show the universe. I like thinkin about something so big I can't imagine the end of it. I feel like I'm livin tall when my mind is flyin like that, tryin to find someplace to land. I feel lightened up inside, maybe it's my heart, I don't know exactly."

Mama could always surprise me, and I stopped short, not getting out of the car, momentarily forgetting my own purpose in taking her away from the others. "I wish we could go right now, Mama, but they're closed."

"Honey, we've got Thanksgiving dinner to put on the table, we're not gon look at stars now." She opened the door on her side. "Come on, let's go get your milk or whatever it is you need."

"I like having time to talk by ourselves." I started gently, but she was already getting out of the car. I threw my words like a dart, it was the only way I could get them out. "Mama, I'm pregnant."

"Come on and let's go," she barked, standing outside. "It's cold."

How could she not have heard? "Listen," I said, talking across the roof of the car.

"I heard you, April." Her voice was flat. "That don't mean I know what to say."

I didn't know how to engage her. She wasn't moving, so I moved toward her. "You're going to meet the father in a few minutes."

"On Franklin Street?"

"At the apartment. Corey."

"You told me you didn't have no boyfriend cause you don't have time."

"I didn't. I don't. I'm not going to go into the details, but . . ."

"I know the details, I had you, didn't I?"

"I didn't think you'd be mad. I didn't know what you'd be, and now I feel like an idiot for not knowing you'd be mad."

"I ain't mad." Mama walked away from me, and I followed not quite beside her, giving her a little space because that's the clear message I was getting. She was honest when she said she wasn't mad, but she wanted distance all the same. She talked without looking at me.

"I can see you sittin at the table in your pajamas, about six years old, starin at your breakfast cause your grandma made you oatmeal, and me knowin you hated the taste of oatmeal, always have. Used to throw it up against the wall and scream your head off when you was a baby. You looked me in the eye that mornin and said, 'I'm gon be a doctor when I get big.' I laughed, Lord I laughed. We were barely hanging on. Me with no husband, and my mama takin care of you so I could keep a job. I laughed, I didn't know what else to do. That mighta been the first time I hurt your feelings, and you no more than a baby."

"I don't remember that."

"It's a blessing children don't remember their hurts."

"What's got you thinking about this?"

"Are you gon give up school to raise your baby?"

"Absolutely not."

"I thought you'd say that. I know your heart, April, but I don't know how you're gon do a residency, not to mention if you specialize, when that baby's not even two years old."

"I'll do whatever I need to do, same as you did."

"Same as I did." She made a snorting sound before stopping to look me dead in the face. "I'm gon tell you something and you might hate me for never tellin you 'til now. I can't do nothing 'bout that. I'm tellin you now, that's all I know to do."

"Are you going to make a confession here in the street?" I laughed awkwardly.

"As a matter of fact I am," Mama said, and her hushed tone made me know she was more somber than I had ever seen her. "I've asked myself 'bout a thousand times if you need to know this, and right now, I believe it's more for me than it is for you. But this feels like a day for honesty to me. It's in the air."

I didn't respond. I was cautious.

"April . . ." She stopped herself momentarily and looked at the ground before resuming. "You had a brother. Thomas. Born and died in the same month, two years before you were born."

"Why are you telling me this now?" I felt strangely angry with her. Not for what she had said, but because I must have decided at some point in my life that my mother was forbidden to have secrets.

"It's your turn to be mad," she said, willing to leave off there.

"I'm listening to you." I wanted more.

"I left Thomas with your daddy one afternoon, your grandma was supposed to come. I wasn't gone but an hour. When I came back, he was dead in his crib."

"Was he sick?"

"No. I don't know. I never will. Your father was there. Sittin on the porch asleep."

"Drunk," I snapped, seeing myself at five, hiding under the bed with my hands over my ears. Drunk. I had never used the word to describe my father to my mama. But the anger of years can live on its own, and it reared up, serpentlike and punishing.

"He probably had some beers, maybe more than that. He usually did. I knew that about your daddy when I married him, only I didn't know it was stronger than both of us put together."

"He killed his own child."

"Honey, don't you know that me hatin your daddy would have been the easiest thing in the world? If I wanted to, I could have stoked that fire enough all this time that it would be burning right now, and burn me up with it. Listen to me. I left my baby in the hands of a person I knew full well couldn't take care of him. If it's anybody's fault, it's mine."

"That's not true. You said Grandma was coming."

"She was, she did. But I was that baby's mother. I was the one . . ." Mama choked on her words.

We held each other while she cried. For the first time ever, I felt I might be a small comfort to the woman who had spent her life comforting everyone else. There was a long space, space for breath, space to regain footing once we had hit the solid ground of revelation.

"I can be a mother to my baby, Mama."

"Can you?" Mama looked up with bloodred eyes. I didn't know then that I would hear that question often, inside my head, posed by myself, to myself, whenever the choice for motherhood required me to answer yes, even if I didn't necessarily feel it. It was Mama's own constant, never-ending "yes" that forged my life, and my own "yes" would have to be every bit as strong, resilient, and long-suffering.

"Yes, Mama, yes." I kissed her, and she touched my cheek, moist with a mixture of her tears and mine.

She pulled back from me, relieved by a promise that I had hurled into the future with all my strength. "There's something else," she said.

"Now? I think I need a break."

"That was about me. This is about you."

"You're going to tell me something I don't already know?"

"Do you know where your name come from?"

"The month I was born in, that's what Grandma said."

"Well that ain't right. There's another reason, and the only other person who knows it is Margaret Clayton."

"Why?"

"She was the only one ever asked me, including your Grandma."

"Tell me then."

"When I was a girl and your Granddaddy was alive and well, I loved to go to his store. All of life was in that store, comings and goings all the time, seemed like it to me anyway. I might as well have been in New York City."

"It was torn down before I ever saw it."

"Well it was something, and he was proud of it, I tell you that. One day in spring, before Easter, I stopped on the way home, but Daddy wasn't inside. The boy that helped him said he didn't know where he was, but he left me a note. When I opened it there was a map inside, not a real map, but one he had drawn with thick crayons, giving me directions. I followed that map all over the yard and finally to the back of the store, and there was a long box lying in a wheelbarrow with my name on it. Daddy jumped out of the storage room and scared me so bad I screamed. He said, 'Girl, go ahead and open it, can't you see it's got your name on it?' He never could keep a surprise, no tellin how long he was hiding back there waitin for me to find my way with that homemade treasure map. I've never been no good at directions."

"And?" I prodded, realizing I sounded impatient. I couldn't imagine what it had to do with me.

"Child, I tore into that thing so fast it would make your head spin. At first all I saw was wadded-up tissue paper, but when I pulled it all off, I found what Daddy had bought for me. A kite, all different colors, the prettiest thing you ever saw. Daddy and me, we took it and ran straight across the road to a mowed down field and flew that thing all afternoon. It was like I was meant to fly a kite and I hadn't ever touched one before. Daddy kept chasing me and whenever he got close, I went even faster, pulling the kite so high above our heads it wasn't no bigger than a sparrow up there in the sky."

Mama looked up and took a deep breath, like she was trying to see whether if she looked long enough it might still be flying, lifted by an invisible wind.

"Daddy had a heart attack on Easter Day, young as he was, and died the same night. I flew that kite all spring, every day except when it was rainin, most of the time all by myself. When you was born, I looked at you in the face and I said, 'April. Those were my flyin days.'"

I was going to tell her it was beautiful, I was going to say thank you, but instead I found her eyes, lingered, and drank her in.

"Stop starin at me, girl," she said. "You got somethin to say?"

"I don't."

She looked back to where we had parked. "I'm gettin colder. I shoulda brought my scarf." We walked again.

"Mama, I will figure this out. You know I will."

"What about Corey?" she asked, hopeful.

"I'm not going to marry him if that's what you're asking. That's what he wants, but I told him no. He wants to help support this baby though; he's offered to put it in writing."

She didn't comment but asked, "Do you ever wonder if we make life harder than it needs to be?"

"Is that directed at me?"

"Baby, it ain't directed anywhere. Only wondered about."

I moved in front of her so she had no choice but to stop walking. "Out of all your pearls of wisdom, I think about one. Do you know what it is?"

"Brush your teeth or they'll rot out?"

"That too. But you told me that the only way to live was to act like what you believe is already so."

"Is that right?" Mama replied, appearing triumphant.

"It has not failed me yet," I said.

Mama turned the collar of her coat up against the gusty November wind as a substitute for the scarf she didn't bring.

"Look at you," she said. "I sure named you right. You're flyin still." I hugged her in the street, holding her longer than she expected me to. She pushed me away and added, "I was gon say 'you forgot your milk,' but I thought I might sound too much like your mama."

We didn't speak once we got in the car. It was getting close to dinnertime, which, as I had earlier explained to Corey and Jasmine, actually meant lunch to Mama's generation. They had already set the table by the time we returned. Taking off our coats, we warmed ourselves in the kitchen, still heated by the overworked oven. Jasmine joined us first, Corey followed, his eyes searching mine for any indication of what had or had not been revealed. Mama perceived the distress signal before it had even fully registered with me. She offered her hand.

"You're Corey. I know you," she said. "My hands are like ice, I'm sorry."

I watched the muscles in his jaw and neck relax. Mama's knee-jerk diplomacy consisted of erasing the borders between neighboring countries by simply deciding they need not exist. Armed with steaming serving dishes, we returned to the dining area and sat. Our plates and napkins were a mismatched effort at graduate student elegance, but they added to the lack of pretense that welcomed Mama and me to each other's Thanksgiving and made us all comfortable partaking freely of the staggering feast of her presence.

CHAPTER TWENTY-SEVEN

MARGARET

Lorraine is sitting in a big chair near me, talking. I am watching her mouth. Her lips open and close in slow motion. On the other side of the room, there's a woman in here who keeps trying to take my order. I don't think it's time for supper, but she's asking what she can get for me. I haven't answered her yet. But I'm thinking, "She's not really asking me what I want. Nobody asks what you want here." But there she stands. Big too. She's got a head full of blue-black hair puffed up in a bouffant, and a little white cap on top, wearing a pale yellow dress with a plain white apron, no ruffles. She looks overworked, and I know waitressing is hard work. I haven't done it myself, but I've known plenty of people who have. On your feet all day. Have to be polite if you expect to get any sort of tip, and have to clean up after everybody's mess, except in the fanciest restaurants where you only have to take the order and they've got other people to do the rest, even down to serving the food. Clearly this woman has to do it all herself.

I don't know where my bed is. All I can see is lots of stools along a bar, and then I'm at that bar too, but I'm not sitting at a stool, I'm lying in bed, but the bed must look like a stool because it fits right in line with the other stools.

"You're gon have something to drink in a few minutes." I can barely make out Lorraine's words. Did I ask for something to drink? I don't remember doing it. "What do you have on special?" I say to the waitress woman with the pad and pencil.

Lorraine says something about a cup of ice—she sounds frustrated, I can't hear her very well. The woman with the pad talks over her which surprises me, because not many people talk over Lorraine. "We have Salisbury steak with gravy on special. That comes with two home-made vegetables. We also have a fried catch-of-the-day," she says, tapping her pencil on her chin, then using it to scratch her head, without damaging the construction that is her hairdo.

"When did y'all start taking orders?" I ask.

She coughs and answers. "I don't take everybody's orders. But I'll be taking yours whenever you can make it here."

"Have you seen me here before?"

"Does it look like what you know?"

I look around me. I have to be honest. "This is not my room. So where?"

"Your drink? I told you it's coming. I told you, honey." Lorraine sounds like she's shouting, and I'm not even talking to her.

I like this new waitress even though I don't know her. I feel like I know her. Something about her reminds me of somebody, maybe it's her nose.

"Well I want you to relax," she says. "Take your time and enjoy yourself."

"Are you going to serve in the dining room?" I ask.

"No ma'am. Right here. It's a simple place, but at least it's mine."

"I don't know how I'll find my way back here."

I look down and there are car keys in my hand. Something is jingling. I think they are keys. Or loose change. Maybe I've dropped them. There is a white sheet or something like it in my car. It's soft, but it's tangled around my legs. I can't move. "My daughter can drive me," I say to the woman. "I know she can find it, she's good at finding things."

"Have you made up your mind?" She touches the pencil point to her tongue, then licks her lips and swallows.

"Yes ma'am I have. I'm going to pass on the specials. I think I'd just like a cup of coffee and something sweet."

I turn to Lorraine. "Don't you want something sweet?"

"'Scuse me?"

"Just tell her what you want," I say.

"Who, Miss Margaret? I'm the only one here." Lorraine leans down to my ear.

I do not like her tone of voice, so I choose not to answer. That is my choice.

"Here, eat one of these. I'm going down the hall for a minute," someone says, and whisks out of my room. I like a shoe that makes some noise when you walk. Lets people know you're coming.

I take a Fig Newton off the tray that is suspended across my lap and try to have a bite without crumbling it. I'm lying down too far. I never said I wanted to lie down. I much prefer sitting up in a restaurant. I'd like to be sitting.

"Let's go on down to the dining room directly." It sounds like Lorraine's voice, but I am already in a restaurant.

CHAPTER TWENTY-EIGHT

LORRAINE

I pull my chair close to the one where she's dozing. A squeak on the floor tiles makes her open her eyes. "How long have you been sitting there?" she asks, halfway mad but welcoming, as usual. In what looks like slow motion, she grabs at the air around her head, like she's tryin to catch a mosquito.

"I've been waitin for you to wake up to feed you dinner," I say.

"Ann's not here."

"No honey, just me, just Lorraine."

"Yes, and she won't come back unless I call her."

"You know that's no such of a thing," I remind her. "She comes down here near 'bout every day."

"Well I don't see her."

"I'm not gon argue with you right now, Miss Margaret."

"All you want to do is argue with me ever since I've known you."

"I'm not gonna argue with that either." I laugh, she has always liked to hear me laugh. "Here now, let me help you eat something. You barely ate anything this morning except a couple mouthfuls of cereal." She is grabbing at air again; it's almost graceful, like she's dancing sitting down.

"I've never seen so many strings hanging in my life, Lorraine." She makes a sweep in front of her face and mine. "You all need to clean out in here, get some scissors and cut them. I can't see one thing through all these strings."

"Don't worry so much. We'll keep everything straightened up for you." I tuck a napkin into the neck of her pajama top.

I have learned after many years that being truthful isn't as important as being present. I could tell her there ain't no strings, that she's imagining or dreaming, but that's only gon agitate her. She's not gon remember any of it in thirty minutes or less, so why should I upset her? I know that some doctors say we ought to tell them the truth all the way to the end, don't ever let up on the truth. That's not my opinion. I think the truth matters a whole lot less than the value of something. What's goin on right now is eatin; strings are not worth talkin about. I have mashed up some meat loaf and reach to put it in her mouth. I can see she's not happy from the frown that wrinkles her top lip.

"You want me to give you the fork?" I say, and she doesn't answer but takes it from my hand and guides it into her mouth by herself.

She chews mighty quick for someone who has no teeth except full plates. "This is real good. I know you didn't make it." She's smiling, she can't help herself.

"I wouldn't cook for you if you paid me."

"Lorraine, I love you, but damn you."

"That's all right," I say and I mix some mashed potatoes and meat loaf onto the fork and hand it to her. We repeat this a few times, not speaking at all.

She looks past me towards the door. "Let's find him a chair."

I look back at the door, even though I've learned that there will probably be nobody there. This is the hard part for me. I wish she'd argue with me, fight me, lash out, anything she needs to do to stay with me.

"Who?" I ask.

"Daddy will be back anytime. He's got a box for me. It's not a kitten, but that's what I want."

"Where are you now?" I try to bring her back. She doesn't answer. "Where are you, Margaret?"

"The same place," she says softly, still staring at the door. "It's all right that it's not a kitten. Maybe next year?"

"That's right, maybe next year, you never know," I say. "You never know what might happen next year." I focus back on the tray of food. "I know you want some of this yellow cake."

"Yes ma'am I do." She sounds like she could cry.

"All right then. Let's have us some cake."

Her hands are folded in her lap. She doesn't try to take the fork. I almost believe someone was there who's gone now, the room is filled up with a sad blue fog. I put a forkful of cake in her mouth. She chews but stops before swallowing. "Have some," she says. Cake crumbs spill out onto her breast when she tries to say more.

"I b'lieve I will." I take a bite of yellow cake. It's soft and good.

She swallows again and can talk better. "How long are you going to stay here, Lorraine?"

"I don't know. I'm not gon leave 'til you finish eatin, I know that."

"No, no, no, how long are you going to stay at this job?"

"I been working here more than twenty years."

"A lot of people would be sick of it by now."

"Is that what I said?"

"No, it's not, but are you?'

I hear myself sigh. "I don't know. No, I'm not. You can get tired of anything, but I'm not ready to leave. And when I get ready, you nor nobody else will stop me."

She is silent. I think we're through talking and she's gon doze off again, like she always does after eating a big meal. She lowers her head.

"Don't leave here before I do. Give me that."

"I'm not leaving you." Our eyes settle on one another. I feel like I'm gon choke. "I'm not leaving," I tell her.

"I'm tired. I wish you'd turn off that blame TV. Nobody around here does a thing I tell them."

I take the remote and switch off the set. "Nobody around here but me will put up with your mouth."

"Is that right?" she says. "Go on and let me rest. I'll make another appointment with you later on."

I take my sweater off the back of an armchair. "I might not be available, you better check my calendar."

"I *am* your calendar!" she calls out, and I laugh in the hall. I know she can hear me and she's laughing too. That's all right for today. That's fine.

CHAPTER TWENTY-NINE

MARGARET

There's either too much light or not enough light. I'm tired, I think I sleep too much, but everybody tells me that it's normal at my age, so I've given into it. There's a woman in my room. I think it's that black-headed waitress back in my room. Why are there stools along the wall again? There's not enough room for all those stools in my room, I could have told her that. She's opening curtains, letting in too much light. It's already too bright. I'm taking a headache. I'm going to ask her for some aspirin. She is moving tables around. This is the same dining room, but she has put up new curtains. There's a menu on the table in front of me. Well they've gotten themselves all fancy haven't they? New curtains and a menu. We never got a choice about anything before. That woman is not a nurse. She probably doesn't have any aspirin. Why am I the only one here?

She sees me looking at her and speaks. "You're a little bit early, but just give me one minute and I'll take your order."

"You act like we're in a restaurant." I laugh.

"I think it's more of a diner."

"Are you new? I'm sleepy."

"Honey, you look wide awake to me. And no, I'm not new, you know me. I've been here forever." She nods at the menu. "Have you made up your mind yet? Everything's good, I promise. Make it all myself."

I open the menu. It hadn't occurred to me that I was hungry but when I start looking at all the choices, I am starving. "Are you a cook?" I ask.

"Cook, waitress, and owner. I'm here to serve. Lot of people don't see it that way since I own the place and all, but that's what it is, pure service twenty-four hours a day."

"You don't work twenty-four hours; no one does."

"It feels like it's constant. I'm not good at keeping track of time. I suppose it's a good thing."

"Maybe you ought to slow down," I offer her and glance back down to the menu a second time.

"My customers would lose their minds if I did that. They've come to depend on me even for simple things, not only full meals. Not to mention that I created all of this, so now should I step back and let other folks run it however they want to? No ma'am, I've got to keep my hand in it."

"Is my daughter Ann in the ladies' room?" This must be someplace she knows about. I do fall asleep in the car a lot.

"Nobody's here except you, it's early."

"If she's not here then who's going to take me back?"

"I expect *you* will since you're the one who drove yourself in, pretty as you please, in a big Plymouth."

"What's my car doing out there? Ann told me it didn't even run. I sure as hell didn't drive it here."

"I don't mean to be contrary, but I saw you with my own eyes."

"They don't let me drive, I'm ninety-one years old."

"You've lived a long time, haven't you?"

"How far away from the rest home are we?"

She is wiping countertops with a damp rag that smells slightly of lemon and ammonia mixed.

"I don't think we're too far, sometimes it seems far. It didn't take you long to get here, did it?"

"I don't know."

She stops wiping. "Honey, you look all agitated. Calm down and let me serve you something. You won't be disappointed."

"I don't think I've got time right now."

"Well come on back anytime you want. I don't ever close."

"I couldn't find my way here if I wanted to."

Lorraine is talking, but her voice sounds like it's in a tunnel. "Now you know I take you everywhere you need to go. You're not gon get lost in here. No need to want to stay in your room all the time."

"Where did you say we are?"

The waitress is walking to the kitchen. "It's only a crossroads. There hasn't been a town here for a long time, and I feel like I've been here forever."

She picks up a tray and goes through swinging doors into what looks like a big silver kitchen.

"Are you coming back?"

"I'm listening to you, give me time. Now what's all this?" Lorraine is close to my ear. She picks up shreds of torn paper from my lap.

"Lorraine, please pull those curtains. I'm going blind in that sun." She doesn't answer me. "Why are y'all moving things around?"

"Nobody's moved one thing. Were you dreamin?" She throws the paper shreds in the trashcan by the bed. "You've had yourself a good old time in here with this paper. I'm gon bring you somethin to eat."

"I already looked at the menu."

"Did you?" Lorraine sounds surprised. "Well tell me what's on it because all I saw was pork chops on those trays in the kitchen." I can feel Lorraine's hands around my shoulders, she is putting something like a blanket around me.

"She said she would take my order."

"Honey, ain't but one waitress and that's me."

"I was taking the headache with all that light."

"You usually like sun in the afternoon."

"I told her to close the curtains. She seemed nice but she kept right on with what she was doing."

"I'll be back with your tray. Do pork chops sound good to you?"

"That's all right. And a Co-Cola. I want to stay awake, I'm groggy."

"We'll sit and have us a good talk when I get back. Sit up straight now, I'll be back directly."

CHAPTER THIRTY

LORRAINE

I been putting lilies in vases with some sprigs of green and then tying them up with pink, blue, and yellow ribbons, one of each color. They're gon dye some eggs later on and we'll spread em around on the tables. I told Ada Everett I didn't think that was a good idea because people will be trying to crack and eat em and they might get sick, but she said we just have to watch everybody and make sure they don't. She ain't gon be watching, you can bet on it, so that means me and whoever else is in here at dinnertime. She also said she didn't want the decorations to be too religious. I do understand what she means, everybody's different, but then I think it's Easter Day and with an Easter dinner, and I don't see no way around that. Either you're doin it or you're not. The lilies are as far as we'll go, everything else on the walls is about all kind of flowers and spring bunnies, and little yellow chicks. That's all right, it looks real pretty. Cheers me up and I ain't even sad.

Miss Margaret don't want to come down here and eat, Lord knows she already told me in what words she could, half asleep as she is. They changed some of her arthritis medication too and it's not doing her any good, so it might have been the medicine talking. Ann came first thing in the morning, before church, and said she would have skipped that if it wasn't Easter Sunday. She said she was sad she had to miss this dinner here, but she'd be back in the afternoon. Even if I can get Miss Margaret down here to the dining room, I'm probably gon have to feed her every bite she puts in her mouth. That's all right. I know what she likes. She hasn't had good luck holding a fork for a few weeks. Trembles all the time. Ann said the doctor says it's natural, not a palsy disease or anything, just gettin old. Gettin old. She knows she's old.

I finish up with the napkins and plates. Mean-tilda offered to help me but I told her not to mind, that I was about finished. If I wanted it to look like a bulldozer decorated the room I would have taken her up on her offer. She was trying to do something nice, and sometime I need to let her. Maybe she'll help with the clean-up. I take me a short break, the one I'm allowed to have, and have a cold soda and a dough-nut. I get both out of the machine in the break room. April asks me why I eat this mess for snacks when I could have fruit or yogurt right there in the kitchen. I tell her I eat it because I want it. A banana is not the same as a doughnut, and I'd rather eat a Krispy Kreme any day.

"I don't drink and I don't smoke," I said, "so if some sugar is gon kill me, then go on and buy the casket. Make it a nice one. Metal, not wood, I don't want nothin rotting with me inside it."

April asked, "Have you been shopping for a funeral or some-thing?"

"When I do, I'm gon take you with me," I said. Truth is, I had looked at a brochure I found in the trashcan. About a month ago, there was a young man in here, real suntanned like he was livin at the beach. He got himself past reception saying he was on pastoral calls, then started makin rounds room to room, one by one. If the person inside was awake, in he went and opened up a satchel and showed color pictures of all kind of caskets, inside and out, and he had scraps of material taped to paper so you could touch em if you wanted to. He also said that the latest trend was to do away with a display room full of big caskets, and instead, line the walls of the funeral home with little cross sections. That way the customer could see the wood, the lining, hardware, and whatever else a person might want to look at in a casket without ever havin to open up a full-sized one. He said it was also better for the family because it wasn't like they were looking at *real* caskets, so the whole experience might be a little bit more pleasant. He would take an order right there for anybody that could give a cash or check deposit, nonrefundable by the way. After a few stops at rooms where people weren't alert enough to give him the time of day, he made it into Miss Margaret's room and started by introducing himself and reading some scripture. She was all right with that, she liked a little Bible reading as long as it didn't turn into hellfire and damnation talk. But he bit off more than he could chew cause when he tried to slip from scripture reading to showing funeral pictures, she told him to get the hell out right then and buzzed the nurse station. There couldn't have been any better time for Mean-tilda to be on duty, and down the hall she come flying. Course he had done left Margaret's room but she found him and said if he didn't leave the premises, she would call the police and hold him 'til they got here. He didn't move fast enough for her, so she slammed her medicine cart up against the wall and took a step towards him when I think he saw for the first time that he was outsized by a long shot. He turned tail and went straight out the emergency exit with her right behind him as fast as she could go. I had to go to the administration office to get a key to turn off the alarm.

Ada Everett's announcement for holiday dinners is the only time anybody ever talks over the intercom unless they have a medical emergency. She is cheery like a bird, as always, in fact her voice sounds like a bird. "Good afternoon everyone, and happy, happy Easter. It's a beautiful spring day, and I'd like to welcome everyone to the dining room for our annual Easter luncheon. See you there!" You got to give her credit, she sounds happy in her work.

I check on several of my patients who don't need my help to make sure they're dressed and ready to go to lunch. When I get to Miss Margaret's room, she is in pajamas, sitting in an armchair with sunglasses on. I don't have no idea whose sunglasses she's got, maybe her daughter's or somebody who came to see her and left them, in a hurry to get out and back to whatever they were doing. "I thought we decided you were gon put on some clothes," I said.

"*We* didn't decide a goddamn thing."

"I know you're not gon talk like that on Easter Day."

"I'll talk whatever I want whenever the hell I want to, Lorraine."

I know when to back off. "All right then, Miss Margaret, I'm gon leave you be 'til you can talk to me like I'm talking to you." I start for the door but she stops me.

"I can't get up from here. I don't feel like it, and I don't have any clothes fitting to wear."

"I told you I'd help you."

"You can't help me. You think you can help me? You can help me go to lunch with a bunch of people worse off than me. That sure sounds like a happy Easter, doesn't it?"

"Would you eat something with me by ourselves?"

"In here? Mama and Daddy have already left, ages ago." Her mind's skipping some.

"I haven't seen them, honey, but they're all right wherever they are. I'm talkin about with me. In the dining room. I been puttin out flowers since breakfast and I made a table off to one side. Ain't room but for two people."

"I don't want to see them, Lorraine." Her voice breaks, weaker now. "They'll look at me and think, 'she can't do anything.'"

"The only one looking at you is gon be me. I have to look at you whether I want to or not." I try to pull a smile out of her.

"Don't say what you can't promise."

"I promise. Now take off them sunglasses." I reach for her hands, and she raises them as high as she can, not quite to shoulder level, but enough for me to take hold below her wrists and pull her to her feet so

I can pull down her pajama pants and underwear. I sit her back down, it's painful for her, then take off her top. Her bra looks brownish. I know she has clean bras. I know Ann does her laundry every few days and brings it down here herself, so this means somebody sorry didn't put a clean one on her. I get her changed and then take a few different things out of the closet so she can pick. We're gon be late but this is more important. I want her to know what she's doin and know what she's wearin and know that it's Easter, and she's not going to if I don't let her be part of the little things that go along with it.

"I like the pink, Lorraine. But it might be too young-looking . . ." She was waiting for my opinion.

"I think it suits you real good." We struggle to get her into the skirt and jacket top and she declares she's gon wear a shoe with a heel. It don't matter cause she can't walk all the way down there anyway. I unfold the wheelchair in the corner. I reach for her hands and she looks up into my face. "Rise up," I tell her.

"That sounds like Easter. Have you been to church?"

"No, I can't go, but I know it's Easter, don't you?"

"We ought to have hats."

"Wouldn't that be a sight," I say, "us prancin in there with Easter bonnets on?"

Our table is waiting like I left it. Everyone else is already eating, so we sit and one of the boys from the kitchen brings us plates. It's ham with a pineapple slice on top, with some garden peas and mashed potatoes. Without asking, I unfold her napkin and put it in her lap, then set her plate in front of me. I cut up the meat into pieces a little child could swallow and raise the fork to her mouth.

"Thank you," she whispers. She opens.

"Chew real good now," I tell her, but she doesn't answer me. I slide my plate to the side and push some mashed potatoes onto her fork. She raises her left arm, reaching for the lilies in the middle of the table. She might knock the whole thing over before we're through, but I'm not gon study that. She wants to touch them, so I move the vase closer to her. "Happy Easter, Margaret. Is it good?" She's still chewing, she has to swallow slow, and only a little at the time. Her sitting here is her thanking me. We're gon take it bite by bite, however we can.

CHAPTER THIRTY-ONE

Margaret

Hey, Mrs. Clayton, glad to see you again." The waitress smiles. She has more teeth than any normal person is supposed to have. Bright shining white teeth.

"Thank you, same to you. I declare I think I could eat everything in this restaurant, I'm so hungry." I haven't eaten one thing I like today except for some candy that Lorraine gave me because it was good and chewy, exactly the kind I'm not supposed to have because it gets all in my dentures. Everybody else brings me some sort of crème-filled old-people candy that tastes like coconut and cough syrup mixed up together inside a chocolate shell. I also have a strong dislike for those big orange sugar peanuts that seem to find their way into every room in this place. Why in the world they make them to look like peanuts I don't know, because there's nothing peanut about them, especially not the taste. "What's on special today?"

"I've got some of the best country-style steak you've ever had, gravy too."

"Is it hard to chew?"

"There's not anything I serve that ain't easy to eat if you want it."

"All right, I'll take that with just a little gravy poured over it and I want some snap beans too. Have you got sweet tea?"

"I'll bring you some tea. But you're not gon have supper 'til five. Just lay your head back and close your eyes."

"She said she had country-style steak."

"Who said?"

"The black-headed woman with the big teeth. She owns the place."

"Who is she? Do you know her?"

"She's running an all-night diner. I thought Bernice ought to have been there but I didn't see her. This woman is nice, real nice."

"Were you looking for Bernice?"

"I don't know."

"It's hard to know sometimes, isn't it?"

"She told me to come back and I said I would."

"That's all right, then. Go on, close your eyes and I'm gon bring you something to drink."

"Who are you?"

CHAPTER THIRTY-TWO

APRIL

I told her several times I would drive her to the hospital. Mama said she could drive herself, but something in her face tugged at me, sending a different message from that of her words. One of her patients is dying. To call Margaret Clayton one of her patients is an understatement because she is Mama's friend, close friend, and they have had intimacy forced upon their relationship by nature and age, yet rather than turn away from it, have walked through it, Mama supporting her all the way, younger in years but somehow older in days. Mrs. Clayton has uterine cancer and refuses to have an operation or chemo, and she is in the hospital now because she has periods of profuse bleeding that are becoming more frequent. She will die, there is no other possible outcome, and she is fighting mad. Mama says her friend has held on as long as she could. She pictures her on a rope behind a ski boat, but the boat is going faster now, and she's falling, and she will have to let go or be pulled under. She will turn loose soon whether or not she wants to, but for now she is still managing to stay on top of the water, shifting in and out of the wake, wherever she can keep her balance. I suppose that, in her frailty, her will is the only thing she has, and she feels anger toward anyone who cannot understand it or will not succumb to it, even over the simplest things. I could have let Mama go alone, but going with her, taking her in fact, was a way for me to say that I understood the weight of the moment, not because someone was dying, an inevitability to which I had been forced as a doctor to become accustomed, but rather, because my mother's friend needs her now.

We arrived at the hospital just after dinnertime. She had suggested we stop on the way at Burger King because it was the only readily available option without taking time to go in somewhere and sit down. We did not talk as we exited the parking deck elevator, through the glass tunnel into a large reception area with rows of industrially upholstered chairs and sofas. I followed her, a few steps behind, and it struck me that she walked with the pace and tranquillity of a Buddhist monk, completely present in each step across the diamond-patterned carpet of pale green and coral. Her shoulders were held back, her neck was long, and her stride was seamless. She knew what she was there to do. Mama believed that everything you bring into a sick person's room is what you leave behind, and she insisted that a person try to keep the chaos of the world and his own heart at bay in the presence of someone not well. In her experience, hurry and general anxiety were two unwelcome accompaniments for the more visible offerings of flowers, candy, and get-well cards. Mama stood at the reception desk with me now beside her. The young black man behind the desk did not look up. She waited, this was not unfamiliar territory to her, she would accept the fact that maybe the receptionist thought, "I am at my job, not here to serve you, and the world is not going to stop just because you've arrived, so you'll have to wait and let me finish what I'm doing or pretending to do at the moment whether you like it or not." Mama was nonplussed. I, on the other hand, did not share her patience. "Excuse me sir, we're here for visitors' passes."

"I'll be with you in a minute." He spoke in a vaguely Caribbean accent. He was crossing off names on one paper and adding them to another.

"We don't want to miss visiting hours. My friend is very sick," Mama added, with cultivated calm. He didn't answer. Mama placed her hand lightly on my arm as if to say, "Don't get angry." She had always seen, even nurtured, the fighter in me and was well aware of the signs of when it began to rear its head. I made no apologies for it. It's one of the things that got me through med school as a single mother with a baby, it's one of the things that steels me against every unspoken judgment of the caliber of the professional qualifications of a black woman doctor in the South.

I was pissed. "I am a doctor," I added, then immediately wished I hadn't. I was ashamed that I had tried to pull rank when the two women standing at that desk ought to have been able to expect common courtesy, whoever they were.

"Do you have a staff pass?" the man asked through rapidly blinking eyes.

"No. Look, I'm sorry, my mother and I would simply like to visit a patient as soon as possible."

"Name of the patient?" he asked in a strangely disconcerting new voice as though we had not had any previous interaction.

"Margaret Clayton."

"C-L-A-Y . . ." he labored over a computer keyboard. How could anyone be such an idiot, I thought.

"T-O-N," Mama finished gently, as though sincerely coaching a young child.

"Room 603." He handed us two stick-on tags with the room number scribbled on them and blinked his eyes several times again without acknowledging when Mama said, "Thank you."

We stepped out of the elevator as a ringing chime marked the doors' closing, and Mama stopped momentarily. "April, she looks bad, real bad. I want you to know before we go in."

"I'll be okay," I reassured her, knowing full well that she had unconsciously said as much for her own sake, to prepare herself, more than for me, her daughter the physician. I had not seen Mrs. Clayton in so long that I didn't know exactly what to expect in her appearance anyway. Her bed was on the far side of the room, by the window, and passing her roommate, I noticed the absence of any cards, acknowledgments, or personal touches of any kind. The occupant of the bed, an ancient white woman with almost no hair, slept, oxygen tubes in her nostrils. Pulling back the curtain slightly, I allowed Mama to pass ahead of me. On Mrs. Clayton's side, there were several vases of flowers of all colors and sizes. From a group of five or six women around the bed, an attractive one in her sixties stepped away and toward us, her face immediately beaming, and reached for Mama, hugging her tightly.

"Lorraine, thank you, she will be so glad you came. She's been dozing off and on, but she'll wake up soon." The woman turned to me. "I'm Ann Clayton, Margaret's daughter." She extended her hand. "Are you April?"

"I am. I'm glad to meet you." Who was that impatient woman downstairs, I wondered, who nearly snapped at having been inconvenienced by a few minutes' wait? Standing here now, I felt exposed, the layer of whatever made me feel separate had been peeled away, and we were here together with someone in need, all of us, even me, a relative stranger, embraced and included, one in the intention of well-being.

"April, you are so kind to come with your mother. I don't know what Mama would do without her." Ann Clayton still held my hand. "She is the wisest person I've ever known."

Mama interrupted. "Well I can tell you your Mama don't think that. She's spent too many years telling me what I ought to do about everything you can name."

Ann laughed. "I know it, what in the world would we do if Mama didn't know everything, Lorraine? We probably wouldn't be able to get out of bed in the morning."

"Is that Lorraine there? I can't see her," a crackly but firm voice said from the bed.

Ann winked and whispered to me, "Speak of the devil," and took

Mama's hand, pulling her toward the bed, where the other women parted to make room. "Bring her in here so I can see if she's gotten fat," Mrs. Clayton barked, to which Mama replied, "Fat enough to sit on top of you if you can't behave yourself."

I faded back, not feeling unwelcome, but rather as a witness to a liturgy that I wanted to remember in every detail, as attentive an observer as I could be. I studied the circle of women, now encompassing my mother as one of their number, young and old, family and neighbors, perhaps single, married, widowed. It is as though they arrived on a timetable, like a flock of migratory birds, their schedule neither agreed upon in advance nor communicated, as much as felt in the subtle first change of seasons. This is simply what they do. They come. They are called to stand watch, oddly, with no male presence. It is perhaps not that the men, with few exceptions, can't take the pain. It's the ambiguity that they can't abide. And there is that to be sure, endless hours of waiting. Surely these stately creatures are the same everywhere, perched around every bed where someone lies helpless. They arrive one at a time, or in pairs, and they bring smiles and stories and concerned brows and open hearts, and most of all they bring time, they have all the time in the world, poured out like water, crystalline and pure. They lower their shoulders, they place their purses on chairs, and they assume their places, familiar by instinct, either sitting or standing, circling the sick with wings of prayer and patience, protectors and mediators, watchers, slow and graceful, with the singular purpose of a great blue heron wading in shallow water, saving all effort for when it is most needed, the split second at which it catches a swimming fish in its beak, finally lifting off in flight, with no regard to the weight it carries, rising, as hope must, lighter than human breath.

CHAPTER THIRTY-THREE

RHONDA

I t used to be in the movies that after having sex people smoked cigarettes or fell asleep. Or maybe they smoked cigarettes and then fell asleep, I don't know. Anyway now I guess the Hollywood bigheads don't think they ought to show too many young lovers smoking cause that's bad for people, especially teenagers who go to the movies. So usually what happens instead is they show us a really hot sex scene with all the right moves and sounds to go along with it, and then boom, the next scene, we wake up in the morning and see the worn-out lovers lying in bed in a perfect ray of sunlight, with their hair messed up just enough to still be sexy rather than look like a hawk has nested in it, which is how mine looks when I wake up. I must move around a lot during the night, so much that in the mornings, Mike sometimes asks me, "How was your trip?"

Well I don't smoke anymore, which I do miss, I'll tell you that right now. I'm not one of those people who acts like she found religion because she ain't involved in the disgusting act of smoking and so she feels the need to tell everybody that she can't imagine how she coulda ever put that foul crap into her lungs in the first place. Puh-leeze. It's one of the worst things I ever did for my health, I know that, even if nobody else acted like it, but I loved every second of it when I was doing it. We all pick our habits, just a matter of what and when. Back when we were still dating, Mike and me got in the routine of getting up out of bed after sex and having a snack. Usually it was ice cream or a couple of cookies if we had any homemade. I don't care if you're not supposed to eat and then go right to bed. Hell, I stopped smoking, I can't stop everything. When my jeans get tight, I've got a choice, either cut back or start looking for new jeans, and since I ain't interested in an assortment of jeans I can't wear, I do without the Edy's for a while. It ain't that hard to figure out. I love that snack time because it's when Mike and me talk. Not just serious stuff like making plans; we talk about whatever comes up. It's the best talking time we ever have, in the middle of the night. It's like we're sneaking around, it's our secret time that the rest of the world will never know one thing about. I hope we keep doing it no matter how old we get.

"Thank you, baby," Mike said the other night, taking out a half gallon of chocolate chip and two big cereal bowls while I sat at the kitchen table. I never heard anybody but him say thank you after sex. I used to think it was weird, it made me kinda uncomfortable, like he was buying gas or something, so one time I asked him about it. He said, "Sweetheart, I ain't thankin you for sex. I'm thankin you for being with me instead of all the other places you could be. Sex ain't nothin but a period at the end of the sentence."

He handed me a big tablespoon. "You want one scoop or two?"

"One and a half," I said. "Will you turn off the light? The stove light's enough."

We took a couple of bites in quiet. I held mine in my mouth and let it slide down my throat seeing how long I could make the cold last. That's the only bad thing about chocolate chip, it doesn't slide as good as other flavors that don't have little pieces of stuff stuck in em.

"What's that?" he nodded to a slip of paper I had put down beside my bowl. "Honey, I love you but I don't think I can go over one of your lists right now."

"I found it in the dresser stuck in our wedding book."

"What?"

"You're gonna think it's dumb. It's a thank-you note to Bernice and Margaret. I am so stupid, I musta never sent this. I wanted it to be perfect."

"Read it to me," he said. I was quiet. "Or let me read it." He reached across the table and took the flimsy folded paper. "Is it okay if I read it?" he asked.

"Yeah. It's fine." I knew exactly what I wrote, it was meant for somebody else to read anyway, not me. I told him to read it out loud.

Dear Mrs. Stokes and Mrs. Clayton,

Thank you both so much for being part of my wedding day. The picture y'all gave to me is sitting in our living room and I will always leave it right there. I will never forget you telling me Mama would have been proud of me, and I feel like she was there because of you. No one ever paid attention to me like y'all. I know that is more than three things, Miss Margaret, but I can't help it because I feel too thankful to reduce it down. Maybe this is a new kind of thank-you note.

Love, from Rhonda

"That's real sweet," he said, half yawning.

"Well it's too late now. Bernice is dead and Margaret's close. That's what I get for waitin rather than just sayin what I thought."

"Honey, you loved both of em. I expect they know that."

"How about *knew*."

"It doesn't go away just because they do, Rhonda."

Now part of me gets sorta pissed when people say things that are either wise or supposed to be. I'm independent that way. But then I think just because I feel a thing doesn't mean it can't be good to hear it come out of somebody else's mouth.

"Thanks for sayin that," I told him.

Mike put our empty bowls in the sink. "You did good, baby," he said and hugged me from behind. When I turned in my chair, his eyes looked bigger than usual, like he was asking a question. Maybe he thought I might not get the full meaning of his words. But I do.

CHAPTER THIRTY-FOUR

LORRAINE

I used to hope that if I went to church long enough, all my inside weight would go away. That ain't right. Jesus may have come to take away our sins, but he left our feelings right where they've always been. I still have inside me some of what I've always had, built up over a lifetime. I just keep adding to it, every day, like everybody else, and hope the stew gets better the more ingredients I put in. My memories come and go now, like my regrets. Sometimes I see them, sometimes I don't, and when I do see, I feel all over again whatever it was I thought had either died or lost its power over me. Time heals, it's true, but it don't erase.

I ought to be singing, everybody around me is.

> *Yet saints their watch are keeping;*
> *Their cry goes up "How long?"*
> *And soon the night of weeping*
> *Shall be the morn of song.*

We all sit when the music stops.

Before Miss Margaret left the hospital, she took my hand from the bed and said, "Lorraine, if you ever see me again, I want you to bring me a fish plate. I could ask Ann to get it, but she won't eat anything fried and she won't have any idea where to go. You know what I want."

"I reckon I do. Catfish?"

"Yes ma'am, and the littler they are the better because they're sweeter. They're more trouble to eat but that's what I want. And I want coleslaw not too vinegary tasting and hush puppies. And if they've got any good shrimp, and I mean fresh, Lorraine, I want some of them too." She was weak as a kitten, but bossy as she ever was.

I told her, "All right then. But you stop sayin things like 'if I ever see you again.'"

She tried to shoo me off with a weak hand, barely lifting it off the bed. "I know, I know. But you listen to what I'm saying. You know what I want."

"You want the same as I like, ain't no need to give me a menu."

"Ann, bless her heart, wouldn't know a catfish from a crappie and that's what I want as my last meal on earth. I have always said I wanted to leave with the taste of something fried in my mouth."

"I don't want to hear that talk right now."

"We're all going, Lorraine." She hardly had any voice left.

"Hush. You and I both know what's goin on here. We don't have to spend the time we have goin over it. Let's do what we need to do."

She died two days later. They knew she wouldn't last, but Ann said she had to let her mother have her wish: to go home one more time. With full-time hospice care, and the comfort of her friends, she passed in the middle of the night. She didn't talk much at the end. Ann stayed with her every minute, the whole time.

Althea takes my hymnal, still open, from my lap. She closes it and puts it in the pew rack. These are new hymnals I can't read because they've got another language printed on top of the English. I thought it might be Spanish, but I feel like I ought to be able to recognize a few words of Spanish. Althea told me it might be Korean. All I can think is that they must have gotten these things on sale cause there ain't no way something this hard to read cost the full price.

The congregation bows their head to pray. They'll be that way for a while. Althea finally stopped singing in the choir, she said her high notes went once she got arthritis. I said her notes didn't have nothin to do with her joints, but she told me I wasn't a singer so I didn't know. What really happened is the new director, a man from somewhere down around Columbia, pulled her over after rehearsal one night and asked her why didn't she just move her mouth when she couldn't hit the notes, and then come back in singin whenever she felt like she could. Althea's feeling was they'd either have all her notes or none of em, and so she said "no thank you very much" and hung up her robe for the final time. I also believe she quit choir so she could spend Sunday mornings sitting in the congregation with me. She mostly likes to whisper about the women's hair and clothes, but I try not to encourage her, especially when preaching is going on. We don't even know anybody up there at the front anymore, the least she can do is be still.

Althea didn't really want to come today cause she didn't feel like it, but when I told her we were having dinner after, she said she believed she might be able to make it. I brought all vegetables, I don't know why but I didn't feel like making meat, they'll be plenty of meat. I cooked us some sweet corn, fried squash, and buttermilk biscuits. Althea said she brought a jar of molasses in her pocketbook just so she could put it on my biscuits, she loves em so good. The two of us are getting so old sometimes I think one day we might have to start sharing a brain. We already share about everything else. We definitely share the chore of getting our bodies to move where we want em to go, one of us always helping the other one, switching back and forth. It's a wonder we still get to church but we do. Althea drives us most days. I don't enjoy driving a car like I used to. I don't pay enough attention to anything except what's on my mind, and that ain't no way to start out on a highway.

Reverend Knowles passed years ago and I miss him, but I do like this young preacher. I can't say his last name, he's not from around here, but he always says call him Kenny so that's what I do. I don't know how much he knows about the Bible, but I swear he knows something about puttin on clothes and fixin himself up good. He's got a good strong voice too. I think he's reading from Isaiah, sounds like it to me. I've always liked the prophets.

I reach for my purse when the offering music starts. Althea is digging in hers too, and she puts her molasses jar on the seat between us so she can get to her wallet, crammed down in a pile of tissues, cough drops, and coupons. Besides my billfold, the only other thing in mine is keys, so I don't have no trouble finding a five-dollar bill, but when the offering plate gets to me, I don't right away know what to do with it. Althea reaches over me, puts a yellow envelope in, and grabs the money out of my hand and drops it in too. I pass the plate on, and Althea whispers, "You got up too early cooking. See, you're wore out, 'bout to fall asleep."

"I ain't wore out," I tell her. "I'm thinkin."

"I'm thinkin too. About dinner." She pinches my leg, and I slap her hand away. Althea has got to learn how to behave better in church, but I don't know who's gon teach her cause I'm too old and so is she.

Reverend Kenny will keep it short today cause he knows not to mix religion with mealtime. It ain't a surprise to nobody which one wins out. "For you shall go out in joy, and be led back in peace," Reverend Kenny reads. I know that is Isaiah. I love to hear it. Margaret Clayton and me took our joy and peace mixed together, all at the same time. As long as I've got a heart that can feel anything, I'll see her as clear as daylight. My friend, alive.

We'll all stand up in a few minutes and go downstairs to the basement where some busy women a lot younger than us have already put up tables and cloths and cups of ice and pitchers of tea. I wish April could be here for the food, my grandbaby too. Everybody in the whole church is goin to ask about her, they always do. They'll say they know I'm proud, and I don't argue. They think it's because she's a doctor, but it's because she's mine.

There will come a day when she will be the one who goes through everything that has belonged to me on earth. She will decide what to keep and what to throw away, she's the one who will judge what was important to me and choose to hang onto what's important to her. She will choose right about some things, wrong about others. And when she looks in my Bible, stuck somewhere in Isaiah, she will find her school pictures from every year, and a torn black-and-white one of my Thomas the week he was born, one Mama gave to me. She will keep it.

"Amen. Let's eat," Reverend Kenny raises his arms and a crowd gathers in the aisles. Standing together, Althea and me are swallowed up by the faces and the years.

CHAPTER THIRTY-FIVE

APRIL

Mama said, "We couldn't have asked for a prettier day," and I felt, with her, that those words made for a new beginning, morning light pointing to a new world unfolding, one minute at a time. The simplicity of her optimism was in the power of her ability to choose it. Even before she retired, osteoarthritis had begun to take its toll on her body, but her mind did not relent easily to discomfort, or even pain. In the coming years, she would be in for an uphill climb at a time when she was by many people's standards still young. I learned long ago that her passions would not be quieted by inconvenience alone. She would have to learn to limit her battles, not bothering to wrestle with demons she couldn't see and focus instead on what was in front of her, the groceries to buy, the shut-in visits to make, even her grandson. I waited while she went to the bathroom, knowing that my time was limited as sentinel only, and that someday I would be supporting her weight, unfastening her clothes, lowering her body into a position to relieve itself, and helping her again to her feet. Gravity would become her greatest enemy. Her defenses would arrive one at a time: an aluminum walker, a cane for days that were a little better, an elevated toilet seat, and a handrail to be installed in her hallway. If life is a concert piece, structured in contrasting movements, then the last strains are an invitation to dance with the most long-standing partner, mortality. We hear the end of the music coming, like a coda that says, "it won't be long now," only a few more well-defined and recognizable chords, and then the earned release, the comforting silence that, far from being empty, resonates with all that has preceded it. The only question becomes how good a dancer you are and if not, whether you can learn.

"April, make sure everything's turned off!" Mama was calling to me from the bathroom.

"I already did."

"Where's Taylor?" Mama loved saying her grandson's name out loud.

"You know he's at school," I answered. "We'll get home about the same time he does. Do you need some help?"

"I don't need you watchin me like a hawk. Please get my pocket-book so I don't forget it."

I had known months ago exactly what I wanted to do for Mama's birthday this year. I took two days off because I thought it would be too tiring for Mama to make a car trip, even a short one, in one day. I'd pick her up and she could spend the night with me after our outing before going back to her house. My partner would be on call for emergencies. I was never good at keeping surprises. I think about the way I blurted out that I was pregnant. Maybe it's more that I was never good at surprising *her*. Her life had given her a sort of sight that was beyond vigilance, beyond knowing, and revealed itself neither in agitation nor worry, but in a spirit of calm that said she had seen much and that consequently, the needs and motivations of people no longer surprised her. Instead she looked around and, in looking, found a small part of herself in everyone else. She called it "looking hard" at another person. I learned that it was compassion she was living, a desire to see and be seen fully, which is the work of human life. Is that part of what it means to let go, to release the white-knuckled grip on whatever pulls us along, if we're lucky, for seventy or eighty years? Maybe we figure out that the only thing we wanted all along was that simple and elusive kind of revelation in which all is known, all is forgiven, and most important, all that's left is celebrated with a victory cheer.

Mama reminded me that we had our picture taken at the Old Well on the day I graduated from medical school. It was the most famous landmark in Chapel Hill and she wanted to see it again.

"Do you feel like walking a little?" I asked.

"Child, I could walk to heaven on a day like this." Her eyes smiled, and I couldn't help thinking that she talked a lot less than she used to. The daffodils alone, scattered with a planned haphazardness across the old quad, made my breathing change. The grass was more like perfect carpet than something that could possibly grow in ordinary dirt. I used to come here with Taylor and spread a blanket when he was a baby. He would fall asleep, I would study, eventually taking off the light sweater I had worn and letting the sun warm my torso, feeling my heart expand with its touch, like warming up for a workout. At the time I had never been more tired in my life: raising a baby, being in med school, and working when I could fit it in for the extra money. I parked by Hill Hall, the music building. It was Taylor's favorite place to play outside when he was little. If we were lucky, the Carolina Choir might be rehearsing with the windows open, the music inside procreating with sounds of nature. "I want to go where the songs are," Taylor said whenever he saw me round up a blanket and start to pack a bag with books and containers of food.

The azaleas were borderline arrogant in their display of fuchsia and white, prideful and not giving a damn what the rest of the world thought about their flamboyance. Mama clasped her hands and rubbed them lightly together against the slight chill of a spring breeze. "You know, April, I never wanted to go anywhere. That's the truth. Only thing I ever wanted to see was people. But I am glad you brought me back here." She squinted into the sun at the Well. "This here is like a sign to me."

"What kind of sign?" I asked, wondering whether she might say something less than lucid.

"My daughter's a doctor and the University of North Carolina says so. That's one big 'Why Not' to me. Why not a doctor? Why not anything?" She patted one of the columns lightly, looked up at the sky with her eyes closed, and said without looking at me, "What time is that show?"

I had not thought to tell her what to expect at a planetarium, and I had not had the time to look at what the particular program offering might be. It had never occurred to me to think of it as a show. To me, a show is something that has real people in it. There was a part of me that didn't want to leave the perfect outdoor world for an artificial one of stars and planets, created to show us ourselves in the galaxy by looking at it above our heads, fixed and controlled, manipulated for our wonder if not edification. I've always been aware that it's not a real sky. The real sky doesn't place us at the center; it is so clearly apart from us that there's no mistaking that it has anything at all to do with our small minds.

We took our places in the angled seats when Mama struggled to cough up some mucus into several tissues, which I carried in my purse at all times when she was with me. I remember being young and thinking that carrying tissues around was an unappealing mark of old age. I was right, but they are essential. Feeling better, she leaned back in her seat, and I had the image of an astronaut strapped in and ready to go, in the final seconds before blasting off. "I like this chair, April. I don't think I can get out of it, but I like it."

"I don't think you would want one in your house, Mama."

"Don't never know. I might change my style."

"Shh. They're turning the lights down." I don't know why our conversation concerned me because there were at least fifty schoolchildren around eight years old to our left, and even with four adults at the helm, their voices were at an excited pitch. When the lights went completely out, there were a few short squeals and giggles, and then surprisingly, quiet throughout the room. Slowly a night sky appeared over our heads, the stars gradually becoming brighter until you could almost believe you were lying on your back in a field with no artificial light for miles around. I looked up and thought of so many summers at my grandma's, in the orange last light before a fiery day would be cooled slightly by blue-black darkness, waiting for Mama to come home from work, having already eaten my dinner and gone back outside to play some more, building forts for dolls out of scrap wood.

"Keep your eyes open for black widows, girl," Grandma said whenever she saw me by her woodpile. "I don't need to be goin to no hospital right here at bedtime."

Any time after the sun went down was bedtime to her, leftover from her days farming with Granddaddy before they had the store, when they started their back-breaking work so early that they couldn't keep their eyes open after dark. Unless she was on the night shift, Mama would come in around dusk, it was the job of the day shift to oversee feeding the patients dinner then get those who needed help into pajamas or whatever they slept in. I could hear her car before I saw it. She always tapped the horn to let my grandmother know that she was pulling into the driveway. I ran to meet her before she got to the porch steps, that was my game every night. We went inside, she ate a little something, and if she wasn't too tired, we would go sit outside and look at the sky until mosquitoes wouldn't leave us alone or I fell asleep nestled in her warmth.

"Find me the Big Dipper, baby," she said, and I could always find it. Always. Then she would show me the North Star. I don't know how Mama knew the North Star, but she had a reverence for all stars, like they were the million eyes of God looking at us all the time.

"What are they made of?" I asked her more than once, sensing that she didn't know the answer.

"Stars are places for your dreams to land, baby, when they can't find a home down here," she said, holding me close. I think of the sky over her head spangled with her thoughts and dreams all the time, sparkling like keepsakes in a giant scrapbook. By looking into a clear night sky, she could hold all of them without ever touching any of them. I took her at her word, and for years, I have pinned my own dreams to stars overhead when no human ear could or would hear them.

A woman's recorded voice, a soothing alto, began narrating the changing visuals overhead. She began by telling us that the planetarium isn't simply the building, it's the name of the huge telescope-like machine in the center of the room. On cue, the apparatus turned slightly as chimelike music mixed with the sounds of otherworldly wind played from speakers on all sides of us. Shooting stars raced across the sky. An explanation of a galaxy followed, specifically describing our own Milky Way. Mama had raised her hands up slightly, palms open, fingers spread, almost like when she was in church. I alternated between watching her and the ceiling, wondering why, for my whole life, I always believed she saw something different from me, even when we were looking at exactly the same thing. And I wondered whether, when the time came that she could no longer live on her own, she would see that too in her own way. Her retirement from the nursing home had been sudden. She had announced it to me over the telephone, out of the blue.

"Did something happen?" I asked, certain that her decision must have been provoked by something specific.

"We got bought by a chain of nursing homes. They said I could have early retirement."

"You're gonna take it?"

"I'm old and they don't want me, April. It's all right. I'm gon take a break from sickness and dying."

She didn't do anything of the kind. In the time since, she may as well have worked full-time between church obligations and volunteering at the county senior citizens' center. When she first mentioned that she'd been to the center, I assumed it was as a participant, her age certainly qualified her. I soon found that she was in fact "staff," doing much of what she had done in her old job, sustained by her interaction with all sorts of people, minus the more grueling aspects of having to deal with bedpans and personal hygiene. I could always tell when one of her new set of charges had to go into the hospital or a home. Her ordinarily unflagging spirit met with some manner of depression, invisible to most but evident to me, that lasted a day or two, before she recuperated by making plans as to how she was going to visit her friend in his or her new surroundings as soon as humanly possible.

"Isn't that beautiful?" Mama whispered, nudging me slightly. "It looks like somethin I'd like to make a dress out of." We were looking at a tremendous photograph of the Orion nebula, a reddish-pink "space cloud," the narrator's recorded voice called it, pointing out that what we could see was only a tiny part of the whole, and one might think of it as a birthplace for stars. "Baby stars, April," Mama snickered, "how 'bout that?" Mama talked freely, if quietly, during the narration, it was her way of savoring the moment, not letting anything pass unmarked. The disembodied voice further informed us that nebulae are composed of gas and dust. "Hmm," Mama grunted. "I ain't never seen dust look like that. If I did, you wouldn't see me clean house again, I tell you that much."

From every direction, the hypnotic presence told us in stereo about the sun, the center of our solar system, around which everything revolves and which holds everything together. The voice explained that "apparent magnitude" is how bright a star looks to us here on earth, based only on what we can see, regardless of how far away it is, but that "absolute magnitude" is the true indicator of a star's brightness, if all the stars could be viewed as they really are, at the same distance, as though lined up side by side. The dome above us burned fiery orange and red, and Mama's face looked like it was glowing bronze from a furnace inside her chest. She laughed at the explosive surface of the sun and turned to whisper, "That right there is something I would like to see. I sure never saw it like that before, did you?"

"We're too far away," I answered.

"That ain't gon stop me from looking harder."

The continuing commentary brought back memories of science class in junior high, words I hadn't heard in years. Blue giant and white dwarf. Supernova. Asteroid. Greek and Latin constellation names. For Mama, it was like finally having a translator to bridge a language gap between old friends, friends from a foreign place she had visited countless times in her imagination.

The car ride to my house took no time at all given Mama's exuberance after leaving the "show" as well as the reward of my own satisfaction. She talked the whole time about the universe, especially the stars being part of a map so big you could never see the whole thing. As we pulled into the driveway, Taylor was shooting baskets, tossed the ball onto the grass, and came running to her side of the car. I had trained him well, I thought. Already big for his age, he grabbed her in a smothering bear hug before she could get the car door all the way open. With long lean arms, he helped her to her feet, and she made a sassy comment, as she always did, about how big he had grown. My son, my hope. I could see the man he would become, was already becoming. Watching them, I could believe in life, and God, seeing in them that age could be fashioned into a gold crown in the hands of love. And I could be assured that my mother's wonder had rooted itself in me, so deeply that I would feel her presence always, in the dignity she bestowed as carelessly as rainwater or falling stars.

CHAPTER THIRTY-SIX

RHONDA

The sign on the front of the shop looks perfect. I love it. It's exactly what I wanted. Nobody's hardly gonna ever see it because the shop's in back of the house, but I told Mike, "I want a sign with my name on it. I don't care if the only ones lookin at it are you and me." He said, "Honey, it's your dream, and by God it's gonna be exactly like what you see in your head." We're making the inside colors a kind of peach and lime green. I told Mike I wanted it to look sort of like Key West in here. Kinda exotic. I know damn well I ain't gonna be doing any exotic hair-dos but I've always liked an island feel. I think it makes people relax, and if you can't at least relax when you're having you're hair fixed, then I hate to tell you but you're hopeless. Plus I like feeling like I'm on a little vacation when I come to work, even if it is only out our kitchen door and across the yard. Mike put some miniature palm trees in pots inside too, but I said, "I love em honey, but you know I can kill a plant by lookin at it, so these are your babies." Hell, I thought he'd be taking em right back to the nursery, but do you know that man comes out here every morning before he goes to deliver the packages that everybody's pulling their hair out for, and he waters any of those plants that need it? He doesn't know it, but I heard him talking to em one time. He said, "Do your thing now, I'm dependin on you. Make her happy, that's why we're here, right?" I found myself a good one, didn't I? Or maybe he found me, I'm never sure how that works, but I do know enough to be grateful. I'm sure Connie would be more than glad to take credit and that's all right, she earned it.

I don't go to the nursing home now. Sometimes I think I will again, but then there's life. Just life, you know? I didn't want to be there much anyway after Margaret Clayton died. That was the hardest part for me, I'd been meaning to get to the hospital but I didn't make it. Then she was gone, it wasn't like I didn't know it was coming, but the longer it takes, you feel like the longer you have, and that ain't the way it is. I did stop at Ridgecrest one time to see if anybody I knew was still there but I didn't recognize a one. A young nurse, a jock sort of guy with a suntan, told me Lorraine Bullock had retired. She was one of the last people I knew there. He'd heard her house had burned down but that she wasn't in it. "You've got to be careful with those old houses," he said, "all the wiring, you know?" I answered, "Yeah," thinking about how old my own house was and whether I could start a fire and not even know it. He didn't know where Lorraine was now, maybe living closer to her daughter, and asked if I wanted him to try and find out at the nurses' station. I told him no, that was all right.

I do miss my ladies. I put their picture out on the coffee table so every day I can look at the three of us, me standin in between Bernice and Margaret, all wearin Santa Claus hats like something crazy. Connie still asks me if I'm gonna keep it out all year long even though it's a Christmas picture, and I still tell her, "Yes I am, Connie, and the answer is gonna be yes next time you ask too." They wanted me to be happy, those two, they wanted it, and it happened. It's happening now. I feel like they know. And I'd love to think that wherever they are they might bring some Christmas cheer to my old sourpuss of a grandma, but I reckon they'd all have to be in the same place to do that, and there's no way those two sweet things are with her.

So things are good. Really good. I got a lot of people coming to the shop already. Some people who I used to do at Evelyn's followed me out here. Evelyn don't care, she's about half retired anyway, and most of the time you can't even find her cause she's in her car headed to the beach. Mike and me have been talking about having a baby. Connie says I'm out of my mind, kids are for young people, but I tell her last time I looked I didn't have one foot in the grave. Connie's like that though. I love her to death, but she always tries to make what she's decided to do the thing that's best for everybody else to do too. It's true that everybody we know is already done with the kid thing, but we might still do it. And if not, that's all right too. I can take what comes. So can Mike. We're the same that way.

Next month I'm flying to Las Vegas to go to a hairdresser convention for three whole days. Mike asked if he could come and said he would take vacation from UPS, but I said, "Hell no, you're not comin. I'm takin Connie. You go on fishin or somethin." He acted like he was disappointed but I know he wasn't. He don't want to do one thing in Vegas except sit at a blackjack table, and he knows I ain't gonna stand around while he does that. Connie will be w-i-l-d fun. She'll do anything and drag me with her. I haven't told her yet that I've reserved us on the Gene Autry Sunset Steak Dinner Ride and Sing-along. I thought it sounded like a bargain. You get to ride horses for five hours through the desert, they feed you, and then they take you back to your hotel. Connie will hate the singing part, but the only other option is a breakfast ride and there is no way she will go on that after staying up all night partying. When we get back we're goin to see Martina McBride at the MGM Grand. She's expensive, but I got tickets as soon as I knew I was taking the trip because I love her. There's gonna be a lot of beauticians around so everybody oughta look real good if you think about it. I hope I come home with some new hair ideas too. I'm always looking for new possibilities.

CHAPTER THIRTY-SEVEN

APRIL

Do you mind if I hold your hand?" I asked, not sure whether he might slap me away as he had his own daughter. He did not answer. I should be used to this by now, but it always felt like something was being pulled up by the roots inside my stomach.

"Mr. Massey, do you mind if I hold your hand while the nurse takes your blood pressure?" I asked again, as gently as I could.

"She's leaving me here!" he barked. "There was not another living soul besides me to raise her after her mother died, but I did it. I did it by myself with these two hands. I don't understand it. I never spoke a cross word to her in my life."

I looked at Mr. Massey's daughter, Denise, a well-dressed woman in her midfifties who, in spite of trying her best to remain composed, was reduced to sniffling and dabbing the corners of her eyes. She did not speak.

"You're going to be taken care of here, Mr. Massey. Denise asked me many times what I thought, and I told her I thought it was a good idea. You'll be safe here, where someone can look in on you whenever you need something."

"Bullshit."

"Dad!" Denise was embarrassed.

"It's normal." The nurse tried to comfort her and exited the room.

"Let him talk," I said to Denise over my shoulder. "That's

right, Mr. Massey. It is bullshit whenever anybody has to leave his home against his wishes. What else do you want to say about it? Tell it."

"She doesn't know," he ranted. "I'm fine by myself. This is all because I forget things sometimes, is that it? It is, isn't it?" He turned to Denise. "I hope no one ever abandons you. I hope you never know what it feels like to be left alone, pulled out of your own house, and not told where you're going."

Denise interjected. "That's not true, I spoke to you about this. Several times, Dad. I'm doing everything I can, you don't see that? But I can't . . . I . . ." She broke off in sobs.

"I took care of you, my only daughter, and for once I need you to take care of me. Is that what you can't do? Can't any daughter who feels anything for her father do that?"

"Mr. Massey." I was still calm but it was time to intervene. "We're all going to do the best we can. Denise and I, and you too. We're going to have dinner this evening, sleep through the night, then we're going to wake up tomorrow, and we're going to do the best we can. We have to try to do that."

"Well I won't stay here. I know my rights and I'll find a way to get out. You will not do this, Denise, not to me. I may be feeble of body but not of mind. No! I still have a mind and I don't intend to lose it in this place."

He had become a caged leopard, clawing to get out, scratching to draw blood; he would do anything if he thought it could change the reality of this day and the life that would follow.

"Denise, why don't you go ahead?" I placed my arm around her. "I'm going to give your father something to calm him until they bring supper. It'll be more important that you come tomorrow."

Denise approached the bed and bent over her father, kissing him lightly on the cheek. She was about to speak when he whispered through clenched teeth, "The kiss of Judas." She had been shot by a bullet that she could not dodge even if she had seen it coming a mile away.

"Go on," I said to her and I gave Mr. Massey a mild sedative. "She'll be back, Mr. Massey. And I am still your doctor, so if you have any complaints or questions or you need anything, you pick up that phone by your bed and you call my office. I am the doctor; all these people are just trying to run a smooth organization and they have to pay attention to a lot around here. The only thing I have to pay attention to is you. So you call me."

"What can you do? You can't do anything for me."

"I can tell you that it will get better, but we're all going to have to work at it. This is a big change, and neither you nor I is stupid enough to think that it will be easy."

"Bullshit," he mumbled, now emotionally spent.

"I know," I said. I would wait until he nodded off.

My mother is at home now thinking about dinner. She will probably reheat the barbecue plate that she couldn't finish yesterday when I took her to lunch and shopping. It's our Wednesday ritual, now that she lives close by. I always pick her up around eleven fifteen in the morning and we drive all the way to Sturgess Barbecue, which has been in the exact same location for as long as I can remember, on a lake in a grove of pine trees about twenty minutes from where she used to live. I try to get her there by noon because that is the time that she feels lunch should be served everywhere in the world, or at least in North Carolina, regardless of what happens in the course of a person's day. I think it's as much about regularity as it is food, although Mama is not shy at all about ordering enough for two people. And she always gets exactly the same thing: a pork barbecue sandwich, chunky and vinegary the way it is done down here in the eastern counties, with french fries, slaw, hush puppies, a side order of Brunswick stew, and always a copious serving of pie, usually lemon chess if they have it. I wouldn't go all the way to Sturgess's if Mama didn't insist. It's not that I don't feel welcome, even though there are not only no other blacks, but no Mexicans, who have become the new Southerners, the new backbone of hard labor. In fact, Mr. Sturgess always speaks to Mama and me by name and puts us at whatever table we pick. And his waitresses, all of whom are white, are nice and down-to-earth. Those are Mama's words, not mine, but I do agree with her. Still, my body feels smaller when I'm in that pine-paneled dining room where tobacco farmers have come to eat since before I was born. I think about the generations of black field labor, Mama's ancestors among them, who never sat at one of these tables. I can feel the ghosts of those who, even now, wouldn't want us here, standing close to the walls, leaned up cross-legged, sneering ever so slightly and looking at us from a distance, wishing us back to another era in which they are the guarantors of where all boundaries lie and content with their chalk-drawn lines of existence. I look around me and there are smiles, warmth. Thankfully the world is not run by ghosts, but I believe they're never far away.

I am grateful for this simple ritual. I want sameness. I want permanence. When I see Mama shuffle as she rises to her feet or dip slightly, favoring a weak knee as she steps out of my car, or the slight tremor of her hand as she raises a spoon, her lipstick unevenly applied, I am aware of change, the time for giving up what is. And I can't bring myself to speak about it. I keep silent before that which scares me, the inevitability of a slowing march, then no march at all, a crawl, infant-like. She will need me more and more. I will hold this fact at bay for as long as I am able, if only because of the visible language of its fierce encroaching. And so next Wednesday I will pick her up again and compliment her on how pretty she looks. And it will not be patronizing; I will mean it, because I will be even more determined to keep her in my heart's eye as she is, a gallery-worthy marble statue of my mother, teacher, my friend, the woman who was the first person to ever love me.

CHAPTER THIRTY-EIGHT

LORRAINE

April was walking ahead of me to get through the crowd, holdin my hand cause I guess she thought I needed draggin or else get lost. I had to yell to make her hear me.

"Honey, I don't want to sit too close to that band. I'm gon go deaf or crazy, I don't know which one."

"I think they're almost finished," she screamed back, and a tall woman beside me laughed so loud it scared me to death while she reached her arm way across in front of my face and took a full champagne glass from a waiter, then handed him her empty with the other hand. I got the idea it wasn't her first time.

"Don't you want something to drink?" April yelled again when she let go and planted me at a table in one corner away from the party.

"Yes I do. I'm 'bout to thirst to death." She started to head for the bar, behind her, crowded with people, like bees in a hive.

"What do you want?" she said. "I know you're not going to drink champagne."

"And you ought not be drinkin liquor this early either, but I know you're gon do exactly what you want to. Bring me Dr Pepper. And not diet."

"Mama, we're on vacation."

"Don't I look like I'm on vacation?" I pulled a pair of sunglasses out of my pocketbook and put em on against the last light of the afternoon.

"They might not have Dr Pepper. Is Coke all right?"

"Yes, and see if they got somethin to nibble on too. They ought to, much as you paid for this trip."

It was her idea that we should go on a cruise in the first place. Now April of all people knows I don't think much of water, and the only time I've ever been on a boat was a ferry at Jamestown, Virginia, that was enough for me. But you can't tell my daughter anything, she's got a mind and will to go with it. She brought in some picture brochures after I got home from church one Sunday.

"Mama, you won't even know you're on a boat, it's so big. You'll love it," she said. "There's plenty to eat and you don't have to walk much. Now can't I make these plans? It'll be a belated Christmas present, we'll spend New Year's in the Caribbean."

"It costs too much. You ain't told me but I know it does," I said.

"Don't worry about that," she said.

"Hmm."

"Oh Mama, come on. Now how about if I invite Althea to go with us? If she will."

"Althea will go to a dog fight if somebody'll take her."

"Does that mean you'll go?"

"I want a room near the lifeboats."

And that was the end of it. April said she had always wanted to take me on a big trip and there wasn't no better time, so I let her. Althea decided she couldn't come at the last minute, she got the flu, but April got trip insurance so she said that was all right, she'd get her money back. I'm the one who told her to get it, she might have on her own, I don't know, but I've read too many articles in the newspaper about people who wanted to go somewhere then they got sick or something and was out every penny they spent.

April came back with two glasses and a little dish of food. "Dr Pepper." She sat down a tall frosted glass in front of me.

"What'd they put this skinny straw in it for? I ain't so old I need to drink a soda with a straw."

"It's just the way they do it, Mama." She pushed the little plate over to me. "I got you some canapés so you don't get hungry. I already ate a couple while I was waiting for the drinks."

"When do they give us supper on here anyway?"

"I'm afraid not for a little while, so eat all you want. We're about to sail away."

"I knew it, April. I felt somethin move and I thought to myself I can feel waves rockin this thing and we ain't even pulled out of Miami yet."

"Are you determined to be seasick by talking about it? It's a lucky thing you travel with your own personal physician, although I think she may have to retire after this trip."

"Don't you worry 'bout me, baby. I said I'd come, I'm here, and as long as we don't drown I'll be all right."

"Good because I've got a surprise for you."

"I hope it's not one of those pictures they took of us gettin on, April. My eyes were closed every time. I wish you'd go back and ask that boy with the camera for that buoy ring or whatever it was he wanted us to hold up while he took our picture. I told him if it was a extra one, I'd like to take it to my cabin. Where was he from anyway, somewhere in France or Europe, that's all I could tell from hearing him talk. Seem like maybe he said Norway."

"There are a lot of Scandinavians in the crew, I think," April said.

"I don't blame em. If I lived anyplace that cold, I'd be tryin to get to Florida as fast as I could too."

A group of waiters and waitresses were all in a clump at the bar, filling up trays of champagne as fast as they could. We're gon have us a bunch of drunks anytime now, I thought. The music finally stopped;

I reckon everybody needs a break sometime. I never heard this music before, but I haven't ever thought much of a steel drum. I know a lot of people like it, it's a real island sound, but it don't do much for me. The bald-headed man with the microphone kept on singing the same words, somethin about red, red wine, and I'm tired of it. I wonder if they're gon play a steel drum at church service on this boat. April told me they did have a church service if I wanted to go but I said I believed I'd pass if it was all right with her.

"I think the chaplain is a Catholic priest," she said.

"Honey, different don't bother me and hasn't for a long time. I'll do my own church just the same."

April also told me I ought to call it a ship, not a boat. I asked her whose feelings I was gon hurt, the captain, who had taken the microphone from the red wine man and was talking about where all we were gon go and that the weather was expected to be fine for the whole trip.

"Don't you want to know what your surprise is?" she whispered while the man in white spoke.

"I figured you'd tell me when you were ready."

"I'll be right back. Close your eyes." April got up and scooted her chair in. "I mean it Mama, close your eyes!"

"In the middle of this crowd of people?" I asked but did what she told me. I love that girl so much I can't stand it, and seein her so excited tryin to do something nice for me breaks my heart. A dark-skinned woman in a long silver gown took over at the piano, and some people started dancin. I folded my hands in my lap and took a deep breath with my eyes closed. The music was light and jazzy sounding, I liked it. My daddy always said he would love to go to New York City just one time and stay up all night going around listening to jazz. If he had lived long enough maybe I would have figured out some way to take him. I like that picture, Daddy and me walkin around New York like we owned the place.

"Open your eyes!" somebody screamed right in front of me, and before I could say anything, Althea was trying to kiss me flat on the mouth, wearing a hat big enough to use as an umbrella. Every time she leaned in, the low brim cut into the bridge of my nose.

"Girl, you're gon kill me with that hat. It's pretty but it's dangerous."

"You want me to take it off?" she looked like she'd been cut to the quick.

"No honey, just keep it on a leash. I see you got over the flu, you musta had a miracle healing."

"I lied in the service of the greater good."

"Uh-huh."

"Surprise," a quiet low voice said behind me. Hands over my eyes, Taylor bent down and kissed me on the cheek from behind and took a step around to where I could see him straight on. "Mama thought she needed my help watching you with all this partying goin on."

"You come here to me right now!" I said. "I ain't studyin no party but you."

I held his cheeks in both my hands and a few short dreadlocks fell down over his eyes. I didn't think I would get used to his hair that way, but I did and I liked it on him. He let it grow out at school when he went up to the University of Chicago. At first April wanted him to go to college closer to home, he even got some kind of a scholarship at Duke, but he had his mind set on gettin out of the South for a little while. I stayed out of it, even when April tried to get me to chime in. I just said, "Baby, that child is your son and he's gon do what he wants and it'll be fine. The apple don't fall far from the tree." But I know how she felt. We didn't see him for months at the time.

The ship's horn was loud and sad, the sound an elephant would make if it could cry. Strings of white lights came on over our heads, Althea squealed like she was sixteen years old, and the band started up again. The crew tossed confetti, snowing in rainbow colors, and we were movin. I knew it this time. For a minute I sat still, waitin for something to happen. I don't know what, some kind of disaster I reckon, but the main thing was I didn't feel sick and April was right, I didn't feel any rockin. Althea had gotten her hands on two glasses of champagne and gave one to me. I took a sip to be polite and set mine down on the table behind us.

"I can't believe you did this, April. You ain't never been able to keep a secret from me!"

"Now how would you know that? Think about it." She winked at Althea.

"Anything worth knowin, I already know, old as I am," I said. "Ain't that right, Althea?"

"You better bite your tongue. You might be gettin up there but I am in my prime."

"Prime compared to what?" I said. I loved to tease Althea so good.

"You look around here at these old women, you couldn't get most of em to dance if you had a shotgun," she said. "Me, I ain't cashin it in until the game's over." She made her way back into the crowd, stubborn and feeble at the same time, putting down her glass and taking mine, still full, raising it above her head like the Statue of Liberty, except black and wearin a church hat. April cheered, "You go, Althea," and Taylor whistled with his fingers in his mouth.

"That woman has dipped a few times but has yet to fall," I shook my head. "That's why I like her."

She's right about one thing though, and I know it. I am old as dirt. There's some kind of comfort in sayin it, and Lord knows it ain't like I don't know exactly what I'm talkin about. I've seen every kind of old there is. And I've had plenty of time to get used to the idea, so I got no bitterness. I don't even think about being young, that's the God's honest truth, except for sometimes when I get to wishin I could live a thing that happened to me one more time, just to feel it again. I never have been much of a worrier, there's plenty folks around who'll do that for you if you're a mind to let em. There's only one thing I worry about and that's getting lonely. Because what I know, what I have seen with these two eyes, is that loneliness will creep up on anybody at any time. You go on doin what you been doin all your life, one day to another, and then the next thing you know, there's nobody around. That's when you know you're old, when all your people start dying and your phone don't ring and you don't feel like puttin up a Christmas tree cause who's gon see it but you. And you don't bother to plant flowers in the spring cause you decide they're too much trouble to take care of. And even though you love to cook more than anything, you stop turnin on the stove. And you don't want to put on clothes because you ain't goin nowhere. And you tell the same stories over and over cause havin new stories means livin and you're not livin, you're sittin in a chair or lyin in a bed with the only thing goin on being what's in your head. And the thing that you never let yourself think about has happened: people have forgotten about you. Without you havin any idea, your days have become like listening to a radio station when you're drivin way out in the country. You get so far off the map that static starts interruptin the music and it's a little bit frustrating but you stay with it, tryin to listen, and then there's more static than music and you might still hang on if you're interested, but then the music is gone and you have to turn the thing off. The silence is better than the noise.

After dinner, which lasted five times longer than any meal I ever ate, we went back up on the outside deck and grouped some chairs together. I had Taylor turn mine and Althea's to look out at the water. From here, it don't even look like water, more like a thick dark bed-spread. Another blond-headed boy in a uniform—they're everywhere you look—brought us blankets. I think he either read my mind, or else he figured old people were always cold or gon get that way soon, so he might as well save himself a trip later on. Althea, worn clean out from dancin with a young white man with sideburns and big arm muscles, then eating enough for three people, fell asleep stretched out in a lounge chair beside me. I hadn't leaned mine back yet. I wanted to look out in the distance, I like that line way out there where the sky starts. April and Taylor had strolled over to the railing, looking over the edge and pointing. That's my family, I thought. That's reason enough for me to want to be here. I laid my chair back one notch and tucked the blanket up under my chin. It wasn't that cold, but the breeze made you want to snuggle up. Althea made a loud noise like she was choking, but she wiggled around some and was quiet again, the way a baby ought to sleep, safe and knowing it.

"Are you cold, Grandma?" Taylor was by my chair. "You want another blanket?"

"I'm all right, baby. Thank you though."

"It must be late, we're the only ones out here," April motioned to the wadded up mound beside me. "Look at Althea, bless her heart, she's dead to the world." Althea was talking in her sleep real quiet, her lips barely moving, saying something like "kitty cat, kitty cat," over and over.

"I know it," I said. "Of all people to fall asleep before a party's over. She'd die if she knew. We're gon have to tell her she didn't miss nothin."

"From what I saw, she didn't." April laughed. "Let's go to bed." She reached for my arm to help me up.

"No, no, no," I said, not taking hold. "I just have got myself comfortable good. I ain't ready to go yet. I'm gon stay out here and look at the stars for a little while."

"I'll stay with you," Taylor said.

"You night owls suit yourselves. I'll see you at breakfast. Taylor, get your grandma and Sleeping Beauty back to their cabin." She pulled her thin sweater close around her shoulders and left us.

Taylor yawned, stretching his arms behind his head and looking up. "It's like home," he said.

"In the middle of the ocean?"

"We never see stars in Chicago, too many lights." He cupped his hands around his eyes. "If I shut out everything and look straight up, it's like a long time ago when we used to sit out in the field at your house."

I tried to let my eyes follow his, both of us peeping through cupped hands like little children. We stared together at the patterns of light above our heads, a million stitches in a quilt that didn't look like it was finished. He was quiet, I wanted to talk. "I think those stars might be closer to earth than you are right now," I said.

Taylor didn't look at me. "You know, Mama used to say we're made for the stars and born for eternity. Actually I'm pretty sure Dr. King is the one who said it, but she adopted it."

"What about you?"

"I think eternity's overrated. I know that doesn't sit too well with you."

"Lord knows you ain't on earth to please me," I put my hand on his arm so he would look my way. "Taylor, you know I'm not an educated woman, so go on and write me off as old and simple if you want to."

"What are you talking about?" He frowned.

"Let's just say I'm closer to the end of the story than the beginning."

"Don't talk that way."

"Now, now, now just wait a minute. I want to tell you somethin. I'm old but I do know this. If you ever want to feel full in this life, you're gon have to ask if you might be made for somethin bigger than yourself. And when you can answer that, the only other question is what are you gon do about it."

"I'm not religious, Grandma."

"I don't blame you, it can get you in trouble."

"I mean I don't believe in God."

"Honey, I ain't in that. That's your business. And if you're tryin to shock me, you've waited about fifty years too long. God or not, you got to find your own way to anything that lasts. Most of what we think is important don't have enough glue in it to stick. Have you had enough of my preachin?"

"If I knew a preacher like you I might listen."

"No you wouldn't. You ain't gon listen to nobody too much yet, that's all right. I'm just tellin you now in case I don't get the chance to again."

"I hate it when you're morbid."

"Honey, I might not be doin too good next time I see you."

"I'm gonna try to come home Easter, it's not that long." He sounded nervous.

"Well that's good," I said, "that's real good, but I want you to do something for me."

"Tell me."

"Promise me you won't ever stop talkin to me. I need that."

"What are you saying?"

"And let me touch you sometimes. That's all."

"Grandma . . ."

I didn't let him finish. "Hush now." I pulled his head down onto my shoulder and stroked his cheek. There was the stubble of a beard, the only thing that made it any different from when I held him as a baby. I felt a warm dampness from his eyes on my hand, cradling him while I stared off into the sky. All that open space over our heads had slipped down around us and creeped inside through cracks we couldn't see, making the bigness of it all part of us too. I don't know if I've ever had a revelation, probably not, at least not straight from God. Most of what I believe sort of rises up to the top like butter in a churn after swirlin around inside me for longer than I would like. Holdin my grandbaby, I know that my love will outlive me. That might be all I need to know from now on.

Maybe we'll all be together again Easter, I don't know, a lot can happen between now and then. Come spring April's yard will be full of tulips and daffodils, it always is and she don't do one thing except add more bulbs year after year. She might have some hyacinth too, I hope she'll bring some inside if she does cause those things are sweet perfume to me. I'll try to make us a good ham if everybody can come and if I'm able. We'll need a crowd to eat it. We'll probably go to church, I know I'll want to show off Taylor, and he won't mind even if it's nothin but a bunch of strangers to him and me both. He might have to do me a favor and go pick up Althea, but she'll come as long as she can move one muscle. April will help me with anything I can't do. It won't be nothin fancy, just good food the way I learned to make it when I was young. We'll eat 'til we're full and we'll talk all about this here trip and show pictures. April will have a bunch of pictures I know, she started takin em as soon as we got off the airplane. We'll sit around the table while the light changes outside and tell so many stories that none of us is gon remember what exactly really happened, but it won't matter to us, we ain't gon argue over details.

ACKNOWLEDGMENTS

Many thanks to my early readers and all those who shared stories, hilarious and heartbreaking, of aging loved ones along the way, especially Sally Lloyd-Jones, Karen Braga, Todd Shuster, Christa Rypins, Eileen Lahart, and Nickole Kerner-Bobley. Special thanks go to my dear friend and muse Laura Grooms for unflagging support at every turn. And to Adriana Trigiani, who is surely the world's greatest cheerleader, not to mention one of the most generous people I've ever met.

I would also like to thank my editor, Marjorie Braman, whose insight and passionate guidance were invaluable, and my agent, Wendy Sherman, whose enthusiasm was immediate and unwavering. I am fortunate to work with both of these extraordinary women.

Additional thanks for important kindnesses go to Gail Godwin, Judy Clain, Gray Coleman, Peggy Hageman, Christopher Little, Robin and Peter Ketchum, Liz and Jed Hogan for the respite of Doolittle, Louise and Bill Grooms for the creative haven of Fripp, my colleagues in the Broadway community, and my friends in France who pretended my grammar was fine. Finally, thanks to Michael for faith, as well as to Sue, Kenneth, and Troy Johnson, and all the Laharts and Flemings, who instinctively knew how to be encouraging without asking too many questions.